The Starved Lover Sings

COLIN O'SULLIVAN

BETIMES BOOKS

First published in the English language worldwide in 2017
by Betimes Books

www.betimesbooks.com

ISBN 978-0-9934331-5-3

Cover design by JT Lindroos

Also by Colin O'Sullivan

Killarney Blues (Betimes Books, 2013)

To Patrick Doyle

"The earthquakes alone make it crazy to live there. Look at those fault systems. They're so big, there's so many of them. The volcanic eruptions alone. What could be more frightening than a volcanic eruption? How do they endure avalanches, year after year, with numbing regularity? It's hard to believe people live there. The floods alone. You can see whole huge discolored areas, all flooded out, washed out. How do they survive, where do they go?"

Don DeLillo, "Human Moments in World War III"

"There is something I longed for more than all the rest – without realizing it properly. It wasn't love, heaven forbid, nor glory, nor wealth. It was…anyway, I had imagined that at certain moments my life could take on a rare and precious quality. There was no need for extraordinary circumstances: all I asked for was a little order."

Jean-Paul Sartre, *Nausea*

None of this should happen

I

beat with perpetual storms

1

The thing that startles is the silence. Before the verbal abuse, before the chants, there's this brief and terrible silence, as if you have just entered into a vacuum. This must be what the birth of the universe was like, first nothingness, silence, then the creative burst. Chaos before the ordering.

Several times during the course of a match this occurs. Just after you blow your whistle for a foul, say, after some player has up-ended another, there's a mute moment, as half the spectators gape, breathlessly aghast at the irredeemable sin you've just committed; the other half begin their wicked smiles, and then, just then, the animals let loose with boos and brays.

I am standing in the middle of a soccer pitch on a cold, wet October day. I am a referee, at least for this afternoon. The players that surround me are kids. Youths. Let's call them that. Youths. This is all amateur. And I, too, am no professional. They, however, take all this with exceeding seriousness. Each header or volley of the ball, each crunching tackle is life or death for them, each second fraught and grave – that might be the trouble here, these kinds of games, and other things of little importance in the scheme of things, in this land, despite our perennial afflictions, contrary to the gravity of more pressing issues, given way too much heft and heave.

I wear a crow black uniform: silky shirt, shorts, black socks with two white stripes around the top, just under my knees. My eyes are black, my thinning hair is black and my heart, these days, is not far off that colour too. Notions lately, what started off with light and hope, soon hatched grey and became befuddled. Now these, my very own thoughts, these too are blackening, becoming muck, curdling, taking on the toughness of tar. One day I could, with hope or tenacity, all of me, be infused again with brightness and colour, once more a smiling and serene man, like when Ruby was around. But I must wait. I must somehow endure. They used to say that my fellow countrymen – back when they still spoke of us – were known for our patience. And they still say that patience is a virtue. But they say lots of things.

Faces of the spectators now, all wide-eyed, as if expecting something momentous to happen. They wave scarves and hoot and howl and holler. The noise, even for such a small crowd, can frequently be tremendous. Or maybe it's my ears, lately, filling up as they do, not sure if it's fluid or noise, just that my head feels full, a swampy thickness. The sets of fans – where do they come from, these people? You don't see them in the day-to-day – have recently been separated by barriers, and a few officials mope around in their Day-Glo luminescence, roaming, restless. They are ambling, helpless men, glad to be out and doing something, rather than sitting at home overwhelmed by loss. They are foolish however in thinking that if there was a riot they could actually do anything about it; the people here know well enough that when the levee breaks the flood cannot be stopped. The nation is like that now, poised ever, ever the brink, ever-edge of some event, some catastrophe near or nearing still, another set of waves fast crashing in and carrying off villages,

villages just like this one, or the earth to belch and rumble and open its crack and swallow us up. These things have happened around here. The very earth's rages. Down through the ages. These things happened yesterday, or just the day before, so clear is our memory, then. And tomorrow, tomorrow close and perilous. This is the way we live now. On edge. On edge. We are always on the bloody edge.

I am the worst person in their meager lives at this moment; these frivolous fans, the boo-boys and bray-girls, the nervous, the clamorous, the ill-at-ease. We have an expression here: the girls scream with *yellow voices*. And that is what their collective high pitch is like, a vicious, too-bright, scorching thing. I have, however, learned how to shut them out. I can ignore. A referee learns to do that. A teacher can do this, too. The snide comment that might get whispered when I walk down the corridor: my radar picks it up, my better sense lets it slide. I could challenge them, I could lash out, but that's probably what they want. Instead, I ignore. Walk on by. I shut out the snickering, walk past the bickering. The white noise between my ears is often pleasant too, like static from an un-tuned radio, or a sad satellite drifting in the nether regions of the galaxy. This is how I see myself when I allow myself "poetic moments". As if poetic moments could somehow help blunt the shards of life that come careering. We'll try anything, us lost folk, anything to help us cope.

The worst person in their world, here in this sodden field, they hold me in such high revulsion. And yet I provide a valuable service. If I wasn't here to bellow at, if I was not the verbal piñata, then maybe they'd have no one. Maybe they'd beat their wives or husbands or children or Labradors. Maybe they'd ravage or rape or murder. It's possible. Once I heard – from my wife, back when she spoke – of a whole village wiped out by a marauding madman. Apparently, the savage went from door to door at night, entering through the kitchens of quiet households and savaged the slumbering souls he found within. A whole village full of them. The village's population was only forty-five, granted, a small village for sure, a hamlet, but an impressive number for a murderer – he must've been very pleased with himself, initially. He was found hanging from a tree a few weeks later, a lopsided grin on his raven-pecked face; perhaps he had no one left to kill, even the grim and ragged scarecrows had been hacked down.

What voices ran through him, what pernickety hum buzzed in his bones?

I wonder now who found him. He'd already massacred the whole sleeping community. Who was left to discover anything? Perhaps it was some neighboring villager out on a Sunday stroll, sauntering past the desperately imploring shapes of apple trees, who looked up to the strange fruit dangling and cut the monster down. What a macabre picture I paint. But around here, that is just the beginning. The tip.

I don't know when it all got to be so vicious. This kind of ludicrous violence in football matches used to be British, we were told; we'd seen it on our screens. Or maybe it was Turkey. Luminous bright red flashes and smoke in the stands. Scarves around mouths, concealing. Concealing what? Identifiable faces? Diabolical grins? That is what I am thinking of, football, isn't it? Not war? No, *hooliganism*, they even had a word for it. When was that? A lifetime ago. But it's here now. Ugly. A supreme ugliness. We get some things much later, some trends, some fads; then they stay and fester. What is it with all the rage? With me, here, perhaps these folk get to vent their venom. That may be it. They need to let off some steam. What was that procedure, where they used to drill holes in people's crania to let out the vapours? Centuries ago I'm talking about. I'm picturing the curious, peering onlookers in a Dutch masters' painting, a Rembrandt say (my mother would be pleased, even saying his name). What was that called? That exhibition of atrocity? The baby Labradors stay safe in their soft-cushioned baskets, Golden Retrievers and hamsters unharmed – pets remain popular here, those that haven't already been ravaged by the packs. Let them have it, these angry faces and their furious fandom. Let their rage pour out of their vulgar mouths; vulgarity: the new trend in this dying village (population one thousand eight hundred eighty-nine, by the way, was once a lot more, and I've certainly no energy for that kind of a number; people keep their backdoors locked these days anyhow, must: wolves, vagrants, wolves). The young, evidently enjoying these new emotions, are adept. It's about all they are good for – I sound like an old fogey, a fuddy-duddy, an ancient passing of wind, I'm not actually, just sick and tired of rain on muddy fields, and the rest of the sinking, drowning things of my days.

The elders are good at it too: this is no youthful rebellion, this is no lashing out against a generation; they're all in on it – at least the nation united in that regard.

And I'm in black, the middle of it all, feeling the brunt, trying to concentrate. This is not my proper... my *official* job, I am a PE teacher at the local high school, asked once to referee a game and (must've been good at it) summoned back again and again. They never let you go. They are like the mafia of a bygone era, the authorities here. Or those square-headed terriers – I forget what they were called, those wild dogs – all vice-grip. There is always a summoning. You learn that in your first week of any job. You will be summoned, and you will obey. They will not let you go. You are trapped.

Suddenly I am surrounded by players, arguing with me about that last decision and was I out of my mind? I must not have been concentrating. My mind often elsewhere. *Was* I out of it? *Am* I out of my mind?

I wave them away. My brow stern, no-nonsense. It is a look I have perfected. I have stood in front of mirrors, training the upcurve of eyebrow, the narrowing of eyes that have been described as *bulging*. I no longer feel the need to do this. The mirror may not see me anyhow. The mirror seems to cast no clear reflection anymore. I make no impression in my own hallway.

A player lines up to take a free-kick just outside the box. The opposition makes its wall, players cupping privates, and their goalkeeper shouting at them. Orders are crisp, instructions swift. I spray the white line to keep them all in check, and they take their positions – something in me likes the construction of these walls, the sense of solidarity, as if men lined up and close together could achieve something, could defend against something so fast and sincere. Mostly they appear helpless, these custodians, they leak, they have holes, the ball often skims right past their shins, deflects and causes havoc. I have to do everything to stop myself from laughing. The young player takes a few steps back, then runs and kicks, swerving the ball into the top left-hand corner of the net, the goalkeeper, for all his scrambling, left no chance. Some things in the world you can do absolutely nothing about. Some forces cannot be stopped. The jungle girls, the hysterical birds in the crowd, release their raucous caws.

All my fault of course. Half of them hate me even more now. I get some bizarre thrill out of this: the power I hold in my hands, in my whistle, in my melancholy head. I've already been hurt so much; they can do what they want with me. String me up. It might be a relief. Beyond it now. Beyond hurt.

Small delirious crowd. It's only an adolescents' soccer

game, and yet the losers' faces, the pain, the tragedy that befalls; this is where they put their travails, as if their real ones are far too awful to contemplate.

Heft. Heave. See the way they grieve.

Some of them have gone the opposite way now and have begun to forgive; they have begun to like me because of the fortune I just awarded their humble heroes. These people are a fickle lot. Every supporter is. We are all of us easily swayed, we like it only when decisions go our way, when the universe fools us into believing it is benign, when the waves look like they could be surfed, and not there just to swallow you up.

The player celebrates with his teammates, and I encourage them back to their own half. It was a rather tasty effort, I must admit. I'm not surprised they are celebrating: these alpha-males in their sudden homoerotic happy hugs. But I'm not supposed to have opinions about their goals. I'm not to have any opinions at all. Not supposed to react. Only when there is an infringement of the rules am I to step in. The two colours I see in my dreams are red and yellow. These loom large. Like Rothko paintings, installed in the big white gallery walls of my mind. Red. Yellow. Neat in my breast-pocket (Rothko no longer ethereal or contemplative but suddenly shrunk and vicious) and ready to be pulled out at a moment's notice. Reaching for these cards or reaching for my notebook is as normal an action as rubbing my forehead or scratching my scalp or scratching my blue untouched balls these days. So often I do. So often I do. Habits. Habiliments. Crow black. This is what life is for me. As often... as often as picking my nose at a traffic light, waiting for green. Light, that is.

The lights still work, mostly, though they crackle and sizzle and flicker, disoriented like everything else around here.

Mine is a poker face. My face is stone. See it anytime,

download my pic (if you can get a viable connection); the drones are forever clicking in an already crepitate sky.

Abused, scorned, vilified, and always to stay impartial: me. Nice way to live life, isn't it? So free.

Be balanced. Be fair. Mollify when necessary. Make no mistakes. Make no mistakes!

I wag my finger. That's another one, another habit. Like it's from another age. A grandmother remonstrating with a pie-eating urchin before dinner, appetite ruined! The players take notice though, they do. Like I said, this is all very serious to them. Exceedingly.

Tall order, isn't it? Trying be balanced. To get things absolutely right, in a fair-minded manner, be just. After all I've been through. After all we, *we've* been through, *we*. What's truly fair in this world? What's...

But I got myself into this position, made my bed. I'm thirty years old, I'm a thirty-year-old PE teacher, and occasional referee, though the wrinkles on my face make me look a lot older (we used to be a young-looking race, and giddy-demeanoured; now we are experienced, old); my wife no longer speaks, to me or anyone else, maybe only silently, to passing ghosts; my daughter is gone, my beloved daughter is forever gone; I want women who don't want me, whores and... and I am trapped and often summoned; I've made my bed, now I'm supposed to lie in this shit.

2

Ferocity cuts. Ferocity cuts. Ferocity cuts her clothes into ribbons. Ferocity snips, then cuts some more. She cuts pieces of her skin, she cuts herself. No. She doesn't. She doesn't cut herself. You have to have guts to cut yourself. Guts to cut someone, anyone. And she is not there yet. She has thought about it – cutting herself, or cutting others: her anger, her constant despising – but instead Ferocity cuts ribbons out of an old T-shirt. This is an old T-shirt she no longer wears. It has Mickey Mouse on it, his big ears, his black eyes, his obscene itty-bitty tail. One hundred and seventeen years old, that mouse. It was too tight, that red T-shirt.

Her breasts are getting bigger now. She is proud of them. She is fifteen. She wants to show them off, and why shouldn't she; but that T-shirt was too tight around the shoulders, and that was the problem with it; nothing to do with her breasts, the shape of them, the ever so gentle upcurve; she is proud of them.

T-shirt issues, mental issues, Mickey Mouse issues – if she has problems, she knows what to do: cut them out of her life. Cut them out. Scissors hold a great fascination for her. The long blades, so sharp. The handles, so easy to manage, so easy to function – you just slip in your fingers and away you go, snip snip: there, there, in ribbons before you know it. And anyway, her new T-shirts (self-made, homemade) are much better. The one she wears today says "I Love ARCK" and has a cute, smiley face (her own face, sketched with permanent ink) at the bottom of it, around where the navel is. This T-shirt is sure to provoke outrage, sure to upset people, sure to make people throw her scimitar looks – she enjoys the fact that these little rebellions reveal who she really is, where she comes from, and all this passes the lonesome time in the lonesome village. They don't like their neighbors because their neighbors don't like them. This is how she comprehends the politics of it, local and international. She breaks things down to their essentials, she's good at that, cuts out the crap. It's one of the reasons she hates adults. They don't cut the crap at all, but instead strive to pile it on. She is not sure if she'll even make it to being an adult – though it's only five years away – and, anyway, what difference does it make? Few ambitions survive around here. The world has embraced the big one or has been bullied into submission, and the barnacle that clung to the bow has been dislodged and discarded – no more cars, or computers: they were falling apart, all re-called, malfunctioning, becoming obsolete. Made in ARCK (The Amalgamated Republics of China and the Koreas) is easier and cheaper on the world, so the world takes it and thank you very much indeed, would you like a receipt with that? So many speaking their new tongue. So many navigating its new forests of strokes and slashes. No one in her neck of the woods wants to see ARCK on a T-shirt, and that is why she wears it (even though the weather is not T-shirt friendly – she will just have to wear it inside a heavy woolly cardigan), that is why she has gone ahead and made it for her free weekends. Red. Yellow. "I Love ARCK". One-man manufacturer. One-girl firm. It's fun doing this kind of stuff.

There isn't much else to do in the village on a Sunday. There used to be a thing called "Punk" in the last century. You can see clips of it, if you can be bothered to do a search and if you can still get a proper connection. The fashion, the abrasive music, it seemed like fun, that "Punk". That was seventy years ago. Ferocity doesn't have a leather jacket nor does she put pins in her nose. No one does that. So maybe she will, sometime, maybe she will – she thinks she might like the sight of the blood, the red red blood, sure to make her best friend faint. She doesn't play guitar and she doesn't beat drums. Ferocity likes to make things, cut things, stick things into holes.

"You look good. Very sexy. Panther sexy," says Velocity. Things are either *Panther sexy* or *Bear scary* or *Panda cute* for her; these are her yardsticks, cartoon animals in her hazy head. The greatest creature of all for her is the Lesser or Red Panda. The epitome of cuteness. Animal perfection. Perfect like cartoons. Unblemishable (real people have the blemishes). She hopes one day to see one, maybe even stroke one. A stuffed representation would suffice. Velocity doesn't ask for much. Not yet at least. She would like her parents to stop fighting. Stop the midnight quarrels, the sounds of slapping and thudding – is that fist on chest? Knuckle on skull? – she hears when trying to get to sleep. Her nightmares are filled with mustachioed men who crash and thud with every footfall, but she longs, longs to dream of the cute and furry.

"If I were a male I'd be staring at you all the time," says Velocity.

"You stare at me all the time anyway, you little lesbian."

They laugh at this because sometimes they *are* little lesbians in the bedroom, like this now, when they have nothing to do and are feeling slightly, or very, horny. Sometimes Ferocity will start it off, for she is the taller and stronger of the two and the one with most ideas. She will move towards Velocity and take her chin in her hand and then kiss her hard on the mouth, her thicker, fuller lips crushing up against Velocity's thinner, subservient ones. Or sometimes this is all done softly, depending on the mood. And then fast as you like she will whip off her own (homemade, sloganized) T-shirt and then just as fast, pull (roughly) Velocity's T-shirt off too, lifting her arms over her head like she is a little child. There will be breast-play and then soon enough they will be completely naked and there will be vagina-play too. Ferocity usually has an orgasm. Won't give up until she gets it. Velocity has yet to experience that. Perhaps that's why she gets tense and fidgety. But all this passes the time in the small bedroom on a Sunday, with its lurid, peeling pink walls, worn white carpet and creaking doors and windows. Everything creaks in the room, with every step or movement the room lets out a soft but baleful sigh, as if it has had quite enough of containing them and their useless junk, as if the room simply awaits an onslaught from the sea, for it to rise and roar and ransack, the whole lot this time, the whole damned village, leave nothing at all behind but white bones and the loneliness of barren soil.

The girls have only ever seen a penis or two and want more of it. Neighbor and half-wit Daisuke showed them his without any hesitation at all, and they gave him some money to get a new notebook in the convenience store, because he lost his, because he always loses his stuff and is a bit on the slow side, even though both girls like him and use him – in fact, they think they might give him a call later and get him to show his penis again, erect, fully erect this time, it looked feeble last time, but that might be on account of the drugs – you can tell by the glazed look in his eyes, to the gills he is loaded; life makes no impression on him and he makes no impression on life, his own or anyone else's. Poor wretch: to the gills he is loaded and full. They've seen their own fathers' penises in the bath, back when they used to bathe as a family, or were in a family *onsen*, and they all dipped into the hot spring together. But the penis–viewing so far has been minimal – they need to up their game. Their hormones boil and they know it's best to be in control and not be overwhelmed. Mostly they talk about boys and are not really lesbians at all; it's just curiosity and moments of quick relief when they flick each other's switches. Yes, it's boys that they are really interested in, even the scrawny scarecrows that sit beside them in school, all boney and lonely. And music: they love to sing and dance in their room. And having fun, they love that too, and coming up with new ideas for having fun. And cutting up things and spreading them around the room in batshit montage. And passing time in the village.

"Your breasts look bigger than even yesterday, much bigger than mine."

Ferocity thinks this is true (Velocity's are still pretty much buds, have yet to truly make their mark), but she cares not to dwell on the fact; it's a conversation not worth having, many conversations with Velocity are not worth having, but she is her best friend, and so she has to see them out. She'd like something more exciting to happen and therefore plans must be hatched. Exciting plans, forthwith (she twirls the scissors in her thin hands, left to right and then back from right to left). The village: shrinking, half-washed away, declining, has little to offer them and so they must stretch it out to see how far it will go. How far do things go before breaking? If these two are to remain in the village until they graduate from the local high school, and then flee to the Capital, or somewhere foreign and hot – a much better plan because it's better to be in a place that won't sink – they may as well get the most out of what they've got around them. Stretch it out to see how far it will go. Time moves very slowly in a place like this. When their homework is done, and it doesn't take all that long for two sharp girls – well, one sharp (Ferocity), and the other no slouch but then no genius either (Velocity) – to get bored and fidgety and looking for something interesting to happen. How far do things stretch before snapping? Sometimes they go to one of their devices or call up images on the WaSc, but they'd much prefer for something to happen physically to them, in the real world (a hand to delicately touch their delicate skin, a finger to push upon their lips saying, *shh, shh, it's all right, it's all right*). They could just call Daisuke and experiment some more with him. Stretch him out to see how far he will go. Ferocity thinks she might like to put it in her mouth, it really wasn't that big. It really looked quite thin and ineffectual. Goodness knows how these things can do so much damage. What does it taste like anyway? Does it taste like any other part of the body when put in the mouth – a thumb say, a toe, skin taste, does it taste of skin? Or does it have an extra taste dimension, the wetness at the top? Are they right in thinking it might be wet at the top? Velocity twisted her mouth in doubt when they tossed the notion about, said she's still not ready for that, her mouth still more receptive to chocolate or nougat or sweet soft caramel.

"Do we have any snacks?"

"Of course we do," says Ferocity, and from under the bed she retrieves the snack box (which she calls the "Snake Box"), which is a very large box indeed and full to the brim with all kinds of sweets, sugary breads and chocolate bars. Sugar fuels them. There has been less manufacture of these goods recently, and the prices get continually hiked, so these goods (mostly stolen) have become exquisitely rare, luxury items. The snakes – only truly likeable in animated or gummy edible form anyway – once ingested, kill off all the other tapeworms and the other boredoms for seconds at least, and there is sugar-thrill enough in that, they make a day worth-while. There is nothing worse than bedroom boredom.

Velocity digs in, her pursed mouth suddenly wide and gaping and cramming in as much as she can take, her sharp little teeth like those of a swift predatory dinosaur that cuts and tears and ravishes.

Today, as they play in Ferocity's cerise bedroom, with very clean-faced, girlish ARCK boys looking down on them from flickering wallscreen (WaSc) images, they call themselves Ferocity and Velocity. These are two words that Ferocity (Shiori Takeyama) found in an English textbook, and she liked the meaning and sound of. Velocity (Maki Mikami) likes the names too, but has already forgotten the meanings and never wrote them down in her English vocabulary notebook. But it doesn't matter all that much, because they'll come up with new identities soon enough.

3

Egg goes splat.

Almost empty car park, the few remaining cars pulling out, and an egg goes splat on the windscreen of my small white Suzuki. It's one of the last puredrives, one where I get the pleasure of actually steering, putting my foot down, feeling as if I am in control of something. But it is faulty, old and rickety, it hiccups and coughs like an emphysemic grandmother, its innards gurgling the exorbitant gas – seems impossible, but they still manage to extract some. I'm forced to feed it.

Then another: *splat!*

I should really have gotten a different-coloured car in the first place, have it dun, like me, like my days. White always shows up the egg smears and the crow shit, making my car an announcement: *This is my life! I started out pure and clean, but that didn't last too long, now you can leave your stains all over me!*

The perpetrators scamper off as I walk towards the mess. I don't know why they are in such a hurry. It's not like I could do anything about it. I could be standing right next to them as they crack egg after egg over my windscreen; they could make an omelet there – how on earth would I begin to dissuade them, this gang of four with injury and malice drawn across their mealy mouths? They could crack them over my very head if they pleased.

I sigh. I sigh at my little life.

I open my sports bag to take out the bottle of bathroom cleaner and the rags I always carry after each game, and I begin to wipe down my misfortunate machine. If this car could speak, I wonder how dejected and forlorn its voice would sound: a wounded caribou calf mooing in some lowly trap, motherless and stuck, or a new-born bat in some clammy cave, frightened at the inhospitality of the environment in which it finds itself: so like my own, this petrified voice; it is only on the playing field that I am able to pretend and summon tones of gravitas and austerity. Only then I act. My car and I, such... failures.

A human voice behind me then from nowhere, a reedy, familiar voice, but I don't take my eyes off the job at hand – I already know the couple that has arrived to taunt me, and I sigh a little more.

"Scrambled eggs again today?"

This is Hide Miyoshi, and by his side, as usual is Takashi Nakazawa. These are the two I have to "work" with, these are "assistant referees", though they are turning out to be more a hindrance than anything else, this strange couple, like twins, both with mean, foxy faces, and the same unruly hair. Same height even. Two lampposts. Only they don't shed much light on anything. It's always these two I get stuck with in matches. I don't know why. These are the two that get summoned, just like me. Perhaps there are no other adult men willing to volunteer their time the way they do, the way I do. I am of course being sarcastic, because *volunteer* is one of those English words we use that has lost all traces of its true original meaning. By *volunteer* we mean *forced* to do something. Even in our school, they round up the troops (that is *students*) on an occasional Saturday morning and tell them that they are going to clean up more of the debris that's still left on the stricken shoreline, volunteer-work to help the community – such spirit, such altruism. But I cannot imagine one student who has actually ever gone along with this of their own volition; the typical teen, like any teen anywhere in the world, I presume, would rather be in bed on a Saturday morning, or idling with some other dubious, skiving mate. *Volunteer!* The barefaced lie of it. Don't get paid a penny. *Volunteer.* Like these two, these weird twins I am forever lumbered with. Three volunteer referees we are then, out in all weather for the municipal good. The municipal good, no less!

Only their eyes are different from each other. With Hide you can hardly see his pupils, so severe is his vicious squint, a fox in some gruesome folktale, illustrated on the page with a simple swish of the brush, whereas Takeshi is all wide display, those clean brown irises – whether they are innocently beautiful or prettily vacant, I haven't quite made up my mind.

"Nothing new, Hide, nothing new."

They could have spoken to me in the dressing-room of course, but they like to keep their taunts till after, when I'm cleaning up the Eggmen's eggs.

"Are you going to join us for a few beers this evening? This is only the twentieth time we've asked you. Surely you'll oblige us this time. Don't you know we're always great fun?"

They giggle together then, like they are an old stage duo, vaudevillian, hitting each other over the heads with their hi-jinksy hilarity.

It may well be the twentieth time they have asked me, and will surely be the twentieth time I will say no. I could not stand an evening in some lifeless *izakaya* with these snickering buffoons, their grubby tales of grubby events in their grubby lives. It is enough to hear them, as they lace their boots before a game, sniggering about their escapades – not for me, an evening sucking on a watery beer and flipping green beans into our gobs as they rattle on about the exhilarating things they have done or are about to do. They are a little younger than I am, and probably just as unmoored, though they will no doubt tell you differently; they will no doubt tell you that their life is nothing but the stability of their homes peppered with the frivolity of their hobbies. That is the main issue when conversing with these two, no matter how you term it, they will almost certainly convince you of its opposite.

Not many people drink anymore of course, beer production has decreased, most people cannot afford, and there certainly is no feeling that any occasion warrants celebration.

"I'm not much company to be honest," I say, the understatement of my day. "I have a lot to deal with at home. I don't really drink anyway. I try to avoid the bars... you know how it is."

How it is. Do they know *how it is*? (I think that was even the title of a book my father used to read, an actual book, I remember the smell of the old yellowing paper on his hands, such an anachronism: but do I mean him or the books?)

They look at me, waiting for me to go on, waiting for me to squirm and explain myself further, or dig myself a deeper hole, knowing I will never really join them – they carry on the charade regardless; this is what people, even in what's left of this shattered society, do.

"Getting eggs on the car is one thing, but I really don't want to get them splattered all over my face. If I set foot inside a bar and the father of some..."

But already I am running out of steam and can explain myself no further. I think I've been through this argument before, and they, too, are beginning to tire of it, of me.

A look of forgiveness comes across Takashi's face, he's always the first to bend; yes, my colleagues will leave me off the hook again. They'll let me scurry back to whatever life I claim to possess.

"That sexy sister-in-law still coming round to your place?" says Hide, a glisten of spittle at the corner of his mouth, the cartoon fox not far off licking his cartoon chops.

"Have you not given her my number yet? Tell her my wife won't mind, every referee needs a mistress, to take the post-match strains away. You won't forget now, will you? To give her my number?"

"I won't forget. I'll see you later."

I get into my car and start its engine. It harrumphs into life. The wipers smear albumen across the windscreen. Is my vision always to be this way impeded; the phenomena of the world in crafty conspiracy, and all too aberrant.

Hide.

Takeshi.

I'd be happy to see them both…

Cursed be thou, thou ancient wolf, that having
more victims than all the other beasts of prey, can't find no
bottom to thine endless craving.

Dante's Purgatory, Canto XX. I used to read a bit once. My father was a teacher of literature in a university, a university that once stood tall and proud, actually… just stood. My mother was an art teacher in a different school (that also collapsed). Both were incredibly gifted intellectuals who nourished me and made me the moody, angst-ridden man you have before you. Is that why I became a PE teacher, instead of lounging in the Arts? A lame rebellion. I could have just followed in their footsteps, just did what they did, I had the intellectual capacity. The ivory tower might have suited me. Philosophy and cardigans. Tepid tea and meandering discussions about writers and their oeuvres. All might have suited me quite well. I could have used words like "uproarious" (for comedic works that are never very funny) and "triumphant" (for books that don't herald very much at all). Instead, I blow the whistle on bitter afternoons. Instead, black, and occasional red and yellow. Instead, melancholia and screams of pointlessness.

They were wonderful, my parents. Could not have hoped for better. However sighful my life (all our lives) have become, I cannot blame it on my childhood; I was well looked after. Those days, those sunny afternoons were all good, those people too. But they were washed away. They left me with some terrific bookfiles, endless download suggestions and even a few precious paperbacks that had survived the torrents in sturdy metal crates (he was old-fashioned that way, my father, a collector), and memories, of course. That's about the size of it. That's all I have left of them. Doesn't seem like a lot but it's enough to cling to.

I used to read a lot, spent some time downloading things (the aftermath, one of the aftermaths, call it mourning): things they had known and referenced in their speech, out of plain curiosity, in my own time, off my own bat. I used to, yes, used to read a lot, but for a short while only. It was a search. A brief flurry. I used to memorize lines, too. Had them come flashing off the screen like my father used to do, thought it would help me better understand the world (I think I was ambitious once). Now I can't be bothered to read or scroll or remember. It's best to try and forget things.

I will not give him my sister-in-law's number. Why would I ever be so obliging?

I know how tenebrous all of this is; you ambling away, already disappointed, melancholia and pointlessness indeed, but there may yet be some heroics, before the next flood, why don't you, like the rest of us, linger, I ache for some company, there might yet...

4

A girl walks the shoreline on and on and sings something about the bottom of the pit and on and on, shoeless and forlorn and on and on, and on and on and on

5

The 13th says it will only get better, but in his eyes you can see the lies, it will only, naturally, get a lot worse.

The 13th will not apologize for the bungling and the fumblings and the crumblings of the State and steely greets the camera properly attired, neck-tied and be-suited and be-quiffed and trying to look like a man who has no knives circling him and no fateful sword hanging by a thread over his bewildered head.

He is the 13th Prime Minister in only twenty years or so and the number is an embarrassment to the nation. Actually, numbers have gotten to be so outrageous they no longer matter, they are ignored, or commonly shunned, avoided in conversations, anathema. Numbers simply got too big: millions unemployed, millions of babies needed if the melted economy was to somehow reform into a workable shape, millions over sixty-five, millions carried away again and again by waves of destruction... so millions dead.

Millions dead. Millions carried away so millions dead.

The people don't really know his name, this spokesman for something. He is only one of a line, a sequence, and though his name flashes large across the screen, they do not really see it anymore, don't recognize it as a word or symbol, it is a blur, like their lives, out of focus, almost invisible. Yes, the 13th is mostly invisible. A wraith. Like something glimpsed from the corner of a teary eye.

The ghosts that walk to and from the waves at night are also invisible. All the suicides, all the suicides too. So soon their names forgotten.

The populace has become nameless. The populace numberless. This sounds like an oxymoron. This is the country the 13th addresses.

The wolves thrive. When the flesh lay across the stones and mud, the wolves came quick for the carrion. Down from the sultry hills they came, animals thought long extinct (Ezo Wolf, gone since 1889), resurrected somehow – where had they been hiding? – down from the high forest thickets, from the thick mists and humid airs they came when the scent of the rotting flesh got all too much.

As baby numbers dwindled – still dwindle, the fires of the populace's loins unkindled – the wolves only grew in their hordes, packs multiplying, growling and howling in the gloaming. The people lie on their floors pushing plugs into their ears trying to block out the cries, sucks and slobbers of the meat-eating ravishing reveries – listen carefully, what's that? Teeth on bone? The very sound gnaws into their fevered dreams.

The 13th says more should be done to remove bodies at a quicker rate when disasters occur, and more international assistance requested, post-haste, forever post-haste. But no one hears the calls, not the human kind. Only the midnight howls at every moon abound, those that grate and sadly those that resonate.

Canis lupus hattai – my, my, where have you been so long?

The 13th says something should be done. He looks into the lens, calm, be-quiffed, while the clucking claque of faceless yessirs that surround him nod to his pleas and his decrees.

The wolves.
The wolves at night. Something should be done about the wolves.
And the waves.

6

The girl came out of her mother red and glistening. I was there to see her shine like a jewel. We both knew right then (that peculiar telepathy of those deeply in love) that even though her name had been decided (Kurumi) that we would always call her Ruby.

Our jewel, our gem, our precious...

I try to talk about her sometimes, I try to talk about Ruby and...

My house is a cold, dark house. Take a walk up the incline and see it still standing, almost neighbourless, a tall, slender structure, gothically grim, remarkable only in its ornate dreariness. It is only imposing in that it stands alone; everything around it fell and decayed when the grumpy ground shuddered for the umpteenth time. Take that walk and see it rise up to the grey sky and ask yourself if it seems the kind of abode that would give off any warmth at all, and if only the bravest dare-acceptor would open the door and care to spend a night inside. It's wintry to look at, whatever the season, and when the door opens and you enter into its spookily quiet halls, even in the height of summer, it stays cold, a place of draughts — we never knew such winds could whip around this little hill until all the others came crashing down around us, and we, *it* at least, stood tall and defiant, and we were to take this as some stroke of good fortune. Even when the kerosene heaters sputter and whiff in every room it still feels full of spiky chills, as if spirits are forever waltzing around here tracing their frigid fingers on every surface as they glide by.

My sister-in law tries to fill this place with her heat. She is here in front of me now, always managing to make herself seen, always here or hereabouts and liking to be noticed. She is an attractive woman, solidly built, with lively eyes and a knack of making foolish heads turn – the foolish heads of men, I mean, of course.

She cracks an egg on the side of the pan, *splat*, there it goes again, phenomena, the splat and ooze presented to me once more; it must surely symbolize something.

The mini-WaSc is on in the corner of the kitchen where we eat. Though the reception isn't what it used to be – it crackles a lot, often a cackle too, a miniature coven must dwell within – and Marisa continually lambasts it for its inefficiency. Too she shakes her fists at the oozing plant six hundred kilometers away that rattled when the earthquake yawned the land open and made us vomit, choke and die. Some of us. Some of us drowned and died. Some of us are still here of course, steadfast, cockroachian.

Her meals are prepared fast, everything she does, she does with speed, and everything comes out tasting good, too; she is a woman of considerable talents. We eat in the kitchen, even though it is small and cramped. The next room is a perfectly acceptable (though also small) dining room, but for reasons unknown we remain here. The women made this decision long ago, without me, which is the way I like a lot of decisions in life to go.

She puts the plates down in front of me, an array of

different bites and samples and tasties, as varied as she can muster. She places a glass of milk in front of me too – a few un-diseased, radiation-less cows of the north still producing, apparently – and then gently the lacquered chopsticks are laid on their rest, a show of style when everything else is dull. She stops then and waits for me to smile in appreciation.

I smile in appreciation.

The 13th is saying something on the crackling screen, but neither of us is really listening. I live so much in my own head, it hardly matters what any other being is taking pains to gibber about.

"She hasn't had such a bad day. Slept a lot in the morning. I took her to the toilet twice. Hasn't said much. I leave the radio on for her most of the time. Gives her something to listen to. If she sleeps, I turn it off."

I keep eating. This is the usual run of things around here. She keeps talking and I keep eating. We never properly converse. That's my fault. My eyes are always on her; my eyes always on her tight skirt and her thick thighs and buttocks. This is the run of things around here.

"How was the game? I suppose you enjoyed yourself. It's great that you have a hobby to keep yourself interested. And it is good exercise, isn't it? Good that you can get out and get fresh air and exercise and…"

The air around here? Fresh? When last could you have said that?

I keep eating. I let her rattle on. She can talk and talk and it's rarely in any way noteworthy, anything she ever says. But she means well. That's why she is here. Helping out. While her sister lays in bed all day and refuses to budge and refuses to speak, this good woman, Marisa, single and energetic and full of the qualities the rest of us seem to lose day by day, stays the course and sets about the house and puts things in order.

I am glad of this. I am glad she keeps things the way she does. I have never been that house-proud to be honest, could easily leave the dust pile, forget to throw away the rubbish, the milk turns sour; this woman is good for me, me and my pale predicament. I feel guilty for looking at her the way I do. Ogling. An ogre. Cartoonish again – the people of this land continue to grow up on animation, maybe it distorts the way we perceive the world, but I can't help but see myself google-eyed, hunchbacked and slobbering, knock-kneed and acned. She is my sister-in-law. But she is a good-looking woman, ample, and aware of it, and when she bends and turns around in my kitchen I somehow feel a right, a sense of ownership – this sounds unfair, misogynistic even – but then she catches me looking, and smiles, and my feeling changes from one of guilt to embarrassment.

"Dessert?"

She once said she thought me admirable, for holding down the job and making the most of things, and for even being that man in the middle of the soccer field trying to keep things balanced and fair, not, the despairing husband of her beached sister as I have come to regard myself. I have come to need and rely on her more and more. I know that this is pathetic. My challenge is to keep my urgent thoughts to myself, and to never act on feverish impulses, I am a man, naturally, and...

My wife's name is Asami. She's upstairs dying. Dying of something. Heartache, I suppose. It's hard to be sure. She lies upstairs waiting to die while we try to work things out down here, like oarsmen in the galley trying to keep the ship a-sail while furious storms are ever looming. Asami: such a sweet name, though when she first introduced herself to me I thought she said "Hasami": scissors; whatever mistimed breath puffed out – not that I was ever the type to make anyone breathless,

I was, *am*, an average man and not too far off hideous, with eyes that earned me my nickname, Tombo, dragonfly, and a faint greeny insect-like pallor to my skin, too, hardly the stuff of Hollywood yearnings. I am muscular though, years of training and PE runabouts everyday with the kids have kept me trim and taut, and of that, I guess, I am proud enough. She was as light and breezy as the sound of her name when we first dated, giddy and jocular, spontaneous, with a sassy stride, forever singing the latest pop songs and dancing merrily regardless of who saw her. You wouldn't have expected her to drop into such depths of despair. It's not a very good place to be, this cold house. Not the greatest of situations for any of us. You could conjure up a lot happier homes for sure, even in this ransacked region. Still, as we bungle along through life, we can't help but contain a sliver of sanguinity, a glitter within us, something minute and bristling with the idea that if we continue to endure, things will improve as they unfold, or at the very least our existential dread lessen.

Marisa cracks a glass off the side of the sink and it breaks. She holds up the jagged piece to show me. She has the look of an innocent child about her, waiting to be consoled or scolded, waiting to be taken away and hugged or flogged.

"Sorry," she says.

This happens often in our house, this breaking of things: cups, saucers, bowls, shards everywhere; turns the place into a treacherous terrain as we walk in our socks, or in our bare feet in the sweltering summers, her painted dainty toenails dancing across the floor, so at odds with the heavy…

Hearts too, she breaks them, if the builders' wolf whistles are anything to go by when she saunters along the narrow roads (this is another vulgar trait picked up from foreign shores, we used to be polite once, we are not who we once were, took the bad influences upon us, took them to our bosoms. It is as if we no longer have any trust in our own selves, our own culture and sense of worth, casting off our virtues like skinny-dippers disrobing and plunging into some fortifying lake. An illusion of course. We kept borrowing, a phrase here, a fad there, and the young savoured those, fed and nurtured upon them, suckled; no wonder those on the Right get stroppy and keep calling for a shutdown, an isolation, like centuries before, it's not like many came to help us when... some bridges burned, blame PM 9, 10, 11).

Marisa has no man in her life, and tells me so often, as she prepares the meals, or scrubs at the floor in a vigorous rush. No one at all, she says. It's one of a series of mysteries I haven't yet begun to fathom, how such a sexy woman could not attract a host of suitors. Or maybe she really does, but is too picky to settle on one, the rich and the svelte and the hulking and the lascivious all surplus to her requirements, their bids and barters ignored, and thus does she remain alone.

"Are you all right? No cuts?"

"No cuts. I'm fine. Sorry."

We say this word a lot in our lives. *Sorry.*

I am sorry for my life. I am sorry for your life. I am sorry for all the lives on the planet. I'm sorry that Ruby never came home. What happened to Ruby on that day? I am sorry for the sick air that we breathe, the sicker breath we throw back out at the world. I am sorry for the multitudes that have died and the multitudes that have to go on living. I am sorry that I struggle and that Everyman's life is a struggle, I am sorry for the way things are and the way things aren't. I am sorry for almost everything and I wish that I was not this way. I wish I was a million other ways.

"As long as you have no cuts, then everything is fine," I say, and I want to hold her, and I want to grow hard in my pants and have it up against her and shock her with my continuing pulse.

She smiles at me. She is beautiful. Everything is not fine.

"So I'll be off then."

This is a little later, as she puts on her jacket, as she buttons up slowly. This is what she always says, every night, as she buttons up one of her trendy coats, the usual run of things. I don't know where she gets the money for such items. Fashion is no longer a concern around these parts. It's a wonder as to where she even buys these things, the stores I pass in the village are dull, wanting affairs – even the mannequins look disappointed with the grim regalia thrust upon them. Maybe she gets them sent from the Capital. Maybe she…

I'm watching her carefully, every little twitch of muscle that moves on her face, the eyelashes, top and bottom, that softly meet and depart from each other again like butterfly wings, the tongue that darts in and out of her mouth, a tiny fleeting private thing, at odds with the rest of her meatiness, the bounty of her body – if I paid as much attention to all my business.

Then, when buttoned, she'll say, "Give Asa-chan a kiss for me and tell her I'll see her in the morning."

I wait for her to say it. Our lines. We never fluff. No corpsing ever on this particular stage.

"Give Asa-chan a kiss for me and tell her I'll see her in the morning."

"Of course."

She stands at my door for a moment, about to make her exit, her night flight from this natty nest. She looks up to me as if expecting something. I always feel awkward at this moment, but I try not to avert my gaze. Eyes on eyes.

Someday one of us might do something about all of this. Someday someone rash.

She nods then and flies for certain.

As soon as I know she is gone, far down that lonely road and on her way to her lonely – is it lonely? – house, I button up my own jacket and head down the hill. At night I do this, I go walking, in search of my girl, my lovely missing girl.

Ruby disappeared two years ago. Our jewel, our gem, our…

Try.

She was eight years old. She had been walking home from school, her hard leather *randsel* schoolbag strapped on her back, walking in that slow, slouchy way she had, long legs, like me, long strides on the footpath, kicking stones into the drains, blowing the fluffy heads off dandelions – no, she was too old for that, why do I paint her a little girl, why such innocence, and what was the season? Fathers and their little girls. No, no dandelions. When did I last see flowers of any description? Even in spring, do they bloom? Or have I just not noticed anymore? Surely it must be that…

And then the rumble, the massive rumble throughout the land, as if the planet had given up its ghost and was preparing to say goodbye to its place in the solar system and spin off its axis completely; a belching, a rupture, then the plates rubbed against each other, like giant palms in gleeful anticipation, and the waves started on their course towards us. Ruby must have ran, she must have seen or heard the monstrous wall of water, a girl as bright and strong as mine, she must have…

Sometimes I dream that she was taken, kidnapped. Some man in a van, some guy snatched her and threw her in the back and drove off with her and somehow… even though taken by some soulless troll… she might still be alive. Or it might have been a hero came to her rescue, or a heroine from those picture books she used to pore over, and still that lovely, soft lady is taking care of her in some secluded spot, maybe further south where it is hotter, where bright fruit weigh down the branches. Sometimes I dream that she is still swimming. That she didn't get pulled under at all but has managed to keep afloat, after all this time, and is on her way home. My girl.

My ears hurt.

The night is feral. You only have to look into the bushes, behind the bins, see the green eyes gleaming back at you. There's always some animal there, some four-legged thing, some mangy cross-breed that cowers and coos, dying of starvation most probably, its lungs half filled with dark fluid, liquid that it never managed to spew back out – there's always some poor creature.

Or else it's human. Those too. Us, I mean. One of us. Lying in the ditch there. Could be dead. Would be better off if it was. Far better.

On my rounds I usually see a raccoon dog. I encounter this beast often. How he got quite so plump in these trying times is another riddle for me, must be a good scavenger, I suppose, or else it is fast or sly enough to evade the prowling packs of wolves. This is a confident creature. It sits there on a dustbin, nonchalantly staring at me. In fact, when we find each other, we both stare, stock-still, eyes locked. Neither of us moves for a minute. It's like a game we play. Who will be the first to flee? His eyes – I say *he*, I don't know why, maybe I recognize a fellow lost male – are never revealing, it is impossible to know what an animal thinks; in his eyes... perhaps he sees some kindred spirit, a comrade that didn't get washed away, and still engages the night, on a mission, on an epic quest – I do so want to be the hero of this tale.

And then one of us does. One of us breaks the bond.

Decides to move on. Has had enough. As if one of us has got to *be* somewhere. One of us has a life that is important and worth salvaging all of a sudden. Sometimes it's me that makes the move – off to search for Ruby. Sometimes it's him, Mr. Racoon-dog, off to forage elsewhere, for whatever it is that sustains him. He looks at me unafraid, has grown used to being around the urban male, the urban male and his pathos.

Marina is standing by a lamppost on the corner of a street. Always the same girl, always the same street, always the same lamppost – a twisted metal thing that got bent over in the floods but managed to stay standing, mostly upright, like myself. I like to think this a scene in some late night noir movie, something French and melancholic, it piques the imagination, *she* does.

She holds an umbrella. She usually has one, a defense against the rain, a defense against a certain class of idiot who tries to get too cozy too quickly. She has the point of it sharpened, must have seen it in some old *yakuza* flick. I think she is of the type unafraid to use it on a trick.

I approach her as I always do, with a smile, because I like her, and I'm assuming, after all these nights of loaded chats and standing beneath her umbrella (until she says I am interfering with business), that she likes me too.

"You should have brought your umbrella, Mr. Wazka, it looks like rain."

"It always looks like rain. And anyway, I don't mind getting wet."

"The dogs lose their scent in the rain and get confused."

She often says wise-sounding things like this. Amazing for what – twenty-threee? Twenty-four years old? She could've been a philosopher, but instead she's a whore. I say this with the utmost respect. I have always admired the profession, secretly intrigued, ever curious, but sadly, I meekly admit, I've never partaken.

"When you come up my apartment with me? I give you good price."

She often says things using incorrect grammar too, or English, if she decides to speak that language – it's adorable.

"Someday, Marina. Someday for sure. Too busy at the moment."

"Ha, Mr. Wazka, you always say that."

Wazka, she once explained, is Polish for dragonfly. Though when I first heard it, it sounded like the English word "walker", as if I am Mr. Walker, the man who goes out walking at night – why am I always mishearing things, is it that I don't pay enough attention, or my ears are so far gone? I'm just glad she speaks to me at all, in any language. One night I left her rattle on in some old-world European tongue, as if I understood every word. I just stood there grinning, delighted with her incomprehensible gusto, until my balls grew sore with want.

She lights a cigarette, inhales deeply, blows a grey stream to the late sky. A couple of moths dance around the streetlamp's burn, the sound of their wings hitting off the plastic like spits of static. Oh how they dance and dice with death, crazed with their own diablerie: I think of Marisa in the kitchen, our stifled domestic drama. Sister-in-lure.

Marina thinks I'm a detective, because I once told her that I was solving a case, a mystery, and that these evening strolls help me to think. Of course I *am* on a case, of sorts, so it's not a complete lie. Where did my daughter go exactly? To what other realm? My quest is often spiritual, often soul-searching, often I go to clear my head of Ruby, and often I go to think of no one else. (My father used to lock himself away in his study, informing us beforehand that he was deeply ensconced in a

philosophical work, in the vein of Cioran – another insom-
niac, huffing through the night hours in a hazy garret – it was
lyrical and profound he said, blaring his own trumpet, no one
taking him seriously at all. Although sometimes he retracted
the entire thing and said it was not a philosophical work at all,
but a long poem, though maintaining the fact that it was lyrical. I once saw snatches of it on his surrounding screens, flashing there. It seemed to have no cohesion at all, though I was
barely a boy and could have offered no critique, all jump and
jitter it was, the way my own fantasies flitter now, and only
occasionally landing on something study-worthy. "Towards a
Theory of the Beyond" was its intriguing title, and on several
of his surrounding screens furious aphorisms flashed. Raging
inside, raging with his own intellect, and yet he wanted no
one to read it and never seemed to finish it – he should have
locked his study door then, we all know young boys are as
curious as kittens. I'm sure he was no philosopher or poet,
just a man who read and wrote and made as much, or as *little*
sense, as any man. But he was good, and he was my father, he
was good, and I am his son.)

    I like Marina. She's not attractive, though she's not unat-
tractive either. She's perfectly ordinary. She turns one or two
tricks a night; seems like it's enough to keep her fed. She's
only a slip of a thing anyway and probably doesn't need
much feeding. I don't need much either, don't really need all
the tasty dishes Marisa offers up; I need fuel enough only for
the PE classes with the kids and the weekly, or twice-weekly,
refereeing appointment, and of course my nightly rambles.
Food has lost all its taste. The ruined people here in my village, the Giacometti-like walking stickmen that look blasted
and bereft, need only a little sustenance, their recognition
buds long destroyed by the continuous saltiness in the unas-
suaging air.

A cat leaps out of nowhere onto a wall, and, perfectly balanced, saunters along on padded paws. Another animal. Another actual living breathing furry creature. How have the wolves not torn it asunder?

Marina and I see a couple kiss and then unlock their front door and enter a dilapidated house. We are jealous that they have somewhere to go, that their embrace is heartfelt, even if their walls are none too steady. Some people get lucky, I suppose. Some people do not get pains or cancer or Ebola or fall down ladders and break their spines and...

The rain spatters on her umbrella – a jazz drummer's brushes on the toms. Again she has me thinking of last century's music and film, though I was alive for none of it. I was not born until 2015 – already the films had become crude and boorish, our foolish makers putting the "melo" into every drama; noir and jazz were almost a century before, but it's that European flavour she brings; I hope she speaks more ancient tongue tonight.

The police ignore her. Or maybe they never see her, so quickly she slips away, a cat herself, through the flaps and cracks. I don't know exactly where she's from. Once she told me she was Czech, and a few months previous to that she talked about her family in Poland. She does have an Eastern European accent, as far as I can tell, but she could be Latvian, Estonian, Lithuanian, how would I know? Geography was never my strong suit. I'm not sure I could identify any of these places on a map. I think she just makes it all up. What difference does it make? I enjoy lies, the construction of selves. The government opened up the country to immigrants about twenty years ago, further relaxing its strict laws and allowing a mixed and varied workforce to gain a foothold, the idea being that they'd support the economy and give the nation renewed hope, boost industry as well as morale, and our generally suspicious nature even went for that idea of adding spice to the mix – what harm could it do? But the laws became too soft, the monitoring got lax, and the floodgates opened to folk from all over the world, some illegally entered the country – Marina? A child brought in and then abandoned? – and the normally (simply) suspicious became resentful, felt betrayed. This was just another bureaucratic mix-up, mess-up, fuck-up – the same dour dealings that have been going on for centuries; pale politics that need strong and clear rules and demarcations, picture this: instead of German Expressionist's thick black oil, we get a wan watercolor wash, this is our back-drop; no one taking responsibility, pass the buck. (My mother would've been pleased with such artistic analogy, she would, I'm sure. Why am I still trying to please my mother? My tender heart still skips to the immature rhythms of a boy.)

No one wants to come to this land anymore, it's too dangerous, the archipelago a-throb with threat. The world knows the names of the nuclear plants, those operational and those at risk. No one would dare take the chance. Fancy a sojourn on our shores these days? Are you out of your mind? The foreigners fled and some clever natives naturally followed and...

What difference does it make where she is from? I'm simply happy she's here. Marina, and her ilk, certainly add spice to my doleful days. And who knows, maybe I will go up to her apartment someday. Why not? She give me good price.

Home. Or let's just call it "house".

Up slowly now, up the wooden stairs, passing the portraits on the walls of a family of three: Tombo, Asami and Ruby. Turn into the bedroom and see a figure in bed, back turned, just a hump under the covers. Cannot see her face. I miss her face. Always turned. I want it, her lovely face, I want it, her songs and spontaneous dance, I want it her lovely face, I want.

I start to undress and hang up my clothes neatly in the wardrobe, careful not to chime the metal hangers. I then put on my beige pajamas, buttoning them to the top, more like a soldier preparing for battle than a man retiring for the evening.

Trepanning! I've just thought of it. Drilling the skull and letting out the vapours. The word just came to me. Oddest moments.

I sigh as I pull the covers over my body. I sigh, I sigh at my little life. The night is chilly. October warning us that winter is only weeks away – be prepared.

No other sound then but my wife's laboured breath.

She in bed. Heap. Heap of life. Heap of sleep. Heap of grief. Wheeze, disease? Breathe. Breathe. Heap of meat. Heap of she. Heap of she. Heap.

The clock says it is one minute to ten.

Asami breathes heavily. Cannot see her face. She never turns. Never notices. Or notices but cannot be bothered. I want. But. Heap. Heap of she. Heap of grief.

I move to her in the bed and kiss the side of her head.

"Goodnight sweetheart."

Her hair smells sweet enough, today a day when she must have washed it. Or Marisa did it for her. Strawberry? Some berry.

There is no other sound in the room, only when the hand of the clock ticks over to ten. In such silence the time ticks cataclysmic.

My eyes stay open for a few moments as I stare at the ceiling – where did she go on that day? That last day. Where were any of my women that day? My women? *My!* Do you hear me? Where was I? My ears hurt. Then my lids, my heavy eyelids, over my bulging, exhausted eyes, they shut.

T ink and Tank both like to make plans. They are walking down the wet road towards their high school and they are both pondering. They are pondering – furrowed brows, pursed lips, a parody of concentration – because this is what Tink has asked them to do, and they are in no rush, because the trudge along the time-and-time-again-flooded-and-thus-pot-holed road is long and tedious. Like sentences.

Tink had been looking at images of Tinker Bell on her phone the previous night, and though the connection is no longer consistent – the images often flicker and break, as if mirroring the disintegration of their own fractured lives – she has decided that it is image enough for the day. Tinker Bell was a lively cartoon character, and Shiori remembers seeing old animated movies in her toddling years: Tinker Bell in flight trying to repair things, rallying the other fairies when there was trouble, a feisty female fairy. The skimpy light-green outfit was an added bonus of sexiness, and Shiori likes her blond hair. So today's moniker would be "Tink", in homage, cute yet piercing. And her partner? They could not think of any of the other fairy folk, so Shiori came up with "Tank", as a kind of match, and anyway, if Maki keeps eating snacks (the Snake Box's delectable treats) the way she does now, then that's how big she will become.

They'll have to go through the usual rote of tedium before they get to carry out their plans: morning assembly in their homeroom with Mr. Matsuyama, a benign but zombie-like human, forever letting his sentences trail off into nothingness: what start out declarative and promising, soon become crippled and limping, then fade completely; the girls pay little or no attention to him or his efforts. Roll calls. Roll calls. Line up. Stand correctly. Don't slouch. They have had quite enough of all this. How are they ever to endure? Plans. Forthwith.

At some stage in the day they will want mischief and they will want naughtiness (if not downright nastiness), but they will have to wait. The thing about successful criminality, they well know, is that it requires patience, patience and timing.

Their first lesson of the morning is to be Mathematics, which upsets them both. They never have the patience for the solving of equations. Tuesday is a more amenable day with PE up first, and that will certainly not fail to get Tink excited; it is only twenty-four hours away, so she will be able to see her quarry then – that is if he doesn't pass them sooner in the corridor, mulling over some piece of paper or fixing off into the middle distance with his bug-eyed stare. All this, the current mind-hatchings, she will now relay to her devoted chum.

"I thought about Tombo last night. As I lay in bed."

"The PE teacher?"

Tink is nodding solemnly. Most of the teachers have nicknames and most of those names discourteous.

"Yes. He will be the chosen one."

"Why have we chosen him?"

"Keep up."

She means with the story. She means with her pace too, because Tink's long legs naturally move faster than Tank's, and this will always be the way. Tink's school uniform skirt is hiked up to show off her thighs. Her legs are long and smooth, and she is as proud of them as she is of her firm breasts, and her eyes (colour-contacted but wide and glaring) and her lips are, she knows, commendable, too – a neat package all in all, and she would say so herself. Tank's shorter legs are hairless too, smooth, with muscular thighs, though her knobby knees are bruised from falling clumsily in PE lessons, or simply from trying to navigate the desks of the classroom, the lockers of the locker room, the general hard-thingness of the world.

As they approach the school, they pull down slightly on the hem of their skirts – there are still school rules, but these, like the rules of the nation, like the peeling cream-colored façade of the school building itself, are falling into disrepair. As the authorities, the nation's buglers, call more and more for decorum, the disaffected youth search only for distracting decadence. There would be more *bosozoku* – the loud motor-cycle gangs, the reckless tribes, revving up their engines to drown out the wolves at night – if only there was enough fuel to go around. The rude boys are kept at home, grounded, un-biked, if they haven't already been drowned.

"Tombo is the epitome of man. He is muscular. He *is* man. We need to see his body, in full, naked, his thing erect. He will set the template."

"The template for what?"

"Keep up. For our lives. If we are to find the perfect part-ner in the future, we need to know what a perfect man looks like. This is all practice."

They pass a bicycle shop. An old man pumps air into a tyre. But he is at least eighty years old, and his movements are slow and cumbersome, whatever is pushed in seems to leak back out, the tyre may never get hard at this rate.

"Tombo is not perfect. He's a little ugly."

"Yes. But only a little. Not hideously so. That will do. In fact, that's better. When I find my man in the future, he will be as strong and manly as Tombo, but better-looking, and that is how I will achieve perfection, my sexual nirvana. We must always strive and push forward. No going back."

Tank is not sure she is keeping up with the logic of the story, but nods to relay that she gets it. Her legs, too, pump hard on the ground.

They pass a man attempting to load a heavy wooden box into a van. Seeing him struggle, a woman, possibly his wife, runs to help him and together they heave the item into the back of the vehicle. Tink nods at this, impressed.

"So how are we to get him?"

"We will ensnare, we're good at that."

"Yes, but *ensnaring* Tombo will not be as easy as ensnaring Daisuke. Daisuke is an idiot."

"True. But that will be the challenge. And Daisuke isn't such an idiot, actually. It's mostly the drugs."

The girls abused their friend again the previous night in the name of research and reconnaissance.

It went like this:

Loping, shaven-headed Daisuke Karino stops to answer his phone, and through the crackling realizes that he is being summoned by those two girls in his class, summoned to the woods again. Near the girls' houses is a wood, no, less than that, a copse, and they have fiddled with him before in the middle of this craven place. He liked the feel of it the first time, even if the drugs stopped him from being the *man* he wanted to be. So he decided that yet again he would go to that copse, and this time he would please these wicked girls who wanted to be pleased so badly.

They are already waiting for him, leaning against either side of a tall, almost branchless tree. They have come here by bicycle, and they must have just arrived, for the front wheels still spin where they have flung them – Daisuke deduces all this, which means his brain is working quite well this evening, despite the pills; somehow he has overcome his daily foggy dullness and is more alert than usual.

It was a government initiative. In order to fuel the loin-fires of its males, the Authorities decided to introduce cheap energy vitamin pills that would improve stamina in all areas of life, making for an efficient, improved workforce, but more importantly would spur the lagging libido of men who were too tired after work for anything that remotely resembled coitus. The drugs were even distributed free at the beginning of the experiment, and Daisuke and a few other males in his class found them an excellent way to stay up at night and watch more 4D animated features on the WaSc or on a PHS (personal hologram show), and not be too tired the follow-ing day on the trudge to school. Free medicine. Life enhance-ment. What could go wrong?

The drugs should only have been taken once a week. They were supposed to spur not spoil.

The drugs were intended to be used sparingly, and the leaflets containing the advice about side effects were supposed to be studied and firmly adhered to.

For Daisuke Karino, it all got a bit too much. What could go wrong? He took too many. He took them at the wrong times. It was no use complaining to the authorities. It was all his own fault. His mind became scrambled. He was declared, by several senior officials in the prefectural offices, to be an utter moron. And even his pampering mother found herself inclined to agree.

"We want you again, Daisuke-kun," one of them says to him, the taller, more forceful one; he cannot remember their names.

What could go wrong?

They come to him like wolves, flashing their teeth, their tongues lolling. Daisuke knows all about the wolves that howl around the hills at midnight. Everyone knows about wolves.

These two might be something from a vampire tale, all teeth and tantalize, and Daisuke can't help but submit to their silky touches, their wicked whispers.

Soon they have him bare-chested. It is cold in the copse, but he endures. He needs to be good at this for his future. Needs to be able to satisfy females. Females have power now in the nation. There is even talk of the 14th being a woman! Imagine! Imagine that! He will let them do what they want, and when it comes to taking his turn, he will not disappoint.

Soon he is naked in this cold copse and they fondle him and they bring him to the state he needs to be in. The state they need him to be in.

"My, my," says the shorter one.

"My, my, indeed," the taller one, taking him in her mouth.

Daisuke smiles through all of this. It is about time he has had some success. The pills have made his mind mush and his grades have plunged abominably in a short space of time. It is a good thing then that he can do this correctly. Standing there tall and erect in that lonely wood. He doesn't mind if a whole crowd come now to see him perform. He is capable. He *can* do. But,

but

but,

no,

no,

no

he is becoming distracted

                    no

              no

            oh no

                              he is made sud-
denly stop, a sudden stalling, the pleasant sensations plum-
meting so quickly, so quickly is the decline before he has time
to spill. It is his damn phone ringing! It has dropped to the
leafy, mulchy ground and it is buzzing, calling his attention.

            But

      but

            but

but – this can't be happening. He sees this device at his feet. Its
screen has lit up. The picture on the phone is his mother. His
mother is calling him, calling him to come home for dinner,
to get out of the copse and away from the vampires and come
home. A young boy like this needs to eat his meat and vegetables to grow strong, for stamina. For endurance. That's what
his mother must be thinking about at the gas stove, over the
miso soup and the fish being grilled (better than those suspect
vitamin pills in her estimation: the kitchen is the key). But
he has shrunk and faded and already the girls have huffed in
disappointment – Tink has spat the surfeit of saliva from her
mouth and it hangs from a tall weed, wet and stringy – and
they are mounting their bicycles, their wetness on the saddles
unloved, unappreciated, and are making their way back to the
pink walls and the girl-faced boys, and they will probably have
to take care of their own desires themselves, in the way they
have become accustomed.

That was how it went. The night before. Sunday in the
bosky outskirts of a waning village.

But here they are now, with their itches largely unscratched.
They are nearing the school and they pull down their skirts (a

little) because they know they will get scolded when it rides up around their thighs. They are not in the mood for arguments with teachers and staff. Teachers and staff who have their eyes forever on thighs.

"Ensnare," says Tink.

"Ensnare," says Tank.

They are in tandem.

When they reach the front door of the school they put on their headsets. All students are required to wear these for most of the day. The headsets (earphones with thin slightly raised antennas from the band or crown) educate, they keep the students informed of events and procedures; they are connected to the central government agencies which will warn of earthquakes and possible tsunamis. This is the latest technology (made in their own country, still) and is essential for the survival of the people in this remote village, in any village, remote or otherwise, anywhere. But the headsets often crackle and fail, like everything else, and the leaks, the leaks from the broken plants and faltering factories, still seep, still weep, and they all, students and teachers alike, try to go about their daily business.

Tink is thinking of Tombo and what she would like him to do to her. It could be a long day, this miserable Monday, and a long year and a long life, unless she starts to get what she wants. She does not want Mathematics first, nor does she want History and Social Studies or any of the fuckery that goes with any of these soul-destroying subjects.

Tink rages and roils. Tink has a sea inside her, a hot boiling sea that ebbs and flows and tosses and throws and is rarely calm, and soon she will be in the cluttered classroom with the point of her compass sharp and tearing bits of skin off her knuckles until her edu-tablet spatters with drops of her own red hot blood.

8

CATASTROVOICE I

The mountain has no voice, but what if the mountain had a voice, what would it say? It might say:

I have been here for a long long time and you can't move me no you can't move me.

If a mountain had a tongue it might stick it out.

I bring forth destruction at a whim, for deep in my belly I have fire, molten malice that I can whip up and spew. This is what I say because I am mountain and I am the voice of catastrophe. Me and my friends, my mountain friends, we line along the spine of this land and we are in cahoots. When the plates move beneath us, they set us off, and we simply can't help ourselves. Giddy with possibility, dormant for years, half asleep, thinking of nothing but the salve of soft winds surrounding, suddenly we are alive again, mark the ash plumeful and the skies darkening above your heads. For you are just human and your matter no matter and have no true longevity, your time is almost up, your eras soon erased, and we will still be here, through it all, my line of friends and I, spine of the country, backbone, and we stand strong and are multiple and are magnificent.

Behold the devils that run amok around us: rabid unidentified burdened beasts, bush fires, gaseous lights and the wanton wolves, ever slavering in their covetousness, quick to gather, all these things, all these things terrific in their terror.

Lone pilgrims, frantic you climb up our sides and pray to your numerous Shinto gods in the hope that your nation will not be attacked yet again by some calamity. But your hope will be in vain, for I am the voice of catastrophe, and I am only one in legion, and we will stay, for that is all we know how to do – reign.

9

Sometimes so deep down into the core of your own blackness you sulkily sink that a maniacal laugh begins to emerge, a great growling guffaw at the sheer fucking injustice of the universe. How can some people be rich and have everything they ever asked for, big healthy families, big contented everything, and some ordinary good folk begin to lose what little they acquired in the first place? How do they cope? Sometimes you laugh like a loon, knowing that there's no hope anywhere, that every which way you turn is taut and you find yourself on the precipice of some tragic abyss. This is my comedy. I hope you are enjoying yourself.

I am running – look at my long legs – following the action on the pitch, eyes, all big bulging eyes, not missing a trick: insect, seeing from all angles, eyes in the back of my head.

Behind me two players are tugging at each other's shirts, the usual love, a push and a shove. When I turn and glare they quickly uncouple.

You'd think I'd be totally focused on the game. You'd think that this would hold all my attention, and it does for the most part. But my mind wanders. I can still spot a foul right away. Instinct, I suppose. It all becomes second nature after a while.

How did I get drafted into all this? Same as anything else: someone asks you to fill in, do a favour, wife having a baby, dog having a lobotomy or something, and so you go along and do it. Next thing you know it's once a month. Then every week. No escape. Sometimes I get paid a small stipend for games, travel money more than anything else. Mostly I get nothing at all. Depends on the organization I'm dealing with of course. Depends on the charity of others. I have some money to see me and Asami through. I still have some money in the bank (the bank and bankers were not washed away). The school, for all its travails, still has enough to pay me to come and teach its useless brats, to make them run and sweat and sleep well at night from over-exertion (I am a hard task-master). My parents left me money too. My dead parents. No one has use for money underwater.

It all goes by so fast. Time. Money. Like everything. Everything begins to disappear, or everything starts to get taken away from you. This is the only song I know how to sing. I know the lyrics of no other.

Foul. Blow. My whistle is shrill in the October air. I call one player over and give him an earful. *One more and it'll be a yellow card.* This is a PE class right now. These are just teenage boys and teenage girls playing soccer. The world's favourite sport. I'm trying to teach them about fairness, and to be aware that a referee is always watching them. They're not really getting it. Most of these players are not particularly good, and most are obviously uninterested, not like the after-school clubs, or the weekend enthusiasts and their ever-growing-in-evil entourages. But still, they need to learn the rules, they need to know what's right and wrong, a foul's a foul. There are lessons in life here; they should be paying more attention.

Two of the girls look at me with hard eyes. They have been doing this a lot lately: hard and horrid stares, unflinching. I do not like them much and have scolded them often. I have consulted their homeroom teacher about their various transgressions on numerous occasions. But they do not seem to learn from their mistakes, or care only to expand on their mischief. They have the look of otherworldly witches, two pairs of wrathful eyes, I'm seeing stirred cauldrons in the pupils there, evil lurking – I must watch out.

I think about Ruby, every game, every day. I think about my wife, lying where she does, a heap of grief on sweaty sheets. The doctors that come to examine her try to coax her to exercise. These erudite men with their sound advice, they have been run ragged, so many casualties over the years, casualties from disasters that keep on coming. How much can one land take? Did you not hear the guffaws from the ARCK? As if we have at last gotten our comeuppance. (We were supposed to apologise, PM 1, PM 2, then 3, apologise for things done decades ago, then the 4th, 5th too, then 6th and 7th, and all the others ignored it as well, maybe that's why they have never taken to us…

I am not political though and…)

Comeuppance.

Is that why their laughs grow abominably loud? We have been hurt. All of us. We have. We.

String us all up, then. One by one. Or send us another missile. A proper one this time, to annihilate us all. It might be a relief. Beyond it now. Beyond hurt. The tragedy a family can…

She has sores all over her body, from time spent in bed, hours with the ticking clock, and the rise and fall of the sun, day to day, breath to breath. Heap. Maybe she doesn't even notice those sores anymore, beyond those too. My wife has gone beyond. That's what it boils down to. She does shower, or fills a bath maybe once a week, bathes quietly alone, silently, only the odd water sound heard, gentle splashes, the drain's gurgle, but they reverberate through the silent, child-less house. She hardly speaks a proper word, slight snorts only, as if forever disgruntled with some incommodious ghost.

The counsellor, *one* of the counsellors, said it would even-tually pass. *She is grieving, people deal with grief in different ways.* But it's more than that. Grief needs a dead body, the cold corpse of your loved one laid out and stiff, that's what grief needs to get itself going. You need to *see* first, recognize, then you will be ready to let go. So there's the crux: she cannot. Maybe she thinks Ruby will turn up one day, slouch in the door, head for the fridge, pull out one of those little yogurts she used to eat. She loved those things. Hardly a spoonful, but she loved them. Her long legs in the door and...

Is that what you are waiting for, Asami? Ruby's smile as she opens the door, her beeline for the fridge and the lick of the yogurt top like a famished feline.

God and the astronaut! God and the astronaut! Just thought of it! A Ruby memory. Ruby was playing with her friend in our house. They had dolls, princess dolls or some-thing, little figures all dressed up in pink and purple and bountifully bejewelled. They had a running commentary going, and her friend, – Yuna, I think her name was – was saying: *Oh God above, please let me meet the prince tonight at the ball.* This was their idea of romance, innocence, sweet gos-samer dreams; they must have been about six years old at the time. Ruby creased her clean, wrinkle-free forehead and said: *Why do you say "God above", Yuna? The princesses don't need a god. There is no God anyway. You know that, don't you?* I had my ear pressed to the door, agog at the proceedings, a six-year-old philosophical debate ensuing, the highlight of my Saturday.

Yuna argued that there was a God. There *had* to be. Maybe *gods*. Plural. Why else would we go to the shrines at New Year and pray for the future? Why else would we pull on the rope and ring the hanging bell and clap hands and pray and hope? And my little rational thinker, my clever girl, countered with: *If there was a god up there, don't you think the astronauts would have seen him by now?* I had to put my hand to my mouth to stop myself laughing. Yuna looked crestfallen, the scientific approach of my six-year-old genius had worked; she could think for herself, she would be fine. The princess drama continued, and maybe the fabulous coaches would arrive pulled by elegant white horses, and they would indeed meet the handsome princes at the ball and waltz to all their wonderment. But my Ruby was greater than any princess, better than royalty, better than any god, too, or God, better than anything, Ruby was everything.

We were young parents. Ruby hadn't been planned. Our wedding was what the Americans like to rudely call *shotgun*. Ruby wasn't on the cards, was just the best kind of accident, even to twenty-year-olds who might have had other things on their minds. We could have been enjoying our youth, drinking sweet chu-hai and singing our hearts out in dimly-lit karaoke boxes, a few boisterous friends to hug and co-rejoice in titillation, days of the yet-fresh and frolicsome. Ruby came and changed all that, forced us into growing up fast, adultified us. I was still in my teacher-training days. Asami gave up her junior college studies completely and begged (shamefacedly) for the support of her parents – which she got (both sets of parents went against type, embraced the shame and supported us in every way). Of course, we thought Ruby would be around. We thought our land could withstand the terrible hands it kept being dealt. We thought our lives would take altogether different routes, we thought many things.

A mumble, that's all I get from her. She lets me kiss the side of her head before I sleep. That's the most she will allow. She is a spectre of the woman she once was. I remember Ruby (kindergarten cute) coming in to the kitchen and setting down her school washbag in the corner of the kitchen, a pink toothbrush peeping out. I remember Asami running after her playfully admonishing: *rascal, rascal, you nearly knocked me over.* She catches her and tickles her. I walk into the kitchen and Asami comes to me, looks up into my eyes, takes my chin in her hand and brings my face down to hers, kisses me straight on the lips. Ruby is watching all this, playing with the little red stone of her necklace, smiling. That was a normal day.

The game of soccer continues. Useless: all of them. Class time nearly over, thankfully. I will have a coffee break soon. I will be able to sit in the staffroom and sip at a hot cup and let it swirl in my belly and heat up my soul. The principal will call me in to his office and then talk to me, *at* me: it's Monday, and this is what he normally does on Mondays, for me only this inconvenient summons, as far as I am aware. This principal, he...

I take a look at my watch and I blow the whistle. Game over. No one looks disappointed to walk away from me and my game. Couldn't care less, any of them. And I am just as despondent.

As soon as I am deep in the bowels of the school I see them. Those two girls again. They give me the creeps. I am walking back down a corridor in the school, and they are standing there, their eyes fixed upon me. I keep walking towards them, the recently polished floor squeaking under my stiff leather shoes (I am forever changing my clothes: for PE classes, naturally, I am to be in sports gear, but for other times, especially meetings with the principal, I am expected to be in my suit). We are in that dark, un-sunlit section of the school, the stubborn stacks of trees outside casting impenetrable shade, the corridor all gloom and only a soft light comes from a flickering fluorescent overhead, so they appear as dark figures, shadows, only their eyes glinting with whatever colour contacts they loaded and inserted today. The school has tried to ban these, but they are facing a losing battle. These extra strength ARCK-made color contacts have adjustable features, and when connected to the headsets, means the students can see the class edu-screens from quite a distance, or even an incoming missile from kilometers away.

"Nemoto-sensei, is it OK if we come to talk to you later today?" says Shiori Takeyama, clearly the leader, and clearly unhinged.

These two make me nervous. I try to appear preoccupied, as if I have a lot to be dealing with and have no time to stop and chat.

"What is all this about?"

"We are both thinking of applying to join the defense forces next year and are wondering about the physical requirements and…"

"Your guidance teacher will help you out in that regard."

"Yes, but maybe a few tips about physical training, how to get that perfect body, you know…"

She wants me to eye her body, her tactics unsubtle, so obvious. So I keep my eyes on her eyes. The shorter one is grinning wildly. You could almost sense their pheromones exiting their pores.

"I really am sorry, but I have a class to go to now, maybe I will have time later…"

"But…"

Pheromones from pores like dust and debris from some

star afterbirth trying to form new lavish and livable planets before me.

"No, sorry, I…"

My words go flaccid as I scamper off, my calm not holding up for very long at all. What is it about those two? How come I can hold my nerve with every student in the school, and yet when these succubi appear before me, my nerves are wrung? What evil drive, what…

I get no time to think about any of this because I am summoned. I have to relinquish the idea of coffee and make my way to the principal's office. He knows I have at least an hour and a half before my next lesson and therefore will take his own sweet time with me. This is the type of man he is, a sweet-time-taking man; I'm sure he has a lot more annoyances up his sleeve too. The note on my desk says that I should come to his office for a "brief" chat and I sigh. I have become quite the sigher.

"Our school is a machine like no other."

He always starts his rant/diatribe/confession/lecture/"brief chat" with something stirring or rallying, utterly prepared and practiced, usually pilfered, and most often, irrelevant. As I said before, my father was a literary man who even owned physical paper books and was forever reciting Flaubert, Oe, Kundera, so I know a quote or a half-quote when I hear one. This one is on the tip of my tongue too – it'll come to me.

"Take a seat, my good man."

He seems in sprightly mood today, which is saying something, given that he is over eighty years old and looks the worse for wear. He has refused to retire. We're not sure that this is even legal, his still being here, but he is the type who has always gone out of his way to flout authority. And now, present in this crumbling place, he *is* the authority. The calls for change have been vociferous for almost a decade, as far as I remember – I started here as a twitchy twenty-two year old and they had had enough of his eccentricities even then.

"This school needs the likes of you, Nemoto-sensei. You are the future, not only of this perishing school, but of this damnable country, it is remarkable specimens like you that we need, to give hope to the cretinous youth."

This is mild stuff. He could get all super-fascisty soon. Just give him time to warm up. Flex his foolish thought-muscles.

"Oh yes, a man of might, a man of integrity. But then tell me, Nemoto-sensei, why have you not yet produced another?"

"Produced?"

It takes a moment for me to get the gist of his babble until I (startlingly) realize that he is asking me (yet again) why I have not sired more offspring. We have been through this several times before. First of all it is none of his business, but the older generation feels they have the right to all areas of family planning, and it is not surprising to hear bosses inquire about the frequency of bedroom activity, as if the government offered extra incentives to school employees that are producing more children (I think they do, actually), and secondly...

"It is of vital importance, Nemoto-sensei. If you have children, then you are exhibiting the right way to do things. And kids here need to know the right way, and to differentiate it from the right way."

"You mean the *wrong* way."

"Yes, indeed. That's what I said."

Of course you did.

He looks out the window, the only non-barred window in the school – the jumpers, you see, the jumpers – his long-rectangular face becoming suddenly serene, his eyes watery, like he is giving pronounced ponder to past glories, when the ground was stiff and solid and rarely jittered or jolted, and the volcanoes never showed off to their friends by blowing smoke circles into the air, and the irascible neighbours never started with their test missiles, test missiles that kept on being tested until they no were longer tests at all but warnings and imperious imperatives. The principal claims those islands are ours, and though the disputes continue, he becomes more steadfast in his beliefs of ownership, or right, of sovereignty. But it's not politics he's on today; it's the family, and the route to national resurrection.

I let him rattle on. I know when to stop listening. It's the usual spiel. It's barefaced effrontery, actually, and was I from any other country, I would probably tell him where to go and what to do with himself. But here, still, or just about, despite the increase of vulgar slang and the recent rampages of rage-words (and indeed rage itself, no by-product), we are supposed to respect our bosses; they are always in the right – only a week ago he made a sexist remark to my fellow PE teacher, the glorious Maya, asking of her as to how such a sumptuous woman cannot yet have the wherewithal to make a baby. No one in the staffroom raised an eyebrow to this too-loud and outrageous comment, no one tutted in reprimand; he has the twin advantages of seniority and senility – even in this moribund mess of a place, the old hierarchies persist. Maybe the new vulgar soccer supporters on those base Saturday fields are right. Maybe we should all just cry out obscenities to each other, tell each other off in the new vulgar parlance – it might be refreshing.

While he looks out the windows gathering his thoughts, I look at the walls. I gaze upon the fine wooden panels that are cleaned and dusted every day by his team of meticulous cleaners. I see the fine calligraphy works, the old pictures of the old country: misty mountains, turtles, cranes, red suns, superstitions and ideals; it all speaks of a time before, before there was war, before angst and social turmoil, when the natural world was copious and generous and industry had yet to make its presence felt. That was all a long time ago, before any of us, before this Principal Misawa even, and all that is gone now, but they are calming, these pictures, I can see why he hangs them here, I see their worth, their use. He has a sword here too, a long, gleaming blade that he often polishes in front of everyone, letting his cloth slide along in slow strokes and trying to catch the light of it in their eyes, as if he was nine years old and not nine times that. Most of them pay no heed, tired of his ostentatiousness. He puts his finger to the tip of it sometimes too, testing its sharpness, judging its potential – could it travel deep inside another human (the ARCKers he so despises)? Like everyone else in the fading villages, he is as Far Right as he can go without falling off the map (they have always been like that, the political lost, Left to Right and then back from Right to Left), and he apologises to no one.

"And oomph, there you go."

He must've been explaining the best techniques regarding successful copulation, which is pretty astonishing given that it must have been a long time since he has done anything remotely resembling the sexual act. He smiles, as if he has just presented me with the advice I sorely needed, the message I had been eagerly seeking out. Conversations with him often go like this, like those cloze tests that the foreign A.L.T. might give his class: *fill in the blanks to make sense of the passage,* but there is no *word bank* to choose from; with the principal, you must fill in the blanks as if you are on board with his train of ludicrous thought as it hurtles along on dubious tracks (he even makes me mix my metaphors, the confusion he brings upon me). I'm itching to get out of there, and am relieved when I am finally dismissed, that phantom coffee taste has been filling up my mouth.

"And one more thing."

Naturally.

"Yes. What is it?"

"I would like you to clean this sword for me. Some day the Emperor might visit, and we wouldn't want this place looking shabby. I am sure he is a man who likes a clean and shining sword. We need everything ready for him, for he is divine."

"Clean it? You want me to…"

"Oh no, not clean it. I can clean it myself. Did I say clean it?"

I have long suspected that he has begun to forget things, Alzheimer's perhaps, the words certainly don't come to him as fast as the rest of us would like.

"Do you want me to sharpen it? Is that it?"

"Yes. Good. That's it."

He has asked me to do this before, and I did. I took it to a neighbour who has whetstones and the like, machines to not only sharpen blades but indeed to repair them, rid them of rust, polish scabbards, make everything like new.

He hands it to me then, ceremoniously, the way we do everything around here. I must remember to do this job for him. At least it brings a smile to his face, the doting old codger. I must remember not just to leave it in the back of the car. Who knows what kind of damage it might do if taken into the wrong hands.

No reason to run amok. The coffee swirls in my cup, its good steam rising, its aroma filling the little kitchenette that sits neatly adjacent to the staffroom. All the teachers are busy at their desks, frowning over the ever-increasing paperwork that accumulates before them. They have fixed frowns, scalded scowls, you will rarely see a smile here, these unfortunates are stuck in their ruts, like every grim factory or office anywhere, chained in their labours, pushing for a country that is incapable of budge (the Economists' verdict: we were too slow in the search for new engaging enterprise, too conservative in our lack of drive for entrepreneurships, too slow for change or too lacklustre in seeking out alternatives), they work for families that may care or may not, that may have been obliterated or may be clinging still, it's hard to say. The only thing I notice truly about these people is that their mouths smell of toothpaste in the morning and bile by lunch.

Here's morose Matsuda, History teacher, writes lovely haiku but is painfully slow in conversation – his wife was carried away in the last and most malicious tsunami; he has little left to say to anyone, perhaps his sad three-line poems are statement enough.

Here's effervescent Nakashima, Social Studies teacher, white-haired at thirty, bubbly but trying, I steer clear of him because he likes to talk soccer, and my time is already too soccer-filled; I'd much rather someone told me about bees, or electrical engineering or the reason why Hot Jupiters are hot.

There's the foreigner, the assistant language teacher, down the back of the room, in the corner, which is probably the most suitable place for him, the dunce. He's been here years and can only speak the rudiments of our language, a klutz from Britain or Ireland or somewhere, forever complaining about what ails him, whether it is back pain or migraine, a tedious individual who should have left years ago when the Ark of foreigners was setting sail, all nations' exemplars two by two, the way they came, but faster on the flood out, fearful and trembling – that's when the goon should have gracefully left, instead he married, and his beautiful wife (kudos) is expecting. *Expecting.*

There's an odd word to use around here. Expecting what, exactly? Expecting what?

And then. Then there's Maya. My fellow PE teacher. Now. Let me take a minute to gather myself. Another sip of coffee. Ah.

Then there's Maya.

Paean or pain?

She is my delirium, she is my torture.

Maya started only a few years ago and is therefore much younger than me. I still remember the day she swayed into the school. Maya always sways or sashays or glides, she does not walk. She is like a manga superhero, otherworldly, as if human traits are beneath her. The gait is everything; the gait is what got me (gets me) going. Her eyes are small, narrow, as if always focused on something of the utmost importance. Her lips are bee-stung-full, her high haughty cheekbones severe and yet daring you to reach out and run a finger along them. Her skin is smooth and white. Her breasts are pert inside her colourful sports T-shirts, and she pushes them out as she walks (sorry: glides, sways, sashays), as if daring anyone to be half as perfectly sculpted as she; she moves like the inside of one of those antique lava lamps, all curvaceous effortless bouncings and blobbings. Her legs are neither long nor short, and when she stands next to me – if my knees are not already buckling from the lashes of lust – then she appears to be the perfect height, for me, that is. Those legs go from muscular tennis-calves up to taut full thighs and then... then there is the heavenly posterior. My head spins every time I see this either in front of me – conveniently she will be walking ahead – or anytime she is nowhere in sight at all, because I am still thinking of her, of *it*, anyway. Even, in my guilt, lying next to my silent wife, it is there in front of me, its full meatiness, its round gravity-defying fleshy thing-ness: I have dreamt about this shape, I have fondled and squeezed and kissed and ejaculated upon it in private subconscious nighttime ecstasies. It does no good to my man's mind, no good will come of any of this.

Once, in fact – maybe it was *Bonnenkai*, our end-of-the-year staff party – we ended up sitting next to each other, on the tatami floor of a private room in an *izakaya*. She spoke animatedly. I spoke nervously, trying to contain my sense of delirium. It was different from school – there, in the school storerooms, surrounded by shelves of volleyballs and badminton rackets we speak business, class strategies, test results – but here, she was asking me questions about my wife, my life. I wanted to scream: *But don't you get it? It's you! It's you!* Instead, I spent the evening nodding and grunting monosyllabically. At one stage in the evening she bent forward over the low table, to get soy sauce or some other condiment, and her breasts brushed against my raised thighs, brushed right along me, her pertness *on* me! I'm sure she hardly noticed. The episode was over in an instant. But the electricity that went through me was staggering. How would I sleep that night? How might I ever sleep again after this... corruption? I fizzled like a powerline that had been brought down in one of our typhoons, sizzling and crackling and now dangerous to the touch.

Yes, mind-amok. If the sober mind is a quaint dancer at some elegant Viennese ball from three hundred years ago, then mine is some gyrating voodoo-struck wild creature, crazed around the campfire under a blood red moon. This is the effect she has on me.

I would like to say that when first we were together in the same room, our eyes met, and that there was a yearning, a love-struck fixing upon each other, but of course there was nothing of the sort, she looked quite past me, as if I didn't exist, and still does so, except when school business means she has to address me – *we need new balls*, she says. She means tennis.

Real live breathing women torture me. But the fantasies… the fantasies help me pass my days. My father used to quote a Beckett character in that regard: "Who cares how the days pass, provided they pass" and if…

Kafka! That's who the principal was quoting. "In the Penal Colony". The name just came to me. Oddest moments.

10

The 13th says it will only get better but in his eyes you can see the lies, it will only, naturally, get a lot worse.

The 13th will not apologize for the ugliness of the four-hundred and forty Great Walls – these huge sea-defenses that were erected in the hope of stopping the waves from crashing in and carrying away all the poor folk.

The coastline already had rows and rows of concrete walls for decades, but the 12th had decided that these were not enough, not stern and resolute enough, and the 13th was inclined to agree when he took office (poisoned chalice), and so he summoned his hard-hatted crews, and they took to the shorelines with their trucks and cement.

Millions it cost.

Billions it cost, to build these 14.7-metre walls. Trillions!

But numbers have gotten to be so outrageous they no longer matter, they are ignored, numbers are no longer understood. What's more than a trillion? What's a trillion trillion? Who can count that far? No one. Who bothers to compute?

The people thought that the giant walls would protect them. They were lulled, lulled into a false sense of security as sure as the lapping water outside the walls lulled them into sepia dreams every night.

The 12th, then the 13th, said nothing would break these ugly erections; no wave could possibly be strong enough to blast through such structures, surely.

But the waves *were* strong enough and the waves *did* crash through the walls and more (millions!) were carried off on the cruel crests, their cries lost in the gurgling black torrents and furious foams.

The 13th now thinks that the walls should have been stronger and needs someone to blame – but who will take that fall? For he is not ready to step down just yet.

"Am I ready to step down?" he asks.

"Oh no no no," say the yesmen.

He has a few more ideas up his sleeve. Maybe he can fire some construction overseer, someone who works with, knows all about, and is possibly even *made of* concrete, some blueprint-inspecting incompetent, and ask him (*tell him!*) to take one for the ill-functioning team.

Take one for the team. Fall on your sword! Literally.

The country should be a fortress, not a feather!

No one listens to the 13th. What's his name again?

His name flashes up on the screen, with his age, and they seem to recall his quiff and his impenetrable eyes, his sharp suits and pernicious lies.

Yes, him, what's his name again? What number? Thirteen? Oh my, oh my!

Who is bothering to vote? Who is bothering to walk to the booths and check boxes that put these men in their positions? Just when is the next election?

The young don't vote. The young have never voted. They

sit in the homes of their parents until those parents die. And then they sit some more, un-reproducing.

Let him blame whomever he wants. Let him sack his cabinet and recruit better thinkers. It's all the same to the populace. They have been ripped apart from their morals and their cares.

One hundred years later, and still millions die. One hundred years ago it was Man. At least now they cannot blame Man solely. This time it is the earth, cold cold nature and its wanton weather. Who can point the finger at the weather? What use condemning the whims of the Earth?

The people wish they had God to give him a piece of their mind.

The people wish they had God to give them peace of mind.

What good now the Shinto shrines and the prayers and incantations to rocks, trees, rivers, and beasts? What good, any of it, what good?

Steely, he greets the camera properly attired, trying to look like a man who has no knives circling him and no fateful sword hanging by a thread over his bewildered head. Bigger and stronger walls, that's what he'll build! He will make his country safe!

The 13th says something should be done. He looks into the lens, calm, be-quiffed, while the people of his country go about the business of harvesting what still grows, wading through the paddies and examining the rice, and setting hard iron traps to keep the wolves at bay, and if they do happen to catch a snarling fiend, crazed with pain and dripping blood and rage (a wolf that is, not the Prime Minister), then they will laugh and skin it, and cook its very flesh, and they will call it a revenge.

11

The wolves eat the people and then defecate on the shoreline. The people are now excrement.

The sea washes away the shit and it breaks up into tiny floating, undulating pieces; some of these fall to the muddy bed and will settle there. It is only a matter of time, tide and time, before the bed is rocked awake again and then the surge moves forward to thrash upon the land again and the people, in the form of tiny particles of useless shit, are then brought home again.

And again.

12

The girls have had a week in school and are hatching again on a Friday night. But before they hatch again they rub their snatches again, so that they can think straight. Such grim poetry is their lives.

Weal and Woe.

Weal first satisfied Woe with her fingers, and then Woe pleased Weal (she could not properly let go, but it was enough to sate; they have enough on their plate).

Woe does not go home much, wants not to be alone much. She stays a lot in Weal's house. It's nice there. The parents don't fight all the time; instead they lounge around looking bored and such. Mr. Weal a long, drawn, forlorn look on his face, not yet jowly, but you can see he's not far off, the stubbly underchin-skin beginning its softening, readying to lag and sag; Mrs. Weal, gaunt, gamine, takes on the dimensions of the vegetables she cooks: leeks, burdock root, the sallow hue of daikon radish. They don't throw their plates at each other, and they don't say they are going to the store for something when *really* they are going *somewhere else* for *something else*.

Woe once followed her parents, Mr. and Mrs. Woe, at separate times, on separate occasions, watched them go.

Her mother went out to meet a man in a car and sat with him. It was a cold January night. Snow falling in the hardly-light. Scarves. Frosted breath on the windows. Engine running. The world looked poised. Felt like a planet to her, a planet and not a habitable place, a planet that could just lose its gravitational pull and go off hurtling into even darker space, sunless, frozen. That was how she felt looking up at the black sky, but her breath, a wet white mist, told her that she was still alive, and there was nothing she could do about it. Woe couldn't stomach it anymore. Had to leave the scene. Her feet fast, back through snow-slush and in the sliding door of home – *home!* – kicked off the shoes (didn't kick the dog, she likes the little dog. Another animal. Another actual living breathing furry creature. How have the wolves not torn it asunder?) and up the wooden stairs passed the portraits on the walls of a family of three, and in and under blankets for warmth and disappearance. She didn't get to find out just what they got up to, her mother and the mustachioed man in the car – was that a mustache or just the light casting shadow there? Just what were they up to? Could an imaginative teen like Woe have been mistaken? Had imagination gotten the better of her? It had been cold and it been dark and that engine purring.

And Woe once followed her father too. A hot July day. T-shirt and insouciance. Who? Him. Saw him saunter down the street with a woman, a woman holding an umbrella. Even though the rain had yet to start. The drops came later. A skinny foreign woman, seemed to be at least. Pale. Pale-faced. The light, too, that day. Hot and pale. No, white-hot. Heat. But Woe couldn't get close enough to be sure if she *really* was a foreign woman, didn't want to see her face, if it was prettier than her mother's, or if it was the face of a witch wound up on her land (Woe likes the idea of witches and wizardry and warlocks and wishes and wonderment). Didn't have the stomach for it. Had to leave the scene. Went to Weal's house instead of her own house and hung out there quiet as a mouse, gazing up at the giant WaSc that sometimes flickers but more often than not actually works and gives them hours of pop and insignificance.

Disappear.

Woe is looking up at the ARCK boys now. Such pristine faces. Such skin, plaster-cast white, the kind that no tragedy has befallen (and no one has yet scribbled upon), the kind that knows... knows maybe nothing at all. She likes that innocence. She wishes she could go back to a time, a few years ago only, when she *was* that innocence. It might be a good thing to know nothing. To be oblivious to everything. Just like an animal, running on instinct, with food and shelter and mating their only preoccupations. No, these ARCK boys on the screen are better. Real and yet not so. Maybe their Chinese or Korean parents don't throw plates at each other or try to stick each other with forks after another argument about the places they go to – *somewhere else* for *something else!* Once her mother raised a fork (it glimmered in the light) and brought it down on the back of Father's hand. There was a silent moment before he screamed, maybe he needed that split second to realize that it was actually happening – the wonders of brain, the Cartesian conundrums – and then he let go, a hellish holler, from the depths of his being, from the depths of even his depths. And when he pulled it out, the blood gushed and spread over the table, a fast flood of blood, and her mother fainted, though it was hard to say whether it was from the blood or the volume of the scream or the incredulity of her own depravity, and Woe shocked to her core, said to herself: *Oh woe is me, this is my family!* Maybe there are no arguments in those other places. Maybe it is only here, oh woe! Maybe everyone is too bored or too tired to argue, like in Weal's house, everyone, slothful, and cannot be bothered. What's the point? The waves will get them all soon enough anyway. There are no fights in Weal's house. Such ennui, lots and lots of it, as if inside, the family of three, have extra gravity forcing them down, keeping their heads heavy, eyes downcast, and hardly a word exchanged between them. Ennui, heavy, you could shovel it. But at least, at least they don't throw plates. Or cups. And they keep their tines to themselves.

The ARCK boys on the WaSc have been programmed. They say things to the girls that have already been written (by the girls), and the images are merely vessels of deliverance (for the girls). Look closely at the mouths and the shapes don't quite fit, the words often jarring, at odds, but let your eyes go all blurry (a little lachrymose, say), and it's amazing the effect, it's as if the boys are speaking right to you, to your very core. It's as if... they know you!

Woe is always transfixed. She knows, of course, but she is happy to let herself un-know.

"I have been in love with you for so long, Maki, I do hope that you love me too."

The girls do not program their ever-changing names, they keep to their original parent-given names, less hassle that way.

Woe smiles back at Jin. This beautiful Jin. A boy that looks like a girl and has an ever-so-sweet smile and pencil-thin eyebrows, long lashes. Woe tingles. Woe is all aglow.

"I love you too, Jin. We will meet some day. We will fall in love forever; forever we will be in love."

"Forever" is an English word that Woe likes, and she throws it into the middle of sentences in her own language as often as she can, even if it breaks the staccato rhythms of her own dialect. She knows the meaning of this word well and mouths it in front of her bathroom mirror sometimes, her front teeth flicking off her bottom lip, or in front of WaSc Jin: *forever,* pout, *forever*. She knows lots of love songs and love-saturated ballads, too, in different languages and sings them aloud to herself when her parents fight. Woe can be quite the romantic. (What were they doing in the car? Really? Was that what they were doing? Even on a cold night. In the hardly-light.)

Weal is cutting up some paper. She has been researching dragonflies and has reams of printouts that will help her understand the life cycles of dragonflies. Why are they here? Just why are they here? According to Weal's latest skew-thoughts, if she can come to an understanding as to the ways dragonflies behave, then maybe she can understand her own Tombo.

Her own Tombo.

Woe tells her that it doesn't make any sense, this research, this line of reasoning, because Tombo isn't actually a real dragonfly, it's just a nickname. But Weal holds up her scissors, brandishes them (they glimmer in the light), and Woe has to duck low and is wise to offer no more, only to her own Jin.

"Me and you, handsome boy, me and you, handsome Jin."

Weal keeps cutting sentences and paragraphs and illustrations from an array of magazines and nature photo-books the school library still held in dusty corners, and she uses them as prompts to speak aloud, for solace.

"You eat mosquitoes. Therefore you are doing us all such a good service, dearest Tombo. Ridding the world of harm. Their stabs and our consequent itchiness. You are indeed a hero."

"Someday, Jin, you and me. A little boat with you at the oars. Your muscular arms. Grab them, Jin. Grab them!"

Though she knows the ARCK boys are not so muscular, she lets herself run with the fantasy. It is Friday night after all, and everyone is deserving of a little fantasy on a Friday night, those in dull villages maybe even more so. Those in dull villages deserve medals of gold, for bravery, for the putting up, the putting up with all kinds of things that they shouldn't have to be putting up with. Maybe people in other places don't have to deal with half as much. Woe tucks into the Snake Box. The sugar melts on the tip of her tongue and she swoons. Sweet sweet sugar-swoon: the usual run of things in this pink bedroom.

"Beware of frogs and lizards. And other dragonflies too of course. Spiders and birds. Spiders and birds."

Weal grimaces, doesn't like spiders and birds, oh no, does not.

"Down on the lake, no waves, just a flat glassy lake, and you at the oars and we moving along and your biceps, my goodness, Jin, I didn't know you had such a physique."

"I have been in love with you for so long, Maki, I do hope that you love me too," says mouth-askew Jin.

Quick digital flicker, the picture breaks for a second (the oozing plant six hundred kilometers away that rattled when the earthquake yawned the land open and made them vomit, choke and die), break break, flicker flicker, oh.

The girls need to type in some new words for the boys to mouth. It gets stale. Nevertheless, when the image of Jin rights itself she is ready again, and so she continues. The fiasco. Image.

"Imago. Imago."

"Oh, Jin." Another little rub to Woe's nether-self, digital flick, the sugar makes her do this – all energy now, she's all energy now.

"Odonata. Toothed ones. Large eyes (filling most of the head), transparent many-veined membranous wings, two pairs, a long slender abdomen."

"How fast you can go, Jin! Look at you row row row your boat (Woe once had a kindergarten class where an English teacher came once a week and sang English nursery rhymes and she remembers them all! *Ba ba black sheep*)...where are you taking me now...oh, you naughty devil."

"80% of their brain, or more, is taken up with analyzing visual information. What do you see, Tombo? What do you see? And when you see it, what do you think?"

"I have been in love with you for so long, Maki, I do hope that you love me too," says Jin, alabaster white, long black lashes, such glorious contrast.

"The main purpose, the main purpose, and I read this aloud slowly to savour the words – the main purpose of the dragonfly... its sole reason for living is... to find a mate! This is its main objective... oh."

Weal swoons without any sugar whatsoever. The scissors are dangerously close to her wrists. The veins there, ever wanting; pulse pulse. The blades are always ready. The blades are ready for anything. She cuts up some more paper. Some fabric. Whatever is close to hand. She'll cut up Woe if she doesn't stop talking to that idiot on the WaSc. Or she'll take the point to his eye, gouge it out. What's his name again? Jin.

"And what if we take a little moment, under the hanging branches of the willow? And in that shade lie down and feel the boat rock gently under our backs, under our backs and bottoms."

"I have been in love with you for so long, Maki, I do hope that you love me too."

"Devil's darning needles. That's what they say, isn't it? But we know better, Tombo. We know that you are upon this earth for good, for good only. You would not sew up the mouth of children. Even one as rude in tongue as I."

"And we would rock and rock gently in that boat, and... oh Jin, you are real, so real. Your throb and thrust." Digital flicks.

"I have been in love with you for so long, Maki, I do hope that you love me too."

"Blind stingers. Water witch. Hobgoblin fly. Devil's horse. Snake killer. You are so unfairly maligned. My man, my hero."

She stops cutting because there is nothing left to cut. She could have a go at the sheets on her bed… but she will regret it later when she tries to crawl under. Her wrists are tempting. The blades are always ready, but… instead, she aims her weapon at the WaSc and flings it, as expertly as a knife-thrower at some revolving wheel in a carnival, and it hits Jin straight in the eye. Poor Jin. Poor Jin. Flickers and fails. Woe falls out of her boat, is dripping wet, lets out a sopping wail. The illusion is shattered.

13

The 13th is still in office. Just about. Murmurings in the corridors of power. The usual run. The 13th is still there though. Hanging in. He paces his office. Paces, paces.

14

Egg goes splat.

Almost empty car park, the few remaining cars pulling out, and an egg gets cracked on the windscreen.

It's Saturday again and I've been refereeing again.

You can shit all over me!

Then another one: *splat!*

The three perpetrators scamper off as I walk towards the inevitable mess. I don't know why they are in such a hurry. It's not like I could do anything about it. I am not timid. Don't get me wrong. I have muscle, and my karate skills (which I have to teach at school) are not to be sniffed at. I won a silver medal for this in the prefectural high school tournament when I was only fifteen, half my lifetime ago; I still remember my parents' unease – how were they to deal with it? They were immensely proud, naturally, of their strong boy, but how much greater their pride would have been had it been awarded for a spirited essay on Saramago, Richter, or Krasznahorkai.

I would never be so foolish as to tackle three of them, and so I watch them, almost envious of their camaraderie, but they scamper.

Before I open my rusty door I am approached by a tall,

hefty man. This is Shouta Takamoto, known as Monstaa, for not only resembling in gruff and growling voice an old character from the days of children's TV, but also because the bastard is an actual monster, i.e. terror, torture, mauling and mayhem are his stock-in-trade. It's quite clear that he is in charge of the Eggmen, and in charge of every other lost and gullible delinquent that idles around these parts, and it's also quite clear that he is coming towards me with insidious intent, and that I have no chance to get into my car and speed off.

"Not so fast now, Nemoto-sensei. Thought we'd have a little chat before you head back to your domicile."

"I'm sorry, but I have no time, I must…"

"I've been watching you for weeks now, and the decisions you are making, they leave a lot to be desired. When I'm watching from the sidelines I'm thinking: was that really a foul? Only a slight nudge there. Hardly anything at all. Do you understand what I'm saying, Nemoto-sensei?"

He's one of those people who keep using your name in order to verify your existence, keeping a tight grip on you, lest you suddenly get subsumed into whatever you happen to be leaning against, which is exactly what I am praying for (my grasp of quantum mechanics is less than rudimentary, I should pay more attention to the boring science teachers at school, could do with a helping leap here).

"There's a rule book, and we have to follow those rules, Takamoto-san, you are famil–"

"Oh, you know my name then?"

"You made yourself known to me before, a few years ago."

He has made suggestions about the "outcome" of games to me in the past, which I have always ignored – but you don't get to pass off on guys like these, they'll come back to pester you again, they'll get you sometime. They're as predictable as typhoons in September, and just as unwelcome.

Everyone knows what this man is like. A gangster, he has his filthy fingers in several pies, and when he strides the narrow paths of this (and neighboring) villages, people smile and bow and give him their gracious regards: plain fear, in other words. He's always flanked at both sides by his twin goons, and here they come now, the horrible henchmen, their walks reminiscent of every bad mobster movie you've ever seen, lacking only in the dark sunglasses, the October sun being too uncharitable. They take their places beside him and leer at me; their most frightening aspect – which I am not sure they are aware of – is their unsettling ugliness: noses too flat and expansive, nostrils too flared, untrimmed hairs sprouting there, eyebrows too bushy, lips too big, teeth too crooked; too much *too* of everything. Both of them. Double the ugliness. Diptych of dire.

"I have an unfortunate and wholly unjustified reputation around these parts. But don't let the rumours fool you, Nemoto-sensei. I'm just a businessman, and like yourself, I have to make a lot of decisions, sometimes snap decisions. It's about time we did some business though? Properly this time. I mean, I've left you alone for so long, because you were doing such a good job. But I'm not so sure your head is in the game anymore. The decisions are just a little... wayward, for my liking."

He picks up a twig from the ground and breaks it in two.

"You understand what I mean by *snap*, don't you?"

I say nothing, just reach out to the door handle of my car, keen to get the albumen off the glass, keen to get back home to the troubles that await me there.

"Am I wasting your time, is that it? Somewhere to be? Home to your bedbound wife, or is it the slutty sister-in-law?"

My head suddenly reels, like he has opened my skull, dipped his hands inside my head and given my brain a brutal squeeze.

"Oh, I do my research all right. Very thorough. You have to be very thorough these days. You have to be prepared, don't you? Know your nosey neighbours, know your enemies. Times are tough. You need to know where your next bowl of rice is coming from. Am I right, Nemoto-sensei?"

"What is it you want?"

His henchmen, not liking the fresh tone in my voice, sidle up to me, their height and bulk a warning. One of them has terrible breath, it stinks, or maybe it's both of them, Fetid and Foul.

"I just thought a few decisions could go our way. You understand? There's a game next Sunday, away from home. And they tell me you will be the man in the middle again. The man in black. Very popular you are. So I was thinking that if I gave you a little something to tide you over, then you might be more considerate and have a few more decisions go our way. As simple as that. Red versus Blue, isn't it, next week? And you know which side I'm on."

"Red."

Fires of hell red. Satanic red. Evil incarnate red.

"Correct. You're not so in the dark at all, are you, Nemoto-sensei? All the referees take a little something every now and again, don't they? That's the way the world works. And who can blame them? Stressful job it is. Very stressful indeed. But a little gift never hurt anyone, did it? Helps with the doctors' bills. Helps if you want to take a little holiday, away from it all. You could... you could take her away from all this. Away from this depressing village. Traps you, doesn't it? The small life. Always you feel you want to break out, tear down the walls and emerge on the other side, a free man. Your father was the same, wasn't he? Very intellectual man, very clever, thought he was better than the rest of us. He was only a few years older than me. But he never made it, did he? His papers unread; his books unpublished. So sad. Really, isn't it? So sad. Ambition thwarted."

How does he know all this? I avoid his eyes and stare only at the ground, but I find no answers there.

"Or... wait... now that I think of it... you could, just you and your sister-in-law, head off to some nice quiet place, give her some tender attention on a little holiday island somewhere remote. Away from this dark village to a place of light. Light. Imagine that, Nemoto-sensei. Although, she'd talk your ear off, wouldn't she, she'd drive you crazy, when all you want to do is throw her down and rape her the way she really wants."

His henchmen think this is hilarious and laugh. *Rape*, one of them repeats, apparently finding the word or concept a hoot.

My head still reels. My balls have become constricted. I feel like throwing up.

"Take a little break, you need it."

"I look after my wife. I need no holiday."

"Perhaps you misunderstand. This really isn't an offer. You'll get the money for your troubles when a few more decisions go red, and not blue.

Gambling is another thing, another thing we have tried around here and have gotten to like (we have moved beyond pachinko), even on amateur football games, the crooks will put their money down on anything; someone somewhere is always running a book these days – we never used to be like this, we were careful, cautious in all our private doings. What happened?

"And, if this business transaction we have going on here *isn't* carried out, well, do you see the way I broke this twig in two?"

He begins to poke me in the ribs with half the twig, then the other half. Both hands jutting out at me. It's surprisingly painful, I'm too stiff to protect myself, must be the fear factor. My father once explained to me the concept of fear. He outlined how organized religions all over the world had implemented this notion, and governments were no different in their systematic use and abuse; it was fear that kept people down and obedient, subservient – the mighty in this world still use it as their main tool.

"You get it, don't you? You understand, don't you? No wonder they gave you license to become a referee. So smart you are. So smart."

He takes out a cigarette and lights it, inhales deeply and blows a steady stream directly in my face.

"Don't worry; I'll have a few words with the egg boys. There'll be no more trips to the car wash for you. Your windscreen will be clean as a whistle from now on. No more omelets. Might even get those little bastards to clean it for you themselves. I have a lot of – how shall I put it? – *sway*, that's it, a lot of *sway* around here, you know. I usually get my way."

The Neanderthals nod. And are smiling. Still considering rape, or they are looking forward to my torture. Or somehow in their rank heads they are combining both.

"I'll be going now. And we can all enjoy the match next week."

I watch them walk away, fear changing to resentment inside me.

I take the rag to the car, but the albumen is getting harder and harder to clean off with each week, the glass seems to get more and more smeared and less easy to see out of; it is a tiring job, and I feel like I should sigh. But I'm not sure I have energy enough even for that. My little life.

15

Marisa Hirai is pushing a supermarket trolley around the aisles. She hums as she moves, stopping intermittently to look at items on the shelves. There used to be so much more on the shelves, and so much more in the line of quality too. She remembers the store itself underwater, the screen images of water cascading in, filling the place right up, halfway to the ceiling, loaves of bread floating on top of it, bobbing like buoys, packets of cookies, cakes, bottles of soda, beer cans, potato chips, various fruits and vegetables, lemons and leeks sailing by, apples floating along like it was some western Halloween game, but no one bobbing for them, everyone instead heading to the hills in search of a dry place.

Marisa, too, had headed for the hills that last terrible tsunami, had had some vision of it – was that it? Was that what it was? A vision? Some instinct she had? She had been in her own house that afternoon, not looking after her sister, and she had felt something, not only under her feet, but deep inside her, a premonition? Or was it that she just fled when she saw others outside her windows stampeding past, and followed, followed others, like she had always done, when she could have been more decisive in her life, more forthright and forward, but just followed the mounting hysteria. The rumble came first, the ground hungry again and ready to open up and take whatever sacrifice was on offer. Is that the way it goes? Please the gods, give them fresh bodies every few months. Appease with virgin blood? What gods? Marisa is the type of woman who kneels at her family altar and offers food and alcohol to her dead ancestors. She lights sticks of incense. She claps her hands together and prays to those looking down on her, watching out for her and she misses her niece as much as anyone, misses that good bright girl. Gods in the rocks, gods in the leaves, gods in the barks, gods in the shadows of light and dark she'll light incense for them all. She is faithful, or is it fanciful? She believes in ghosts, phantoms, spirits, wraiths, poltergeists, everything she can't see. She is deep. Or is that gullible? What she has trouble believing is what she *does* actually see: the waves, the waves in angry ascents, the lopes of lupine packs past the doors at night with dark intent, spied from the top window, the smells of shameless wet fur and the iron tang of blood in the air that sits on the tip of her own tongue as if she too craves for the life force – the more she sees about her, the more she feels torment within.

But the supermarket calms her. The rows of neatly ordered shelves make her tranquil. Only certain things in life calm her now: her sister when she is safe and deep in untroubled sleep; the gentle furrows on Tomohiro's brow when he is mired in thought; sweet music she plays on the old upright piano in her living room – how did that survive? How come the gods left that one dry and alone? The keys and wires still do what's required, it needs tuning, but doesn't everything. And the rows and rows of goods, there for perusal, there for consumption, rows and rows of order, neatly stacked. Her people used to love to shop, to take out their heavy purses and fill shopping bags with the latest brands, the latest gadgets, the latest's latest. She gazes at the aisles, half empty, but the goods that are there, what have managed to come out of the manufacturer's hands and into this retail store, remain neatly stacked.

How cruel the prospect of order revoked. How cruel the waves that came crashing through everything, deposing the land's natural good with demonic depositions ensuring nothing proper grows close here or hereabouts. Nothing but the brackish breath of the winds. Winds howling around, like the wolves.

The 13th said on a broadcast that something should be done about the saline deposits and implored the scientists to find solutions as to how to make the land fertile. The 13th waits. Fertile. The 13th waits and paces his office and waits. Not febrile. The 13th has his work cut out for him.

The trolley Marisa pushes has a bad wheel, it takes some shoving. But it will do. She will get the job done. Marisa Hirai is a persistent woman, and unafraid of a challenge. She pulled many live bodies from the smothering muds and floods up to the rooftops, the old and the weary, the hunched and lame, indiscriminate she nearly flung them – such was her strength, using all her muscle and might, just to get them to where they could breathe and keep their lives. She shrugged off the praise, just did what anyone would do, it's the way she was raised.

Mrs. Izumi Shiroto (once wealthy, once important, and once a fellow attendee of free cooking classes at the high school) spots her and quickly tries to duck out of the way, but Marisa has already seen her and is delighted for a chance to catch up.

"Shiroto-san! How are you?"

The trolleys are nose to nose, as yet gapingly empty, almost animated in anticipation. Izumi Shiroto taps on the handle, already keen to leave.

"I don't know how long it's been but you're looking good,

Shiroto-san. Those evening classes – maybe that was the last time. How many years ago was that? All well?"

"Very good. And you?"

"Oh, you know, doing my best. Still looking after my sister, you know how these things are. She's still in a state, the poor thing. Two years now, since, since, well, you know, and she still can't get out of the bed. An awful pity, the poor thing. But she's lucky to have me around. I don't mean *me*, I mean just *someone*, someone to have to look after her, you know. Nurses are so expensive, and there's not anything *officially* wrong…with her, anyway you know, you know how it is, nervous breakdown, I suppose that's what it is. Anyway, I'm there with her every day, so that helps. Nemoto-sensei, keeps on working and staying positive, and keeps refereeing the games too, great with the kids."

Mrs. Shiroto is nodding and fidgeting, her fingers faster on the handle, but Marisa continues her chat-barrage.

"But we carry on, don't we, we just do our best. He's a fine man. Doesn't deserve all that pain and suffering. Who does? He's lucky to have me, a helping hand I mean, since, well, you know…"

Shiroto is smiling and enjoying the blush that spreads across Marisa's face. Marisa talks herself into horrible holes and often cannot climb back out again. She should learn to be more discerning, or just plain quiet, maybe she could learn a little something from her silent sister.

"He's rock solid, doesn't get flustered, he just tries to get on with life as best he can. And isn't that all we can do, you know, when…"

Mrs. Shiroto seems surprised at the opportunity to get a word in and quickly spits it out.

"Oh yes, that's all."

"Jobs aren't easy to come by these days. That's what I

always tell him. You are lucky to be in a good school and are able to make a decent wage, that's what I always say to him. And I'm there every day. I give him his dinner. Did you know that? I have a nice dinner on the table for him every day. He deserves that."

Marisa laughs at her own words, her cheeks redder now. She shouldn't be going on at length about her brother-in-law.

Izumi Shiroto doesn't see the humour in any of this and begins to angle her trolley away, aiming for the packets of dried seaweed further on down the aisle.

"They need us though, those men, don't you think? Don't you think they do? A woman in the house I mean, keep the place in good order. How's your husband? Is he well? You were the envy of the village when you got him."

Marisa is thinking of Satoshi Shiroto, who was indeed a handsome classmate when they all sat stiffly at their wooden desks: broad-shuddered and thick-set with soft, bouncy hair and a surprisingly shy smile.

Mrs. Shiroto continues to steer slowly away.

"It's really time I should be going, Hirai-san."

"Better get the goods home, or there'll be no meal at all ready for him, and we couldn't have that. Of course not. Well, it was nice talking to you. I'm sure I'll see you again sometime soon. I doubt those evenings classes will ever start up again."

"Yes. I mean, no, you're probably right. They probably won't. And yes... well... goodbye."

Marisa is left staring at the shelves. She knows she talks too much. Her sister doesn't respond, so she's left alone to fill the void, her own voice drifting, sounding aimlessly, it's only function in filling the strained silence. She quickly reaches up and puts a box of tea bags into her trolley.

Tea bags. Such a simple item. Such a simple idea. If only everything could be so simple and useful. That's what she is herself: simple and useful. There are worse things. There are evidently worse things she could be. She likes those tea bags. So what if she talks too much. A good brew. Nemoto-sensei likes her anyway, enjoys her dinners. Actually she'll get two boxes, one for emergencies. It's a good brand. Good taste, that tea. She likes it strong herself. Such a simple idea. She is useful.

As Marisa leaves the supermarket she notices two young men standing outside. They stand idly and stare in her direction. It is as if they have no place to go, no place to be, and here, outside this supermarket, is as good as any place to mope, to while away. Marisa pauses for a minute, and then, bravely, decides that she will just walk straight pass them, holding her head high. It would be so easy to turn back inside and take the rear exit – is their idleness that threatening? Then she could walk all the way back around to her car, that way she would avoid the glare of these two youths – is that what they are, youths? But she decides to be bold. Why the hell not? She was once woman enough to turn the heads of gazing and lecherous men, was once the perennial subject of winks and nudges. She is still only thirty-five years old, and thirty-five years old is not old in this day and age, not this century – but women have aged around here, once-smooth faces have wrinkled with rage and perplexity, the onslaught of weather, and the configuring of how to deal with its continuous encumbrances has seen to all that.

The two young men watch her as she passes, her nose in the air, her neck stretching to stand long and noble. (Always proud of that neck, its fine form, the way men ached to kiss it, and the way it held strong when arms clung around it and she pulled them to safety).

One of them, the taller, skinnier of the two, hair dyed a colour that is alarm-red, achtung-red, a long feathery earring hanging from one lobe, nudges the other in the arm. Marisa feels herself being watched and smiles to herself. *See*, she tells herself, *I still have it. I can still make things happen.*

Feather–earring, wanting to be heard, breaks the silence of the moment to speak suddenly and with volume to his partner:

"You would take that, wouldn't you?"

The second young man tries to speak softly but ends up being just as loud.

"No way. Well past her sell-by-date."

Marisa's smirk quickly dies and her features fall to furrows. She hurriedly fills the boot of her car with the shopping bags, almost letting her purchase drop, but managing, just managing, to keep it all together. She is relieved to be cocooned inside her automatic vehicle and to bark instructions to the dashboard, filling it with memorized codes and orders to steer her swiftly away from the scene.

Izumi Shiroto is also filling her car, and as Marisa drives by, she waves to her. But Marisa doesn't respond. Instead she implores the control system to play loud rock music, to drown out her twitchy, testy thoughts. She is concerned with getting out of this parking area and getting on the road to home. Only that. That is all she wants now. Though not *home*. Tombo's house, she means. (Her sister's house, too, of course.) Not home. Not her own empty house. Useful and simple. A good idea. Really? Is she? Is she really of any use? Buying teabags. Is that all she is good for? Is that all? They clung to her neck, old frail women, tiny children, a dog, she remembers a dog in her arms at one stage, and she lifted them all up. She is good. She found a dry place. A high dry place. She is a good woman. Who cares if no one wants to kiss her neck anymore. Everyone ages. Even Satoshi Shiroto must have aged. His shy smile must now have creases at the edges of his mouth, he can't stay young – you can't stay young forever! But she is good. She is decent. Forget those idiots. Just because they no longer have motorcycles to rev at night and annoy the good honest folk, that doesn't give them the right to loll around and upset the people of the village. Like her. She *is* the good honest folk of the village. She asks the music to... no, she *demands* that the music go one decibel louder.

16

CATASTROVOICE 2

M-m-mud slides. M-m-m-mud slides slowly down the sides of the hills ever nearing and nearing still, mmmud slides over houses over people over the very air they need until it engulfs and nothing is but mud is.

The mud has no voice, but what if the mud had a voice, what would it say? It might say:

I have been biding my time, waiting, for I am mass wasting and ooze and flow and will overthrow and nothing can halt me for I know only motion, down down and am about to get you.

I am rainfall, snowmelt, ooze and ooze, I am erosive corrosive and sour in my deed, I am channel scour.

I will take your men and your women and your houses and your pets. I will take your fishermen, your drivers, your teachers and I'll get: your babies, your teens, your brides and your screams.

Your tears will make me stronger: I start out slow enough but with motion I get longer.

I will take. I will take. I will take your fucking breath away.

You do not know when I will come. You do not know how long I'll run. I am one of many, as you are well aware.

Mmmud and water and rock and mad debris, from anything
I'll make my way and move towards and take your right to be.
From scarp to shelf to toe I am near and nearing still.
Near and nearing still.
Till nothing is but mud is.

17

Marisa pulls up in her car, gets out slowly, no spring in her step, laden. I am already there and opening the front door for her, chivalric, if only for this brief time. I can see she is distressed about something: her easy-to-read face.

She smiles at me as she passes, but it is a weak attempt, you can see that she is burdened more with life than with shopping bags. Maybe I have spent too much of my private time adoring her body, subjecting her to my lustful stares; I forget that she is a person and has feelings and not there just to help around the house and arouse its hapless owner; she's not an object, is human and she wanes, I forget sometimes to look at her face, and look at the lines and creases that reveal her every emotion. I am not a decent man.

I reach out to take some of the bags off her and our fingers get intertwined awkwardly on the biting handles – a cynical mind might think I had planned it that way, but not even one as lowly…

I have suddenly become very sorry for her, too sorry to want to touch. Something has happened to her for sure. You can see it in the dimming of her eyes. But what can happen on the way to and from the supermarket? In that short space of time, what could possibly have gone down?

I will not ask. If I were to guess, I would say it's because she talks too much. She rattles on so much that she is bound to say the wrong thing to a wrong someone every now and again, the law of verbiages; she must have upset a sulky someone. But who? Should I ask? Or should I let her be? Take myself out and away to one of my other objects of desire, where things might be more straightforward. (Why so many objects of desire? Is that the question? Why never content? Is it that I feel owed? If one's daughter is taken away, doesn't that then give you the right to steal, or covet first, to then steal, to become an actual thief?

Why?

Is it?

If?

Become.)

The small wallscreen is on in the corner of the kitchen and a drama plays. Marisa tries to keep an eye on it as she busies herself with her chores. She spends more time here now than at her own house. Of course, she doesn't sleep here. She sleeps alone (I presume) at home (I presume).

I can't stand these afternoon dramas. They are far too unrealistic, the ersatz emotions of the actors, the tawdry sets, the gimcrack feel of the whole endeavour. Their emotions are foreign to me: shouts and tears and terrific tantrums and hugs and romantic lunacy: I never see it on the streets, only on the screens. The truth of the streets is a far danker affair, far messier and ever-inchoate, cries and tears for sure, but truer, more honest, all for the real flagging souls that get spirited away. When I do bother to call something on the bigger WaSc in the living room, it is usually a comedy. I want to hear people telling me jokes, I want to let go in rippling convulsions, abandon to the kind of spastic joy that overtakes the body and being, like when a really fine comedian takes you further and further; making your stomach sore and eyes water; it is a rare joy.

Rarejoy.

Joyrare.

I eat what she quickly prepares. I keep eating, my eyes following her as she moves around the kitchen. The sympathy I had for her a half-hour ago has quickly evaporated, I am all animal again – I think suddenly of that raccoon dog, as if he is there nodding at me, or even winking, naturally knowing.

My eyes follow her tight skirt, her thick thighs and buttocks.

I watch her. We have been here before.

Does she know that I watch her? Do women know when we have our eyes upon them? Our focused, one-track mind through two intent, unwavering eyes.

I tell myself I will stop this objectifying, my inevitable pulse and delirium, but I don't… because right now I can't.

She may be all that I have left in this world. She is at least here, and is vital. But she is not mine. I have no hold on her. I have no right to…

She glances over at me and we lock eyes for a split second, and then she hurriedly goes about her business again. This is the usual run of things around here.

Maybe she hears me. Maybe she is attuned. Even when I don't speak aloud, perhaps she hears my silent screams. I'm clearly hoping that she is screaming too.

A dark-coloured van turning a corner. In the interior of the van the driver's slim fingers (he is surprisingly thin and weak-looking) drumming on the steering wheel. The man hums, a jolly tune, like from a musical (remember them? Songs and dancing! So much cavorting. Where did they go?). We do not see his face. He stops and opens the door and in steps my daughter, and he whisks her away; off he goes with her to some secluded spot, maybe further south where it is hotter, where bright fruit weigh down the branches. She might still be alive. (She isn't.)

Sometimes I dream that she is still swimming. That she didn't get pulled under at all but has managed to keep afloat, after all this time, afloat, and is coming home. (Is she?)

Everything in such a hurry. Look at her. Look at her go. I watch her move. I watch her every move. She has suds flying from the kitchen sink again. Such vivacity.

I bring my plates over to her and plonk them into the sink, then I pick up a tea towel and start to dry the glasses, the cutlery, the few things we have bothered to use.

"Leave them. I can do it. That's why I'm here."

Why? Why are you here, really, Marisa? For your sister? For your sins? What sins?

"You are not our servant, nor are you a maid or an employee. You are family."

Marisa stops, her hands in the suds, and stares out the kitchen window. We see each other in the reflection (the night grows in on us, daylight outside making rapid retreat) as if we are afraid to turn and face each other, our real faces. We stay silent for a few seconds, gathering our thoughts, trying to tame their flurries.

"You are quiet tonight," I say. "It's not like you."

She doesn't reply. She just keeps her hands busy, her eyes on the bubbles, the grease sliding off the plates.

"I can stay over any night you know..."

She lets her sentence suspend. I'm not sure I know what to do with it.

A small bubble lifts from the washing-up liquid bottle when she squirts, and it takes off into the air. I watch its tiny revolving rainbow floating up and up. I want to think about it. I want to allow myself time to think about that bubble, to think of multiverses, to think of the dark matter and dark energies the physicists almost have a hold on, can almost ascertain, think of the leaps that they now say are imminent... imminently possible. But I don't. I have no time to think on these things. I am bound here, with my bad faith, my inauthenticity and my kitchen. No time to think about the essence of things.

"There's no need," I say.

"You know what I mean, don't you?"

We continue to stare ahead. Darkness outside, but not yet pitch.

The bubble must have exploded somewhere. Another galaxy gone.

"She's always upstairs."

She pauses and takes off a glove to itch her nose.

"Down here. Us. Both of us, I mean. Maybe... the living room."

I think...

What do I think?

The living room. The living. Room of living. Room where people do things. Where they live. People. But aren't the living just "a species of the dead?" Who said that? At my age, nothing but echoes. At my age! But I'm young! Or at least I am not old. My father's flashing quotes from his old screens; the people he deified: Nietzsche (yes, that last one was him), Sartre. Who else read them around here? No one. No one cared. No one cares. What good would any of it have done them? What point philosophy, what point filling your head with any useless story? What point to it all? None. None at all. They were right. We know how it ends. The girl vanishes.

She doesn't return. This is not the ending anyone wants. But it must be. Mustn't it? It must be. What good any…

I continue to dry, but it's the same bowl over and over, my hands are moving slower. The bowl is dry enough. How many times do you need to circle the bowl? Why do I go walking at night? Time seems to be slowing down but the darkness outside is speeding up; this is an unsteady mind, this mind I've been lumbered with, what luck, an unsteady mind on this unsteadiest of lands.

"You are still a handsome man. Everyone has little secrets… everyone can hide things."

I nod, and still I do not look at her. I look at everything, everything but her. I look at the ceiling, the floor, the walls of the house, the scratches on surfaces, the grain, the many watermarks.

It is her turn to sigh, and it is big. She wipes her hands on the towel and leaves me there alone, in my kitchen – there's the sink and there's the refrigerator and there are the drawers with spoons and knives and forks and chopsticks and there are plates and cups and dishes over there and what use have I for all these things, these solid items that surround, what relation to them have I, here in my…

But they are ordered. Everything in their right place. Stacked and neat and aligned, the crockery.

Wolves howl outside, as if in mockery.

19

(I did nothing. If it was a proposition – was it? – I did nothing. I don't know why. Not now I don't. Perhaps the answers will come to me. Off to the night then, and outside. Off.)

At night I ramble. At night I roam. Alone alone. The streets I comb. Some things you can have. And other things you can't. Some things you can take. Others things are taken from you.

These are my steps, one two, one two, one foot in front of the other, and always on.

And on.

Lovelessness loneliness.

Is lovelessness loneliness, is loneliness lovelessness? This conundrum as I pound on, one step two step and on and on.

I don't know the rules of the world. I only know the rules of the game of soccer. I only know what happens on the pitch. A short timeframe. That's all I can manage. Ninety minutes of…I almost said *concentration*. Then everything else is chaos. Everything else is a confusing mess, so I step slowly, one two, and I try to see it through, and always on, and always on.

I chant as I go: *adhaesit pavimento animea me;* I've

forgotten what this means, or where I read it, what language it is even; must surely have been from Dante, and Dante took it from somewhere else, it can't be Italian; that's the way with those artists, forever pilfering. My father would be so proud, my head full of the ripples of others; words, that's the way he was, as if others could somehow offer inspiration. I used to read, for a short time I took in all those words – have I said all this before? Sometimes I think there is no point to any of it, and sometimes…

My mother would kiss my brow. She was affectionate, more so than the people of our land usually allow. She used to do that, kiss me, right in the middle of my forehead. Nobody kisses me now.

My raccoon dog often rummages here. He tries to climb into the bins. He is full of industry. He will take whatever he can get. *My!* Did you hear that? *My* raccoon dog! Ownership! There's no sign of him tonight. *Him?* Is it even a "he"? Maybe it's a female raccoon dog, out to forage for her whimpering young ones? Their mouths open, their begging cries. That would seem more… heroic, wouldn't it? But no, he has *he* written all over. The same yearning eyes as me, lost. Longing and lounging and looking a little lost.

I walk on.

From out of one of the (last) seedy bars a man is suddenly and violently ejected. Two burly security men fling out this short, stubby salaryman onto the cold cracked asphalt. He lands on the street with a thump. None of this surprises me in the slightest. I've seen this happen to the same guy on several occasions, from the same bar even, the same bouncers too if I'm not mistaken – I wonder why they keep letting him in. Perhaps he is good enough until his money runs dry – it is one of the only things that runs dry around here, everything else is a sopping, drowned wet. Who knows the crime of Mr.

Stubby Salaryman? He never seems to mind, almost seems to enjoy being hurled – has he lost everything too? – or maybe he's used to it, prepared even for the hard landing, like a pro-wrestler from the olden days, or a stuntman. You can get used to all kinds of things.

The man just sits there, blind drunk, muttering away to himself, he seems quite contented there, in his decrepitude, and then, as expected, from around the corner, a tall, thin woman arrives, with what must be a ten or eleven-year-old boy, push-ing a wheelbarrow, one of those heavy industrial ones, used I'm pretty sure, for the making of those ugly sea walls.

They somehow manage to load him into it, and he sits inside it, cradled, and smiling, his taxi home, his chariot. (It could be from Picasso's Blue Period, my mother would have said, something sombre about the whole thing, but utterly human in its bleak comedy. I did pay attention to her; everything she said, maybe it was she who taught me how to see.)

The woman holds the thick handles of the barrow and begins to push. For all her emaciation she seems full of vigour, as if nothing could get in her way – I'm sure she was fast out of the way of the waves, or maybe she commanded them to stop, and they obeyed, as if she was some Greek goddess who had such supernatural command. As if...

The boy walks alongside, holding up his father's limp hand as it hangs over the rim, careful not to let the knuckles scrape along the ground. He shows no sign of despair, this boy, he knows the ways of the barrow, of his father, of the world, old before his time, you can see it in the dark shadows under his eyes, already he has seen way too much of what goes on. Only here, now, only here, now, all this, what we are faced with: this is the level of desolation. It is very funny though, quite the scene, a lot of despair unreservedly comedic that way. They afford me a chuckle, and too, I am envious that they are together.

Imagine being thrown out of an establishment and having to lie (and die) on the pavement alone: it is at least something to be wheeled away by your loved ones in an industrial wheelbarrow. If it were me there, cradled in its grey concave, who do you see pushing it?

The things you encounter on your way. And then there's more. There's always more. You never have to look too far. Around every corner, some other small scene playing itself out. It was never a big village to begin with, but there was always enough going on, should you be in a mood to see something happen. There is still one or two who make it out and make it entertaining. The minutiae: you must look closely, startling what you'll come across, the fish that landed on a roof say, flung from a wave, out of its element, gruesomely gasping, its unblinking eyes unavoidable, and how it slid down and landed slap on a passerby's bald pate, or else some great crane trained its eye upon it and came swooping like a crazed pterodactyl – such monstrosities, as if mere bird is not enough, and the tangibility of the unfortunate baldness – maybe that's why I walk at night: the sheer volume of entertainment, even in a largely empty space.

My father and mother encouraged creativity in me from an early age. Every book and crayon and pen and pencil you could have hoped for. And I used them. Every shade and hue. Paint too. Used them all up. And then came the sports, fostered in elementary school, the joy of physicality, bodies bumping against other bodies, or the speed of the baseball you had to anticipate. This was far more exciting than my father's quotes and inapplicable aphorisms, my mother's pigments and palettes and plaster casts – I took to the fields, the pitches, the gymnasium, from crash mat to basketball net, and my body excelled. I gave no real thought to my mind, if that doesn't sound like antinomy. I had betrayed my parents in a way I suppose, and the guilt still stings, but they never objected to anything I wanted to do. Perhaps they were happy enough that I was able to express myself, whatever the medium, and this I believe to be their true glory, indeed all parents, the letting the child become his or herself, nurture rather than stricture – I'm wondering, if I had had a brother or sister, would they also have been allowed to flourish so freely. Most probably.

I turn down a dark lane and see a youth with a spray can working on a wall. He wears a balaclava and those combat fatigues that never seem to go out of fashion. He works with terrific urgency. I don't know why he hides himself like this, the secrecy, the cloak and dagger nature of his every gesture, it's not like anyone cares, if anything, his graffiti livens the place up.

I stand watching him, as so often I do (and I know my mother would have done the same, fascinated by the creative urge). He turns abruptly, ready to bid a hasty retreat, but when he realizes it's only me he relaxes, and casually nods, then continues again his deft spraying. We have become acquainted, he can trust me; I've been watching him and his movements for some time; I feel an affection for the artist in his endeavor – yes, Mother, yes, I'm still thinking of you. Actually, one of the first times I ever recognized my mother as an artist was when we were walking to kindergarten and I got a nosebleed. They'd often come for no reason, these nasal drips and gushes. It didn't have to be the whack of a football or the wayward elbow of a runner in the playground. Sometimes even the slightest touch to the bridge of my nose would set it off: a sure, steady stream, a shock of red, especially vivid if it was on one of those cold, crisp autumn days, the grey sky a stark contrast to the splash of astonishing red – who'd have thought that even inside the blandest of us we'd have a colour so expressionistic? Back then it seemed I only had to think of a trauma and the flow would start, first a drop, then a succession of drips, then soon enough a red splotch on the ground that Francis Bacon might have happily seques-tered for one of his visceral pieces. Once too, walking with my mother, a dead crow lay before our feet just outside the nursery school gates, its innards no longer in, but spilling gro-tesquely out, with maggots there feeding (Bacon-ish again). My nose started, predictably enough, the familiar plip plop, and the blood mingling with the black feathers and purple goo of the dead beast only added to the carrion – the maggots must've been pleased with the lashing of fresh sauce; I think I saw them wriggling even more, delighted with their bounty. My capillaries – or are they veins? – were finally cauterized, but still, years after all that, even as a teenager, and maybe yet, I associated nosebleeds with crows and ravens, never needed my father's favourite Poe to summon gothic terror. Even in their black hundreds, their murder, as they flocked home to roost in the fading sky, my blood would stir as if in auger, expecting weird portent. I was an imaginative boy for sure, a dreamy adult too, but crows, crows, they are all around us all the time, have learned our ways and are wise to us, maybe closer to us than we would like to think. I remember an expert once on some programme illustrating their wiles, how they can take unopened nuts, hard chestnuts say, to motorways, drop them under the wheels of passing cars to crack them open, then sweep down when the coast is clear. Clever cor-vids: the humans doing the work for them. There was even footage of them making tools out of twigs to pull food out of containers, the kind of intelligence that only monkeys or chimpanzees display. Maybe we have ignored crows for too long, and they are evolving a lot faster than anything else. I say all this now because I can see one perched on a high wire overhead. And there was one also, a big black brute, that evening when those two girls in school were tormenting me about their future – what future? – just outside the window, on the branch of a lopsided tree. Portentous surely, these black signifiers, too high and fast to be gotten at by the wolves, and too clever by far.

"Still a long way to go."

The graffiti youth turns from his artistry, nods to me, then resumes his speedy spraying.

I leave him at it, pleased by his enterprise, wishing that he'd spray more of the village buildings, beautify the dull greys with pinks and luminous greens, have the place pop-bright and cheery, give the illusion that there is hope among the ruins; I walk away.

As I pound the path I begin to think about an old man that used to live near us, right across from my childhood house actually, parallel. He was a nice old man, Mr. Fujibayashi, had lived in America for some time, he claimed, which added to his appeal: it was as if he had been places, seen things. He was retired when I was still a child; if I was ten then he must have been about seventy. He cut hair occasionally, kids' hair mostly, as favours to the mothers, and he was good at it, good because he was accurate with his shears and could talk on any subject, the real test of a good barber, it didn't matter if the kid in the chair was wittering on about 3DS games or action heroes, Mr. Fujibayashi could accommodate. Which war he had served in none of us children ever really knew, just that there had been a conflict with guns and tanks and stuff and that was enough – someone said Afghanistan (wherever that was) but… how could he have fought for our country? Weren't we neutral then? Pre Article 9? Or a peacekeeping force? Or had the Americans drafted him? Was he a *half*?). As he got older he ventured out less and less, his legs weak, and he spent most of the time in front of the ever-loudening screen. You'd hear the news if you passed-by, or the familiar strains of a daytime drama coming out the open window. The little garden he had grew wild and unkempt and occasionally one of us would skip over his gate and tidy the place up, busying away with whatever tools were available to us, until our skinny, tanned arms were soon sore and our soft hands soon blistering from the effort. We missed him cutting our hair, missed the war stories when he clipped and chatted, filling us in on the names of planes and military operations. He may have been making it all up, but it didn't matter, we wanted to believe, that was good enough for a child. I picture him still, inside that dull house – I'd been a few times bringing some hot *bento* mother had made – the old flat screen glowing in the gloom, the ascetic walls. I see him just sitting there, the world spinning round and letting him know its details: more wars, political hi-jinks, terror, hi-jacks, fraud, famine, fighting, fear. What did he think as he watched all that, his legs hardly able to carry him anymore? He couldn't walk away from it. Did he despair? Just switch it off when it got too much? Did he sigh, as I do now, about everything? Was he fed up? Or did it matter to him at all? This veteran, who knew all about action heroes because he had been a real one, said he even had the medals to prove it (and we so wanted to believe, though we never got shown them, they glowed in our dreams). Or was his sigh the knowledge that there was nothing he could do to change anything anymore? He was past it. His glories: past. His stories: past. I think of him too when I am sitting alone and grumbling, knowing I will end up like him, alone most prob-ably, as the sky darkens each evening and I do nothing, nothing but search hopelessly...

So many remembrances as I walk. Maybe that's why I

walk at night: looking back, watching the memories play out across the starless sky, at least the memories remain steadfast, and on, on they'll stay, until my final dotage.

All the feral, out at night, searching for something. On and only on. All the feral, out and about.

Marina is in her usual spot. There's a bruise on the side of her face. "What happened?" I ask her, stunned and looking around me, suddenly fearful.

She just shrugs. She takes a cigarette out of her bag then and lights it up. We've had a long history with cigarettes in this land; we've always been favourable to them. When many other countries put a stop to them we still stuck with the yellow fingertips and the black lungs, how charming. Nowadays not many partake at all, but there are a few who keep on puffing, despite the high taxes that finally got stamped on them.

"You here to pay me for sex?"

As usual I say nothing.

"That's what I thought. You just like to nosey around. Make small conversations. Meaningless. You have no meaning, Mr. Walker."

She has, of course, hit the nail on the head.

"Sorry if I bother you."

"No. You don't bother me. Maybe that's problem. I'd prefer if you bothered me. Pay me money for my time. Treat me bad, like all men. You think you're so different."

"I think nothing."

That's wrong though. I do think. I think a lot. I'm thinking this minute what a courageous woman she is, to be out, night after night, to take on all comers (pardoning the pun) and to survive it all. Even in a country that doesn't want her, doesn't need her. She's out and about, living, making things happen. I could never look down on her, I admire her, and I think I've always been a little in love with her. There was a girl I knew, in my college days (right before I met Asami), also studying to become a PE teacher, who blew my mind with her beauty. I had thought her unobtainable when she first walked down the steps of the lecture hall (it was a rather pretentious lecture on sports psychology, which I was only too delighted to be distracted from). I had been shocked by her instant and devastating beauty, her rows of perfectly straight white teeth, and that crooked, arch smile that set them a-gleam, and her smooth long hair that shone under the electric lights. We became friendly over a few coffees, and I suppose I was desperately in love with her too, ever a sucker for the pretty and pristine. But I kept it all to myself. Hadn't the courage, or know-how, to make that move. Within months she had moved away to somewhere else – I never discovered the reason – and soon we were lost to each other, though I'm sure it was no great burden on her. Nothing might have become of it all of course, had I had the courage to ask her in the first place, I mean, and soon my life was only Asami and Ruby anyway, but a man in his thirties will set about these questions for himself: *What if things had been another way; I wonder what if such and such and such and such…*

I don't understand women. I think that much is plainly obvious at this stage. I am hopeless with them. They do not want or need me, and I am not a decent man. The only thing I can attract is the attention of two weird schoolgirls who have a misplaced crush or something. That's about my lot. And the women I am attracted to…

And my wife…

I do think. I do think. I do think a lot. But none of it seems to get me anywhere.

"Mr. Walker, why don't you watch in my window sometime? You might like what you see. I will leave the curtain open. You can see what life is all about. How unfair it is."

I don't need to see in her window. I already know how unfair life is. But I choose not to argue with her.

She pauses to take a long drag of the cigarette.

"You told me before, that you referee the children's football games. Well, look in my window, see me in the action. See if your red card would make any difference. No punishments for the... how do you say it? The foul play."

I don't know what to do. I'm not even sure what she is talking about. Or I don't want to acknowledge any of it. Should I reach out to her physically, put my hand near her, and would she then accept, my what... my peace offering? What exactly am I trying to do here? Why do I stop to talk to her? Why am I not near my costive wife and consoling her? Crying beside her and urging her to rise.

That college girl. Her name was Ai. Naturally.

I do put my hand towards her, and for a second I think she will try to quench her burning cigarette there, right there on my skin, put it out, brand me. Instead she places it between my fingers. I take a long drag of it, looking into her eyes all the time, it's the closest my mouth can get to hers, this sharing. I cough of course. Spluttering like an amateur. Which makes her laugh. Have I said how lovely she is when she smiles? Impossibly innocent. I should try to choke more often, anything for sympathy. Then I hand the cigarette back to her, placing it gently between her lips. My hand shakes. Nervousness. Loneliness. Lovelessness. Woman. When I am with her (and Maya, and Marisa) I am enrapt. Beautiful women. A beautiful woman makes me want to worship or weep. Have I said this before? My hand with the cigarette, placing it gently between her lips. This is as close as I...

"Where is your place?"

"Back down that lane, up the steel stairs, first apartment on left, blue door."

I wanted to make some joke about a red light, but I'm not that tactless. This girl knows far more about the world than I will ever know.

"So?"

"So what?"

"You gonna watch me in action some night? My big game."

"Yes, I think I will."

She shakes her head as I move off. She does not believe me, but the beautiful and instinctive whore knows all about the pathetic beast in my pants that craves affection. The mad instinctive creature bound up in boxer shorts hasn't been touched by hands (other than mine) for months, years now, that is all she reads in my eyes, on those distrait nights under the sheltering sheath, as the wolves make their rumpus in the hills.

Actually, the last time we were under her umbrella, as a noxious rain fell again (the plant, oozing) I noticed a slight slit in the fabric, and a drop coming in. What use is it: an umbrella with a hole in it? What use a man's life, if there's a big hole in it, what...

I ramble on, through the night, still looking into the bushes or hedgerows of gardens (what's left of gardens, remnants of gardens, they were never much to begin with) to see if... to see if I might see something, anything. I never thought I'd end up a Peeping Tom. No, scratch that, I don't think I *am* a Peeping Tom, and yet, why is it that I am always peeping through windows. Marina is right. Always nosey. Maybe she knows me well enough to offer her window to me. Maybe she can see me for what I am (poor beast come a-begging); but people do leave their curtains open, their bright lights displaying their warm and cosy rooms (as cosy and bright as flickering lights allow), and if that's not invitation then what is? I'm no voyeur, no, scratch that too, everyone...

And here we are. I never thought I'd come here, never thought I'd be this far gone, this far lost, spiritually I mean, never thought I'd *find* myself here. But here I am.

This is Marisa's house that I am outside and looking at now. My sister-in-law's. The one who left me only a short while ago, from my own house, having fed me, nourished me and… what did she mean by *still a handsome man?* Wasn't that what she said? Wasn't it? I haven't imagined that, have I?

Why am I here? I'm supposed to be searching for Ruby, for my raccoon dog, for my sense of…

I look around to see if any neighbours are watching. I sneak over towards the front window and manage to see through an opening at the side of the curtain. Marisa is on the sofa watching something on the WaSc. She is sipping from a glass of red wine and occasionally swiping her hand in front of her to change channel. Lights gleam on her face, reflecting on the control-glasses, and she is transfixed, manipulating whatever image she has there, enlarging it maybe, or changing its colour or texture. I spend very little time at any WaSc since Ruby left, never bother with Hologram Shows or any kind of televisual device, everything fills me with dread, most of all I can't abide happy faces there. The dramas are the worst, especially when some poor prodigal returns and the family is waiting there, joyfully tearful and welcoming and…

I fix into my position, like some greedy gothic gargoyle, intoxicated with the prospect of my prey, eyes wide and gluttonous – of course, I have been to this house several times before with Asami, unloading shopping, stopping in for a cup of replenishing tea, fixing a shelf once! Me! The handyman! It needed nothing but the tightening of a few screws, like most of my students.

I look around again to see if anyone notices me. Not a soul, not a living thing abroad. Marisa stares straight ahead, utterly absorbed. Then, suddenly, she presses the side of her glasses, swipes in front of her eyes and keys in a code, her fingers touching the nothingness, in command. She sits back and sips at her wine – it must be that cheap sweet stuff she gets, produced in the south, where it is rumoured the sun still shines, where Ruby might be; the other nations hardly share their wine anymore; they know we can no longer afford such luxuries. You get accustomed to being ignored.

I move to the very side of the window and angle my neck to see more of her and more of what she is watching, and I get myself into a position where I can almost see the whole screen. What did she mean by: *the living room?*

And my, oh my, this is not what I expected, but this is what I see (I am not sure I am ready for any of this).

She is viewing a pornographic film, and my, oh my, my interest level in the night's proceedings have gone up a quick notch and the hidden (unbidden) beast would surely purr if it could only make a sound.

Marisa stares at the screen. It has two blonde foreign women removing the clothes (with both dexterity and ravenousness) of a tall black man until he stands before them naked and massively engorged. In the year 2023 the government allowed pornography to be un-pixilated, allowed all to be seen, and not before time, according to most of the males in the country (though not Principal Misawa, who thought it a disgrace and a lowering of moral standards). After years of Internet use – abuse? – it all seemed rather trite however, a little late in the day, and the government scored nothing out of it, nothing at all.

They drop to their knees, the two blonde ladies. Marisa moves like she will remove her garments too, participate in the virtual scene, opening the button of her jeans and pulling down the zipper and then… suddenly, abruptly, she stops herself, pauses for a second… and zips back up again.

I confess that I am stumped. But also I am glued. I am stuck. I am gobsmacked. Out of luck.

Marisa seems to exhale deeply, a sad expression on her face, swipes away the whole system to a shutdown and gulps back the glass of wine in one swift motion. She stands up, wipes her mouth with the cuff of her sleeve, turns off the light and leaves the room. I scuttle down low so as not to be seen. I am breathing heavily. I crawl away from the house and mini-garden and onto the silent road. A light goes on in her bedroom and she pulls her curtains closed. She does not see me, I hope she does not see me, and yet at the same time…

I am frozen in the middle of the road. Not knowing what to do. Then the lights go out in the bedroom. Just like that. Lights out. And where does that leave me, this pitiful wretch who has just (technically) become a stalker. Isn't that what I am? Isn't that what I have become? Why could I not have stayed and watched that graffiti-boy do his thing on the wall? What is it that he is painting there anyway, what is the whole thing to become? He only does a scrap of it every night. Painting? It's not painting! Why have I been driven to this? Because no hands have touched me, because a fire has been…

Retire. She just retired for the evening. She did nothing. Marisa did nothing at all. She didn't play with herself, paid no heed to the black man and his frisky friends, she just swiped the porn away. Did she know someone was watching? Do people always know when someone is watching? We often get that feeling, don't we? Eyes on us. I have to be careful now. Tonight I have become more than a peeper, I have become a stalker. There is no way back. Is it because…

unkindled…

a-fire…

I look up to see if there are any drones overhead. I can't see any now, can't hear any either (they have become so quiet over the years, deathly so, as if to spite their name), but I know that they are there. If the police catch me creeping around in other people's property, spying no less, what will they do to me? I have always been something of the voyeur I suppose, always prowling around, having a gawp at this or that. It has been very hard to stop this. Even as my father sat and read in his study, his precious paperbacks in a tall tower beside him, I would peer through the keyhole, just to watch him, fascinated by his concentration, intrigued by the notion of reading. What was the point of it? Why had he spent so many hours doing it? And mother, too, standing behind her back, I used to gaze at her as she slapped paint on the canvas and turned and dipped into the palette and back again to the chaos she was trying to order. Did she see me then? Probably. But ignored me – I was just a curious child. But I kept up this hobby of looking and staring and peeping in on people; perhaps it's just a part of growing up. Sometimes I feel I would rather just be watching, even now still, a sex scene, just watching, than be involved in it at all, on the outside looking in, not getting my hands dirty, so to speak. For all its implied dirtiness there is a kind of cleanliness about voyeurism, a contradiction that is just becoming apparent to me. A fellow teacher from another prefecture, at some dull conference, confided in me once that he had set up a miniature camera in the girls' changing rooms in the school and regularly masturbated to images downloaded from this. He said he had one in the boys' room too, though of course he was free to walk in there whenever he pleased (he was, after all, a fellow

PE teacher, for his sins). I was appalled, sickened by it. He asked me whether I was interested in obtaining one of these secret cameras (*why not*, he explained, *everybody was spying on everybody else – look at the government!*) and that he could set it up for me himself (*ARCK-made, easy to operate, not easily noticeable, though not completely reliable*), we could even watch the movies together and he'd be happy to fondle me! I think I said nothing, my mouth open in incredulity for the entire conversation and my stomach doing cartwheels. He left my side then, putting his index finger to his lips, imploring my quiet complicity – I was now a co-conspirator. The annoying thing was that he thought I was like him! What in my demeanour had given him that notion? What in my...

I didn't rat on him. I am perhaps not the most saintly of men, but I should have reported him, of course I should have, why the tardiness? Maybe I was in too much of a shock. For all my voyeuristic tendencies (and who honestly doesn't have these?), I know when to draw the line. That man, most convincingly, *was* the line. A wrong, crooked one.

Oddly enough, when he was telling me of his dastardly secrets I also had to keep quelling the instinct to reach towards my breast pocket. I wanted to send him off. How absurd. The habits we acquire, the strange involuntary...

Nothing, I'm sure, nothing at all, that's what police would do if they caught me creeping around like this. If I'm not mistaken the police box got washed away in the last flood too. Not sure what happened to the cops inside; like everything else, bobbing on the water, their stern faces becoming soft and malleable, wrinkly from the surfeit, pale from the wave-push and pummeling – their guns floating along beside them for a brief second, barrel-up, aimed at the empty sky and then sinking to the bottom of the sea.

No wonder the village has become so lawless over the years: sans sheriff nothing but outlaws and vagabonds, wastrels, scoundrels and mad chancers (opportunistic as the wolves) nothing but this cast, ever in moral descent, ever hurtling towards the maelstrom. And the cities do not care. The big cities of the 13th are well-looked after, still lively and noticeable, and proud (despite their own battering). From the outside, the country might look stable enough, but it is the small villages, the small forgotten wave-washed towns; there were just too many to take care of, and nothing but old people everywhere, all the elderly, a land of no youth, only wizened faces that have seen too much, the young departed, the young unborn! Worse and worse it got. Even the place I work, a school with hardly any students, forty in total now, it used to be three hundred, better let, yes, best let all these broken villages die off, or put them out of their misery, away, go, begone…

I run. I run fast through the streets. I am either running *from* something or *to* something. No, I am merely running. I am…

A little rain starts to spit on my head and then it gets heavier. So I run even faster.

Ruby!

I'm not sure if this is shouted aloud or not, sometimes the scream is only in my head, sometimes it does not get out, sometimes it must for sure, screeches out, beseeching, and the screech frightens the roosting birds out of the skeletal trees, and they take off from their makeshift homes alarmed, and I imagine their clouds as smoke signals: *Ruby! Ruby!*

My running makes me woozy, a quick sickness overtaking. I look down the grim lanes of the crippled village, into its peculiar icy silence, its ever-fear, and I stand to take a breather on a bridge (a bridge that has remained firm despite heckles from the firmament) and watch the river flow underneath me. So much water. So much of it always going on, unstoppable. Everywhere. Finding its level. Everywhere you look it'll be there, everywhere, in waves, in runs, in rivers and rain, and tears too, their accumulation.

I run again, sweat on my brow mixing with the rain, more liquid, more salt. Back in the centre of town I slow down (breathe, breathe, stitch in my side) and begin to walk.

These runs and walks, these ambles and sprints, whatever I do, these nebulous nights, I am on the lookout for Ruby. I see different things. Find myself in other places.

Is that why I go out at night?

In school they make us sit through meetings. Long, very long meetings. When I am there and the Heads are muttering about something or other – they could be mad masks in some grim ceremony, they blur, even though they are close to me – mostly I just sit and seethe. It's as if I am wasting my time and could be doing more profitable things. Like what? Walking. Running. Searching. Actually, now that I come to think of it, apropos of nothing at all, I realize how little we are involved in the sexual act, all of us I mean, humans. If it is for *homo sapiens* the most meaningful and enjoyable of all pursuits, then why so little of it? (I'm not talking only of my own life here.) If we had not been so tired all the time, couldn't we have made love to our beautiful women and filled the land and…

Why so much time invested in other activities? Why knit for example? Sometimes I think of these things during the tedious staff meetings, and why shouldn't I? Many of us are under thirty, shouldn't we be doing something else, engaging in more satisfactory recreations, some rollicking rutting orgy perhaps – I should speak to Marina about it all.

The lamppost. Where Marina usually is. Not. Marina is not. Is a solitary lamppost, only. Marina is not. Not there.

Marina is not there. Sometimes my head takes time to figure things out. You get so used to things being there, and then they are not.

My head hurts. Just there over my eyes. My forehead. Back of my eyes too. And my ears, filling up, forever they feel like they are filling up.

I stroll down the dark laneway. I climb the steel stairs slowly, trying not to make any noise with my footfalls. I go to her window, voyeuristic tendencies, and who honestly…

Marina is not the type to lie. She says I can look in. I have her permission to do this. That's what she said. Why wait for any other night? Why not tonight? This is her presentation. This is what she wants. What she has invited me to do.

Wide-eyed now, again, a swift torment brewing inside me again, and then, then, when I see (Peeping Tom, me *again*) the two assistant referees on the bed (my colleagues) with Marina (my whore, my whore who I never touch and never pay, not even respect).

Fuck!

The three of them are naked and rolling around on each other. It's Bacchanalian, it's centuries old. Marina is tossing her head back and laughing (her hair snakes, her hands gyrate) and the two men grab and grapple with her (she looks demonic, looks inflamed, looks like she's enjoying herself).

Hide Miyoshi and Takashi Nakazawa. These two sandwiching her. Marina is in the middle (this is not the soccer pitch, with me in the middle, whistleblower, them sidelined, flag-raisers). Like twins, both of them, with mean foxy faces a-slabber a-slobber *on* her. Same height even. And lying on the bed all is equal. Life's great playing field, in microcosm. Bed, the leveller. Their long legs are all a-tangle. I am woozier now, sick to the stomach, my head pounds, behind my eyes, my ears are full. I want to throw up, and I want to die. But I keep watching. You would have guessed as much, for sure my eyes stay, for sure I keep on watching.

This... this is what she wanted me to see? This is what she wanted me to be a part of? *Why don't you watch in my window sometime? You might like what you see. I will leave the curtain open. You can see what life is all about.* This is her presentation. I prefer the ones they do in schools and conventions, with projections and animated images and red laser points to the facts we are supposed to be underlining, highlighting.

More tangles. More snakes. They run their fingers through her hair. My whore, my whore Marina, my love, had I the gumption.

I take my eyes away from the window and sit on the wet ground. Did I mention it is raining again? Has it been raining every day? Hasn't there been rather enough water already? My hands go to my side and I sit in puddles of rain, my backside wet, and if I'm not mistaken those are tears again, on my cheeks.

Ruby. Ruby, if only I could find you. Wouldn't that set my heart at ease? My wife could stir. Finally our breath at ease. I would never come out into the night again.

There is a sudden rattling in the bins further down the block of flats and I see Mr. Racoon dog with some piece of garbage hanging from his mouth. I glare at him and he glares right back at me, unfazed as ever, as if to say: *Want some? I don't mind sharing. We are alike, you and me. We are the longing and the lost, we are just scavengers, like all the rest.* Is that a smile? Is the animal smiling at me?

Sharing.

They are *sharing* her. My colleagues. My precious prostitute. Can I bring myself to look in the window again?

The animal scampers off, successful. He doesn't need me. He. Definitely a he. Written all over. The same yearning eyes as me, lost. Longing and lost, indeed.

Who does? Who needs me? If I were to vanish now, if one more drop of rain was to fall on me and simply melt me into a puddle right here on the cold wet ground, who would care? Who would push the barrow?

I take one more look in the window and then, then, just when you think you've seen it all, just when you think you've seen all there was ever to be seen (wolves waves death destruction empathic beasts), just when you think there's no more in this dastardly world that can take you by surprise (insulting octogenarian principals with swords, attempted underwater worlds, drunk men carried home in wheelbarrows) there appears before you, there comes this:

Marina stands on the bed, stands naked above the two men, her pert white breasts exposed and her meagre frame athletic... and when I look (wide-eyed, agape again), I see, despite the tears in my eyes... a penis... straight and hard protruding from her female body, and...

and...

and the two men reach for it and fondle it, one putting it in his mouth and the other cradling her balls. This is no false... *instrument.* No plastic thing strapped on, oh no toy, oh no. This is the real thing, the realest of things.

I turn and throw up. I throw up from the putrid pit of my being over the railing and splat onto the ground far below. This is Marisa's dinner that has just been hurled, but it is also all my loves and my desires and my pains and my fears and my realizations, yes (I am sorry for my life. I am sorry for your life. I am sorry for all lives on the planet. I'm sorry that Ruby never came home. What happened to Ruby on that day? I am sorry for the sick air that we breathe, the sicker breath we throw back out at the world. I am sorry for the multitudes that have died and the multitudes that have to go on living. Heave heave, more of it. I am sorry that I struggle and that

Everyman's life is a struggle, I am sorry for the way things are and the way things aren't. I am sorry for almost everything and I wish that I was not this way. I wish I was a million other ways), my realisation is in that yellow bile, and my stupidity too of course, my naivety. How could I not, how could I not, really *see*? Is it from the tears that constantly well, or is it the romance in them, always clouding? What are eyes for? What are eyes for? Mother, tell me, please, what are eyes for?

Then I hear laughter from within the room. Raucous laughter and frivolity. I know my ears don't work so well anymore since… but they are working well enough to hear this. It is as if they know I am outside and another one of my worlds has come crumbling down.

All this mockery.

I've just realised, too, that I don't know what they do, these two, the assistant referees, what their jobs are, I mean. I am only ever familiar with them raising flags, lacing boots, coming to sneer at me as I wipe egg-mess from my car front, and now like this? Why have I never bothered to ask, bothered to investigate? Maybe I just don't care. Is this true? That I just don't care?

Solipsism. As a philosophical concept perhaps my father would've…

But why should I care? About anything. About Marina? Does it matter what she *is*, this whore I love, this whore I love and never feel? Is she a *he*? (We had thought all those "new-halves" had gone, back to whatever circuses they had come from. Philippines? Thailand? They were on our screens for so long, so-called comedians, their grandiose regalia, their foolish shtick, a bored nation transfixed as ever, whatever is the foolish order of the day will suffice. I remember them when I was a teenager, laughing at them, and vaguely curious too – how odd they seemed with all those boas and bracelets. And then the quakes came and knocked the TV stations down – the stuffing out of us – and the new-halves ran to wherever they came from, their tails between their legs.) What difference does it make? I only wanted to ever hear her speak in her foreign tongue, hear sounds that made no sense and try to put order on them… I am a married man, I am a married man and my wife… Asami is the name of my wife and…

The door opens and Marina steps out in a garish pink dressing gown, lighting a cigarette. It's amazing to think such colours are still being manufactured. Who needs for such garments? A female whore maybe. A whore with a cock. She looks at my sorry state: I'm squatted there on the ground in the rain, understanding nothing, understanding nothing of the world, with a sticky mess all down the front of my shirt. She does not look in the least bit surprised.

"Thought you might come to have a look. Good timing."

"I shouldn't be here."

"But you are here, Mr. Walker. Come in, have some fun. First one is free you know."

"I'm looking for my daughter."

"You won't find her here."

"Yes, but I must… I have to…"

"I know, it's a bit of a shock seeing your workmates doing things like that, but they're just men having fun. Not up to anything bad. They're not hurting anyone. And they pay well you know. Not married of course, like you are. So maybe they have no responsibilities. Your friends."

"They are not my friends."

"Suit yourself, Mr. Wazka. I only ever hold my hand out to you. I mean no harm. I like you. I like when you come and talk to me, when you are out walking at night. You are a handsome man. I wish we could get closer."

You are still a handsome man. Everyone has little secrets… and… everyone can hide things.

I am not a handsome man. I have no intention of getting close to anyone. To anyone.

She takes an umbrella from inside the entrance and puts it up for us. This one has no hole. A protective sheath. It seems to have no sharp point either, doesn't seem like a weapon.

"A new umbrella."

"Yes, we need good umbrellas. More rain forecast. Streetwalkers always check the weather forecast. I use the other one when I feel I might be in danger, when I sense danger coming. You know?"

I don't know.

She calls herself a streetwalker. So many different names for what she does. But what she *is*. This is what distresses me. I'm no longer sure of what she *is*. There is so much I do not get.

She smiles at me, her face angelic, how can it be that…

"I never thought about that, the weather," I murmur, to break my own thought patterns.

"There are lots of things you never thought about, by the look of it."

Her face gazing down upon me is a mixture of pity and wry amusement; she flicks her head then with authority which is an order for me to rise. Her body may no longer make any sense to me, but I feel I can trust her commands. I could have married someone like this. She would never collapse in a heap. She is the one out on cold, rainy nights, trying to make a buck with a suck; I'm the one with a nice (albeit gloomy) still-standing house and a wife and a secure job. And yet *she* is sorry for *me*. Her body is covered now. She is all covered up and looks comfortable and cuddle-worthy (if I put the fact of her appendage right out of my mind). For this I am grateful.

Marina takes a long drag of the cigarette.

"You want one. A smoke, I mean."

"No. I don't smoke."

"No, of course. You must stay fit to run up and down on the pitch. Need strong lungs."

A groan of pleasure can be heard inside. The laughter has died, it's all groan and grunt now.

"Sounds like those guys are having fun. You should try it sometime. Fun I mean."

Once, my literary father told me about a book he was reading. He used to do this, used to go on at length, and usually with no one at all willing to listen to him – it didn't seem to bother him all that much, maybe we are only all talking to ourselves anyway. The book was all about a guy who just takes off one day, leaves his wife and family and heads off in his car, not really knowing where he is going, or only with a vague sense of direction. My father said that the man's name was Rabbit, which to my young ears (only half-listening) seemed like a very odd name to give a hero. He said that all men wanted to run. It's in their nature, to get away from their mundane existences. There's always that feeling in the breast of man that he can begin again, somewhere else, live somewhere new. That everything will be different, or better, next time round. That book must be a hundred years old now. I wonder if I'll ever read it. No. All that is gone too. Books no good to me. No good to anyone. All we want is a ship that stays afloat, a Noah to come and load us all in and take us away to safety. Maybe that's who I am looking for, Noah, not Ruby. But I do what the book says, I am suddenly that Rabbit man, I look Marina in the eye once, hard and steady, and then I take off running, down the steps and away from the scene. I run all the way home wet with sweat and rain; soon soaked, and soon shivering. When I get inside my house I collapse in the hallway breathing heavily, the walls spinning around me.

Spin. Everything a-spin. In spin. All around me. Like I am

riding on a child's New Year top, set off with the string and sent hurtling at top speed. Top speed on top of the top. I have to calm down, breathe slowly to get my bearing – this spinning head on this spinning planet. Is this the plight of every man? Not just me… is it?

I don't know the rules of the world. I know so little of the games people play. I'm not supposed to have opinions about their goals. I'm not to have any opinions at all. I'm not supposed to react. Only to when there is an infringement of the rules. Has there been? Has there been an infringement of the rules? A violation? An encroachment? Where's Ruby? That's not supposed to be the order of the world. Kids are not supposed to go before their time, before their parents. This is wrong. I reach to my breast pocket, tap myself there, nothing, where are my cards? Why these women and their similar names? What is that all about? To confuse me? Why do they all seem to blend into one? Why is that? Why am I so unfair to them? Why do the fantasies only grow and grow and I have no hold on the real?

That penis, that was real, wasn't it? Where's Noah?

Shakily I get to my feet. I am like a new-born animal, a giraffe say, all sway and buckle, struggling to right myself. I look at my face in the mirror. There I am. A reflection. Not a vampire then. Still alive. But barely. Barely is this wan image I return to myself. The lights are still off so my face appears shadowy, spectral, although I *am* there, here I mean, just, I hardly recognize myself. What have I become?

I don't know the rules of the world. Only the rules of a football game. Only what happens on the pitch. Only within a short frame of time. That's all I can manage. Everything else around me is chaos. Everything else… *my disgust at all existence.*

Up slowly now, up the wooden stairs, with mental effort

to stay on track, to not get dizzy and lose myself, passing the portraits on the walls of a family of three: Tombo, Asami and Ruby. That's us. Turn into the bedroom and see a figure in bed, back turned, just a hump under the covers. Heap. Cannot see her face. Heap of life. Heap of sleep. Heap of grief. Heap of meat. Heap of she. Heap of she. She.

I start to undress and hang up my clothes neatly in the wardrobe. I then put on my beige pajamas, buttoning to the top, more like a soldier preparing for battle than a man retiring for the evening. But I am no soldier, no Fujibayashi, and while the marching in line might have suited me, even the early morning drills, I have never hunched in the trenches, never flew over foreign fields in a thunderous helicopter, never held a weapon. I am a man who only blows a whistle. Could I kill? Could I, in warfare, if I had to, if pressed to, could I pull the trigger? What if…

The clock says it is one minute to ten. My wife breathes heavily. Her name is Asami. My name…

What a day it has been. What a day every day has been.

I know that tomorrow the waking will be the pain. The waking will be the pain. The waking. Will. Be. The. Pain. I'll be. When I open my eyes the pain. Or even before. When I just become awake and a thousand thought-floods burst in… the waking is the pain. No-Ruby will be the pain. Heap beside me is the pain. Air traveling through the nostrils into the lungs, oxygen to the brain is the pain, breathe breathe, disease, for waking is the pain. No solace is the pain. Plans and schedules are the pain. Planners. Meetings. Calendars and pens. Every day is the pain. Without Ruby. No touching is the pain. Beauty before me, in and around me, beauty-no-touch is the pain, like art in the galleries behind the ropes my mother would have loved is the pain, don't touch, look but don't touch is the pain. When was I last touched? Pathetic pants beast. Just-look is the pain. No touch. Stay behind the ropes. Seeing is the pain. Being is the pain. Wake to the pain. Wake to all of this is the pain.

So what should I do? Get up. Get up and get on with it when the time comes. In the morning. This is what they advise. This is what most people do. Despite tsunamis. Despite catastrophes. Despite thunder and the gods shaking their fists in anger. What gods? This is what they do. This is what I must do. Must. Get on with it. Let the oxygen go there and let synapses fire and...get going, get going. Get up tomorrow morning. Waking is the pain for everybody. Why should I be any different? Wake past heap past no Ruby get up and on and make and move and get up and go and make your day and make...

It is only a matter of time, tide and time, before the bed is rocked awake again and then the surge moves forward to thrash upon the land again and the people, in the form of tiny particles of useless shit, are then brought home again. I am tired. Tired of these thoughts.

Let me be the heap. Why is it not me? Why am I the one to have to get up? Why did I not break?

My ears hurt. My ears are full of water since...

I turn to my wife in the bed and kiss the side of her head.

"Goodnight sweetheart."

There is no other sound in the room, only when the hand of the clock ticks over to ten. My bulging eyes stay open for a few moments as I stare at the ceiling. Then they shut.

20

She is barefoot now. What has happened to her shoes? Did they float away and did they sink? She stops a while and rests and looks at her blisters and picks out the sand and grit. Lulled by nightingales, embraced by sleep, she feels close again. Close to home.

When she wakes she walks on and sings something about the bottom of the pit and on and on shoeless and forlorn and on and on and on

21

Sit ups.

Every so often I stop, look at my watch, groan, and observe the droplets of sweat falling from my forehead and onto my thighs. Universes there. Each drop a story.

More water of course. Just when you think you have had enough of the sight of it, you discover that you also need it more than anything: a quick drink is what I need, so a quick drink is what I take, big big gulps and it quenches. Then it's back to the sits ups and the groans.

Pain. My body is full of pain. Waking and living the pain. Breathing, thinking the pain. But I need to be fit. A referee needs to be fit. Even a teacher needs to be fit. Standing at the top of the classroom all day, the pacing to and fro, and hours spent over paperwork, the neck-cricks and lower back bites, the muscular stabs and sears; a teacher needs to be fit, physically and mentally, and physical fitness can lead to mental fitness, and vice versa, there's a theory in that somewhere, perhaps my literate father, perhaps he could have poeticized it, not me, not me for sure, I am only a referee and a teacher, no, I am only a humble teacher and a referee.

My groans are getting louder, there is a theory about that

too, that if you vocalize the pain you lessen the pain. That you should shout out your suffering. Perhaps that's what all of this is. Right from the beginning. A shouting-out of all this suffering. Alleviate: that's why the boo-boys and bray-girls on the Saturday afternoon pitches proclaim their profanities, swearing like moored and insatiate sailors – they are relieving their pain, banishing their existential angst, assuaging their ontological confusion. There's a good theory in that too, and if...

"Big game today."

Marisa is in the room with me now and looking down on me. She is watching me sweat. She is hearing me groan. Sees my pain manifest.

"Hnnn."

One, two, up and down, my stomach muscles tightening – I try to pick up the pace when she is watching, naturally, trying to impress: I am a man.

On the mat, this exercise mat, Marisa stands above me, looking down; this is the curious position in which we have found ourselves today, as if I don't have enough to be getting on with. She looks good from every angle. If ever I was to have sex with her, if ever – this all only fantasy, mind – and I the one beneath, this is the sort of angle I would find myself privy to. A man could get used to an angle like this. A man can get used to all kinds of things.

"Be careful you don't tire yourself out before the game even starts. You'll be no use if you're winded already. Keep a bit of that gusto for running on the pitch. Do you want a cup of tea? I was just about to make one and bring one up to Asami too, even though she probably won't drink it, well, sometimes she does, and sometimes she doesn't. But I'll leave it by the bed anyway, in case, just in case she wants a sip. I think I'll try to persuade her to have a bath today. She might. She might do that. She might have a bath. You want a cup of tea? And you should have a big breakfast, really. Get yourself prepared for the day. Of course you'll need a shower too, before you go, you're all sweaty, just look at you. And then you'll be all sweaty after the game too, and will need another shower. Ha ha. From shower to shower. Still, a man like you sweats, I suppose."

"Hnnn."

I do. I sweat. I am a man and I sweat, from every pore, with every one-two.

She is suddenly beside me on the mat. There is hardly room enough for one human, but here she is beside me on the mat, two humans. Why would two humans be in such proximity, in such a position? We have never been so close before. What has come over her?

"I don't know how you do it, these sit-ups. Right, push over, give me a turn."

The angles I would be privy to. The sights a man could become accustomed to.

Marisa straightens herself out on the mat and then tries to lift herself up, using her abdominal muscles. But she doesn't quite make it. She starts laughing. She twists and tries again, grunting and groaning, and she starts to laugh at her own incompetence. She is already breathless and wheezing.

"Useless," she giggles.

I begin to giggle myself. I forgot how hard these are, especially to the untrained. I guess I am used to this kind of physical activity and must be *in* shape if I am to convince my students that exercise is very important, I can't be seen to be hypocritical and...

She tries again. I see her breasts undulate under her sweater, her large heavy...

"Useless. No good," she says with a gigglewheeze.

I try to stifle my growing erection. I want her to leave now.

I want her to get out of here, right now. Maybe I'll have that cup of tea after all.

"One last go," she says, and she is squirming again, and the momentum makes her turn sideways and clumsily she tumbles on top of me.

"Oh, dear, sorry," she says, still laughing now, hearty and breathless. It is the laugh of a foolish girl, a teenager in a school corridor, I hear it all the time, it is a nervous laugh, a laugh that says she is in the wrong and knows it, but is not in any way guilty, only excited, and therefore it is not really wrong at all, it's just the way things turn out.

I start laughing, too, hoping she has not felt my hardness brush against her. And too, wickedly, hoping that she has.

Upstairs, Asami, on her back in the bed, eyes wide open, is listening to the radio. Signals still come in. Still reach us. The reception is often crackling, static-y, snatches of sounds, souls, reports, voices and music, bleeps and sonatas. When she hears the laughing and groaning from downstairs she reaches out her thin arm and turns it off. Her arm has the dimensions and hue of what we might imagine an alien to possess, something extra-terrestrial seen once in some late movie, a lean monster, slow and rickety from its emaciation, the skin loose and reptilian, and she tucks the arm right under the covers again. She tries to focus on the foreign sounds below her. Concentrating. Avid. She hears groans and grunts and giggling and then laughing. She stares at the ceiling, then her eyes close and she slips into a dream, a dream about a man who kills off a whole slumbering village.

I drink tea. And the tea is good. Marisa always chooses the best tea bags. I must remember to compliment her on this.

I am washed (I was going to add *up* to that, but refrained

– sometimes you must just stop yourself). I am a little sore in the pit of me, overdid the sit-ups, trying to impress, I was really only intent on a few stretches, but I got carried away; this is an expression that comes to mind a lot: *I got carried away*. Imagination. All mine.

Lives got carried away too, the cruel crests of waves, lives that could…

Another story.

The tea is good. The tea is good though. I must remember.

Marisa breaks nothing this morning. Nothing falls to the floor. The place looks in good order, ship-shape. Good. Order.

But just when you think *order*, the universe seems to find a way to redress, thus: *disorder*. This is the referee's bane. For outside the house, just as I depart with my bag (contents: boots and whistles, notebook, red and yellow cards), they are there again, those two students. Those two girls that are forever hanging around. Those two.

I must admit that I am quite taken aback: I have no idea why they are here, and for a moment my mouth simply hangs open, no words pouring forth – this from a teacher who does nothing else but talk and shout all day long.

Then they do come, eventually, words, much needed words, as I fumble in my pockets for my car keys:

"What on earth are you doing here? Is there something you want?"

They say nothing now, these two, only stare straight ahead, their eyes on me, as if lasers trained. My skin starts to itch, insects crawling across my skin.

"Well? Is there something you want? This is my home!"

I almost say their names, I almost scream their names, until I realise I'm not sure I remember them properly. The taller one: Takeyama… Something, and the shorter one… I forget. On the playing fields I remember every student, but

I'm quick to banish them from my mind when the school day is done. This is my private time that they are intruding upon. This has all gotten quite out of hand.

"Well?"

Still nothing. They stand like zombies. They could be from an ancient B-movie, all vacant stare and impassivity.

And then their mouths open. In perfect unison, ghostly voices:

"You are the one! You are the one!"

This is all executed trance-like, monotone, grave.

And again.

"You are the one! You are the one!"

I don't know whether to feel afraid or shocked or disgusted or whether to simply burst out laughing at the farcical spectacle before me.

"You are the one! You are the one! You are the one!"

I turn to see if anyone else is witnessing this. Marisa is. Peeping from behind the downstairs living room curtain, Marisa is. Aghast too, or is that confusion etched on her face?

"You are the one! You are the one! You are the one!"

I decide I've had enough and throw myself into my car, no time for foolishness, whatever game these two have planned must wait, it's a football game I have to referee today and already I am behind time. I am a referee and...

"You are the one! You are the one! You are the one!"

Must get a move on. No time to waste.

"You are the one! You are the one! You are the one!"

They keep up the incantation outside my car as I set my controls; I see their mouths move even as I pull away from the house:

"You are the one! You are the one!"

Rearview mirror: my eyes, their woven hands, their silent imploring, my disdain, a sour taste in my mouth. I am not the one.

"Do you think it worked?" says Nail.

"I think so," says Tooth, "he'll think of nothing but us all day. Nothing but us. We are inside his head now. We are there beautiful. We're in."

Nail smiles and her sharp teeth flash in the sunlight. Her teeth and gums are sore, perhaps from all the candy she has consumed.

There is to be a full moon this evening, already there is a sense of the wolf packs itching in the thickets, warming up for their hideous peals.

Marisa decides to confront the two interlopers. She wants to know what they want, what they are doing here. For some reason, she takes a broom with her (it was at hand, a cleaning implement is always at hand, she works hard for her brother-in-law). They are the kind who need shooing, like copulating cats, noisy and bothersome, eerie and unwanted.

"Look at the witch," Tooth says. "Are you going to fly on that?"

Nail bares her almost-lupine teeth – are those flews on her face, flews that flap and drool with spittle: what horrorshow is this?

"It's not Halloween," says Tooth, and she flashes no teeth at all, just a tight-lipped smirk.

Marisa stands before them, the broom raised now, like a rifle she holds it, aiming.

So which one is diabolical here? The witch with the angry face, broom aloft? Or these two harbingers of doom, these Lady Middays?

Marisa remembers the tales her grandmother told her of the Jikininki, the spirits of the un-gods, those that have passed to the other side but are greedy and hungry and malevolent. Her grandmother said that they take things from corpses, sneaking into sepulchres and stealing whatever valued goods they find there: wedding rings, necklaces, gold watches; while there they are believed to eat the rotting flesh, feasting and gnawing on the lifeless bones and gorging themselves on putridity. This makes them sick of course, her grandmother explained, but not a physical sickness, no, the sickness is all in the self-loathing, they know they have sunk so low and reviled themselves, that is their true disease, these Jikininki. And to worsen things they take on human form, they live amongst us, as if they are actually one of us, you would never know one if you saw one, perhaps you already know one! They might be your friends, your family! If you do recognize one, never look him in the eye, she said, or you could be paralyzed with dread; never think of them in bed. But why put such horror in a young girl's head?

"Why have you come?"

"We have come to see our teacher. He might be able to help us."

"Help you? School hours are ended. This is the weekend. He's entitled to some free time."

"He's the one. The one we need."

"For what?"

"For us."

"For what?"

"Witch, you would never understand."

Marisa raises her broom again, as if to strike.

"You can't hit us."

"Oh, I can. What do you think will happen? The police come to your house? You think that might happen?"

The girls are silent. They know there is no more authority. The streets: sans sheriff. The police boxes floated all away. The police officers too. Their caps bobbing. All away.

"We will tear you apart, every fibre of you."

"Will you?" laughs Marisa. "I've fought off bigger rats than you."

Nail flashes sharp incisors. Her back arches like a cat. Her hair black and sleek as a panther. She hisses. Is there no animal she doesn't resemble?

Tooth takes out scissors from her rucksack and twirls them in her hand, gunslinger.

"You'll need a bigger weapon than that," Marisa says, laughing again.

"We will get our man and we will bleed him dry," says Tooth, eyes narrow, face tightened. "He is ours. At least… he will be."

"Get out of here now, before you get hurt."

The two girls stand mute for a moment and look up to the darkening clouds.

"Ever-threatening storms," says Tooth.

"Chaos blustering round," says Nail.

"Inclement sky," says Tooth.

Bad day for a football game.

Just a bad day.

The girls journey on, pensive and slow, they hold hands, both stirred in their loins, feeling flinches that might need attention, might need to be relieved, all this excitement, all this excitement has gotten the better of them. They will go home to the pink room and the creaking doors and raid the Snake Box. They will go back to their headquarters and figure out where to go from here. Young girls and boys these days need hobbies. There is so little to do in the village. Half of the village is gone. And they are far from the cities. Are the cities gone too? Some of them. But most are actually strong and do flourish, it's the villages that get forgotten, the country has no need to sweat the small stuff. So they need to keep themselves amused. Hobbies then. They might have not got long left, before the next natural assault. If they can only endure another year or two they might have qualification enough to get out, get out of the village, get away to somewhere unsinkable. But for now, hatching, hatching together, to get their man, a new plan, ensnare, ensnare, they are giddy all over, and they need some relief.

Sweat has gathered at Marisa's temples and she wipes it away. She has over-exerted herself. She cannot do sit-ups, and she has not brandished a broom (or any weapon) like that before, her hands were so tight on the handle, what was she thinking? But she can fight off predators; she can protect the home. She can. She can do.

Upstairs she treads (softly, ever so softly) to see if Asami has heard the commotion – was the radio on? – but her eyes are closed in the comfort of sleep and she looks peaceful, she must have heard nothing. Marisa hopes she has heard nothing – was the radio on? – sonatas, arias, sounds of souls from somewhere far, bleeps and murmurings, weather reports, stocks and shares, mutterings and proclamations, drones and interferences and hisses. Was the radio on, static-y or amniotic? It must be nice to sleep and dream so much. Was the radio on pelagic and peaceful? What goes on in those dreams? What goes on? What goes on in those dreams? What goes on?

II
quite abolished, and expire

You, a prophet. You a prophet come a-calling. A prophet come a-calling on a village. But wait. Before you come a-calling you need a name. Your name is Nai. The negative form. As if you don't exist. Maybe you don't. Not there. None. It may that your name had originally been Osanai, and they shortened it. Who? Don't know. Everybody. Possibly. Everybody. Who is to say? Invent. This is you inventing. Who inventing who? Let's start with a fine childhood. Fine. Fast. You did the following: found coins on the road once and spent them on little cakes, alone, ate, was often alone, found geckos and lizards, didn't eat them, found a dead deer and took its antlers, your mother scolded but… doesn't matter. You found things, found God, found yourself, went mad, no one quite knew, you don't quite know yourself, maybe these things are all the same, you don't quite know yourself. Did you hear voices? Do you, now? Voices? Is it only one voice you hear now, only this one? You look quite raddled, you look frowsy, you look like a hobo, you look like a vagrant, a vagrant come a-calling, you have a hunched back, yes, that's it, they say you have a hunched back. Who? Who says such a thing? Everybody. Possibly. Everybody. Or only one. You are trying to get beyond.

Why does this word keep coming back to you? Beyond. Let's put you walking. Where are you going? Trying to get beyond. There is no transport. What year is this? You are on your own two feet and walking. You have blisters from all of it, from all of that walking, the exertion, but that doesn't stop you. Nothing can stop you now. You are a man on a mission. There is nothing that will get in your way. An ugly man on an ugly mission. Ugly? Oh yes, yes, hunchbacked and all warted and irredeemably disgusting. Disease-filled. That's it. But don't worry. You are not alone in that regard. Impetigo too. All these unfortunate afflictions. You poor you. But you can walk and talk. A little .You can't talk much. No. Stop. How about mute? Go with that. You are mute. There. You have only ever gurgled words. Not even words, just sounds from the back of your throat. No one understands you. Poor creature. No one knows a thing about you, only your creator. But you are on a mission. So, let's get you started. Wait. What's the noise? Something downstairs. Not the radio. The radio is off. Sometimes the radio is on but it is unnecessary. Some other noise. Laughter. Laughter? Laughter. A drama on some screen in some room of this house? Is that it? Does this house still stand? How is it that this house still stands? Everything else comes tumbling down. But never mind all that now. What's gone is gone, what's done is done. So, a mission. You will do all kinds of things. You are on your way now. See what? You see what in this village? What exactly? You see…go on then. What do you see? A muddy road. A muddy road you walk down, wet always from rain or flood. Left: hedgerow. Right: hedgerow, and some dilapida-tion. Rubble. This place. From all the trouble. Is there a house still standing? Yes. Some. There are still some houses around here. Go in to one. Enter. Entertain. Fine. You go up to the gate of the first house. It is rusty on its hinges. It creaks when you put hand to it. Sways open. Nearly falls off. Everything is rusty from all the water. But you carry on. You are quite the criminal now. Hunchbacked and hideous and your senses coming alive with the prospect of what you will do. Go on. Go in. Go ahead. The door is open. This is the way things used to be. Wait. What's that noise? Stop a moment. Halt. Who goes there? *Hnn. Hnn.* There. Do you hear it? That's... what? That sound. Coming from where? Below. Is that... who...? Laughing again. That's the sound. *Hnn. Hnn.* Effort. Exertion. Everything takes effort. Exertion. Is that what it is? Never mind. Radio off. Is it? Is the radio off? Continue. You are at the door now, Nai. Your duty. The whole village. The whole lot of them. This is what you will do. No one hears your steps on the floor. You take off your shoes. Holey socks on the wooden floors. Holey socks. Where the mice might have nibbled, anything for a bit of sustenance. They feasted on your sweat when you slept, tickles, gorging on your fungi. Are there still mice? So little these days, so little to go about. Barren everything. In you go. In. Wait. Snores. Is that what you hear? Rumbling. Always rumbling. Bellies. The land. Adenoids. Nothing but snores, and the odd house creak, the odd house murmur, the house just sighing a little, it doesn't want you in it, does it, no one wants you, oh you angel of death, for that's what you are now Nai, an angel, now, Nai, of death, now, Nai, with a mission, now Nai, you may as well just go ahead and do it now. Get it all over with. What the hell are you waiting for? It'll pass the time. All this atrocity. Atrocity passes the time. They do not care anyway. They are sleeping, they do not want to make anything of their lives anymore. Who does? Some would rather sleep it off. Straight to death, in the middle of a dream about ice cream or sunflower fields. They do not want to wake up. Go on. You are doing them all a favour. No. Not the stairs yet. The kitchen first. You need to choose your weapon. A knife will be just fine. Just make sure it is the sharpest in the drawer. There. That one will do nicely. It gleams in the moonlight. You know there are only two souls upstairs. Go on. Go ahead. Him and her. Him and her in the same bed. Head near head. The old tradition remains. It is nice to see the old traditions remain. Isn't it? Is it? What about bodies apart? Even in the same bed, but souls wrung apart? Like the tearing of an old shirt you might use for a cleaning rag. Some have not managed to stay together. Some have not managed so well. Wait. The laughter has died down. The laughter stopped. *Hnn Hnn* stopped. A door closes. A car starts. That car farts, so old it is, one of the old ones it is, how it still goes is anyone's guess, what does it even run on? Work around the house then, can you hear it? Clinkings and clank-ings, cutlery laid down in drawers in the correct order, or are they the chains of old ghosts rattling in the childless corridors? Put them out of their misery, and yours too, your own, when the time comes. The time comes. No need to wait for another set of waves to come crashing in. That'll be soon enough. What year is this? What moon? Anyway. Go on. You have your knife and it is sharp. Gleams in the moonlight, and your slow silent steps on the floor in the silent night. On you go. Only the snores of him and her, him and her that lay before you. This destruction. This creation. Do you need to see their faces one last time? No, you don't. This is all you need. All that matters. Let's call them the Shirotos. For the sake of characters having names. Him and her. He is handsome. But so what? She is not all that attractive, but who cares? You think only of the job at hand to pass the time. You have to take them all out. One by one. Fast and stealthy in the night. With no one else around. Here now. The bedroom. The noise is louder. Both of them snore. You will take the breath from both of them. Take it. Take it away. You are saving them. You are a saviour. You are required. And so you must go on. The knife raised now. You stand, the knife raised over the heart of him. The heart of man. Him first. The tactic. Take the stronger one out first. In case the other one wakes up and puts up a fight. But what fight has anyone left? One might wake up, so, just in case. That is the burden of the village. The waking up. Best if they all don't wake up. Best sleep sleep. Dreams of ice cream and sunflower fields. Best die die. Great, so, the moonlight, the knife, the knife raised over the heart of man and then the... wait. Wait. Wait. What is that noise outside the window? Girls' voices. Who are they? What words do they speak? *Witch*, the word. *Witch*. Witch? What intrusion is this? All the laughing has stopped. It's shouting now. It's not. It's chanting now. What's this? *Fly on that?* Someone says. A girl's voice says *fly on that? Not Halloween*, then. Girls' voices. What is going on? What has come to disturb the order? When all that was wanted was a bit of peace and quiet. Radio on? Is it? Is it on? Or was it turned off? Sometimes it is on and there are sonatas, arias, sounds of souls from somewhere far, bleeps and murmurings, and sometimes the machine is off, but sounds come from outside the house. The house that still stands but should have gone along with everything else. *You can't hit us.* That's the next heard. Then, *every fibre of you.* What? What is? Never mind. Ignore it. Go on, Nai. This is what you have been chosen to do. To take them all away from this. Take their useless breath. They do nothing but weep all day anyway, these villagers. Every village everywhere. What kind of a way to weep all day? Knife raised. Go on, Nai. Only snores now and your heart beating fast. This is the first time you have ever done such a thing. Bound to be nervous. Natural. Now! Now! Now! Now! Down plunges the knife, fast and forceful, into the chest of the handsome man who has just risen up with the sheer force of it, and his eyes have shot open in instantaneous alarm, and no sooner does the pain register than the life is sucked right out of him. His gasping is only seconds for soon it fades and soon is nothing but demise. All a lot faster than you would have thought. You struck so well into the heart of the matter, straight strike, bull's eye, gave no time for anything else. Just did it! And barely a budge from the other side of the bed. Hardly registered anything in the quiet night. Snoring continues. Does not have any idea, no awareness that the husband beside her, beside her of say, twenty years, is now taken away, just like that, so soon erased. So you move, Nai, quickly, Nai, to the other side of the bed, and raise it up once more. Raise it up to the air and down again the terrible plunge as swift and deadly as the first. Such strength you show, such bravery and exactitude. You are the kind of hero we need around these parts. Put an end to all of them and their misery. So much of it. Misery. Every land needs a hero. And you have come to assume that mantle. A prophet. No, a messiah. A saviour. Now, off you go. You have quite a bit of work to do. A whole village full of them. An undertaking for sure. But you are not beyond it. Not beyond. It can be done. And what of the woman in the bed? What about...

can you move to the most gloomy bed and with the same knife
can you please please please put out the light
put out of misery, out of
can you please do it, just do it, just do it
please oh please can you just do

III

the starved lover sings

22

Hordes.

Hordes of fans walking towards the ground. Match day. Whole families of characters and minds, echoes, echoing through the streets. Another chance for fans to scream. Who is there to watch the kicks and fouls and scurryings and scramblings? And who is there just to scream? Let off some steam.

Dressing room. Full swell of man-smell. Get beyond the drain cleaner and there is deodorant and sweat and urine, shampoo and stud-mud, body soap and semen-like wet towel. Hide and Takeshi in the middle of all this. Lacing their boots. They don't look up when I step in, they don't acknowledge my existence.

"I am here."

"Good afternoon, Nemoto-san."

Unnerving unison, taking their eyes from their aglets for the briefest moment and up to my face.

I shouldn't be the one that is uncomfortable. I shouldn't be the one. It's these...

It's these two, these are the ones that had Marina's male genitals in their clammy paws. Even as I think this it seems to make no sense, how could I not have known? How come I never know these kinds of things? Was it not obvious? No, I don't think so, no I don't...

I tell them I'll need a few minutes to prepare and that they can go ahead and warm up. I hand them their flags, hoping they will be on form today, and will not let me down – I get a sudden image of Monstaa too, and know he will be in the crowd expecting. Expecting what? What is he expecting of me? That I just roll over do what he says? Is that how I am to live my life? Roll over? Play dead? And what if I don't? What if I don't comply? What would he do to me? Am I to find out?

Speak of the devil.

He appears at the door, large frame blocking out the light. He nods at me. Am I supposed to nod back? He turns around to see if anyone is listening in, but only his two goons are behind, one flagrantly giving his balls a good shuffle. Nice. We have become such a charming race.

"All OK, Nemoto-sensei?"

I say nothing, just keep my eyes on my bootlaces, but how many times do they need to be knotted? It is an embarrassing thing when they loosen on the pitch, or you lose your boot, or one gets stuck in the mud, causes jeers from the crowd when you bend to do them up. It has been raining of course. Naturally. They'll be sliding all over the pitch, the players taking lumps out of the ground, as well as each other.

"I'm hoping things will go according to plan."

I inspect my studs, make sure they are clean and ready to sink into the soft grass.

According to plan? What does he mean *according to plan*? How should I know the way a game will turn out? How am I supposed to know what way the wind will blow, what way a ball can deflect and ricochet off in another direction altogether? How am I to know when the waves will come again and drown us all? Where was I when Ruby was walking home and the waves, the giant waves came and…

The missiles too sometimes change direction. Were the last ones aimed at the Capital? Or is everything just coming for me? My solipsism and I, we get along so well together, we…

"You are very silent. Looks like you have a lot to think about. Well, I'll leave you to your thoughts, Nemoto-sensei, I'm sure you have a lot to prepare. A lot to think about. I will see you at half-time, just to check in."

Think about what? Check in on what? How am I to know anything? Am I a person or just a tool, a conduit, a…

I find my hands are shaking. My heart is beating fast. This is no way to begin a game. I am supposed to appear calm and in control of things. This is the impression I am supposed to give. I am the one who is supposed to impose order. I cannot be seen to be shaking and sweating already.

Am I then to relent? Just do as he pleases? Roll over?

Why were those two girls at my house? What do they want from me?

My wife. She sleeps. Heap of grief.

Play dead?

Why did Marisa join me on the exercise mat, then tumble on top of me? What was to gain by that? What is to gain by any of this? What is the point? And why me? Why me in the middle of the pitch calling the shots. Why me? Why can't someone else take charge? It's not a very enticing position. Why can't somebody else do it? Maybe there is no one else. Maybe there is no one else, no one else in the whole world; only me out walking at night, the last nights on Earth, me, and a few wild animals. That's all that's left.

Serried ranks of excitable fans singing in the stands. Already yellow voices. What have they got to be angry about so soon? Nothing has happened yet. Already I hear my name and the abuse that goes with it. Some are ex-students, I can see one or two faces in the crowd. I knew them. Maybe I was harsh on them when they lined up in the gymnasium on cold mornings and I shouted at them and I made them bend and move to the radio warm-up exercises. This is their moment of payback.

But I have learned how to shut them out. I can ignore. A referee learns to do that. A teacher can do this too. I am a referee and a teacher and a man and a husband. No, I am a husband and a teacher and a referee. No, I am a father and a husband...

I insist on order. I insist on the order of things. Someday I may have it all sorted out.

I jog and jump a little on the spot. Get my legs pumping. I need to be fit. A referee needs to be fit. Even a teacher needs to be fit. Standing at the top of the classroom all day, the pacing to and fro, and hours spent over paperwork, the neck-cricks and lower back bites, the muscular stabs and sears, a teacher needs to be fit, physically and mentally...

No, I need order, not repetition.

The two captains are in the centre circle with me. They shake hands. They look like they mean business. Everyone takes this with exceeding seriousness. It's just a game. No, it's not just a game. Look at their eyes. They are youths, yes, but they are not children. Exceeding seriousness. This means a lot to them. It means nothing to me. I don't care. I only care about Ruby and Asami and Marisa and...

Forget the order of things. On with the game.

I take a look at my watch. Then over to the two assistant referees. Look at them. How could they have...

It's almost time. All eyes are on me. The place is buzz-ing and it needs me to start things off. I am the centre of the universe for one brief moment. Or *before* the universe, *before* the bang. The silence is momentarily startling. Before the tirade of verbal abuse, before the tsunami of chants, there's this brief and terrible silence, as if you have just entered into a vacuum. This must be what the birth of the universe was like, first nothingness, silence, then...

Blow... begin... chaos... you must keep it in order, the whole thing in order... if you don't blow, if you don't stop them they will kick and elbow the shit out of... screams from the home crowd, screams in return from the travelling fans... yellow voices... Monstaa watching my every move, I can't even see him but I can feel him... run run running the game... blow, foul... already... my fingers to my eyes say "I've got them fixed on you boy"... I've seen him before, nasty piece... I run... I'm running... at night I walk... by day I run... run from my problems... Rabbit... run to my fantasies... run into trouble... Maya... the Maya encomium... run into... I'm watching you too, midfielder... run run running the game... Maya's ass... gait and glide... wait, Maya is not the manga superhero, it's me... I have the ability to stop time... one blow and everything freezes... my father wrote... *but the people here have no spirit for revolution*... that was what my father wrote... Asami sleeps in a heap... my father wrote... what?... reams... reams of thoughts, called it philosophy, called it literature sometimes too... such bullshit... *but the people here have no spirit for revolution*... maybe he was right... furious aphorisms from his screen... or called them fizzles... purloined word of course... or poetry... such shit... those things... nobody... nobody these days... play on... run run running the game... Marisa says she likes space...space programmes on the WaSc... she didn't mention porn... says she likes the idea of nothingness and vastness... blow, foul... enough of that boys... break it up... spray the line... take it from there... blow... kicks it till it finds someone's head and over the crossbar... useless... run run running the game... wasted opportunity... their fathers and mothers must be proud though... their sons giving it all... my girl... giving it everything... my girl is gone... run running running... running the game...at least that's my excuse... blow... take that throw again... screams from the crowd... yellow... why is he allowed take that again? They want to know... they want to know... this treacherous crowd... demanding... was a foul throw... I don't know... not getting much help from the two assistant referees... how could I not, how could I not, really see? Hide shakes his head as if I am... on... running... as if I am making mistakes... how could I not have known? no way, no foul... get up, play on... advantage... run run running the game... Hide raises his flag for offside... what? I didn't think that... but I must give it... must be seen to be in line with these two... these two... the fans are screaming... at least one set of fans... no way was that offside... I think they are right... but I have just given it... given in... better watch those two... have they been gotten to? has Monstaa... run run running the game... who is running all this... right, eye on those two as well as the players as well as Monstaa and the yellow girls... did I put the cards in my pocket... pat... yep... red and yellow... these colours... I see them in my dreams... heap of wife beside me wheezes in her mind-disease... red... yellow... not yet... watch it! got my eyes on you... severity of expression... blow... foul... nope, take it back, back further... back further... spray... lines... don't cross the lines... how do you know if you have crossed a line... you are a stalker... no... technically... you were outside her house... yes... but... not following her... it is clear on the green of the pitch... a clear white line... demarcation... you are... you are a Peeping Tom... no... but... we are all of us voyeurs... blow... kick... ball-swerve... goal! oh my word!... that was a piece of artistry... which side is Monstaa on again? shit... he'll be fuming... I don't care... I am no one's toy... demarcation, what people need... I am... run run running the game... I am a man and... look at my watch... still a long way to go this first half... another flag, Takeshi this time... go over

"What was that for?"

"He was offside. I had a clear view of it."

"Didn't look offside to me."

"Honest."

"Really?"

"Honest."

Really? Really?

Hordes. Hordes murmuring. Hordes muttering. Hordes waiting for the game to commence. Waiting to lambast. That's what I'm there for. Receiver of lambasts. If I wasn't here to bellow at then maybe they'd have no one. Maybe they'd beat their wives or husbands or children or Labradors. Maybe they'd ravage or rape or murder. It's possible. Once I heard, maybe from my wife, back when she spoke, of a marauding madman who...

What is a horde? ...running the game... it can't be a horde, this is only a village... hordes are big... the waves know no demarcations... the waves know only their wave-ness... but big for here... do the waves know when they are coming... imagine if all these catastrophes had voices as they came... what would they sound like? ...because this village is small and is diminishing... what does a mountain sound like? if it could talk I mean... running, running... gasses and ice and asses... what would they say as they planned their terror together? ...what do they want, those two? ...the land eroded ...those two weird girls… get up for… get up off the ground… get out of bed… walk, walk again… everything decreasing… always a something… never nothing… always a something coming for you… or if the mudslides had voices… and everything ceasing then…

But now is not the time.

What is the time?

I look at my watch.

Blow.

Half time.

23

CATASTROVOICE 3

The 11th thought it would be a great idea, but the idea was shit. This happens a lot in politics. This happens a lot in every field, in every half-baked discipline.

The year was 2030. *A modern-day Atlantis! What a splendid idea!* A community of people that would live under the sea, or at least just under the surface. Huge spirals were made (cost: billions, 3tn for each one, and they made two), connecting watertight spheres to the ocean floor (the people were to live in these spheres). Power was to be generated by methane-producing micro-organism factories, and workers could even travel down the spirals to the seabed to mine other materials (rare earth materials that were dwindling on the land above and could be brought up and used as possible alternative energy sources). Splendid.

They estimated that at least five thousand people could live in the spheres and that these spheres could retract when the weather was bad and pull back down under the water. When the sun was out they could go up again and take advantage of the sunlight (solar panels also used for generation within the spheres). Splendid.

What a way to signal the country's re-emergence, what a

way to say to the rest of the world: look this is what we can do, we have thinkers that go beyond, we have the know-how and dexterity to carry this off and soon, soon cities in the oceans will be as common as cities on land.

But it had been founded on the premise that the ocean floor was stable and would not move, and after years of plate shifts wasn't this a rather foolish assumption? The 11th (or was it the 9th or 10th?) was clearly trying to write himself into the glorious annals of a once glorious nation that might (with a bit of luck) become glorious again.

But the plates had other ideas. The plates (and any rational mind might concur) have no voice, but what if the plates had a voice, what would they say?

We have been here for a long long time and we like to move, oh yes, we do like to move. Just when you think we have settled in our place we are off again, rubbing up against each other for all we are worth and having a great old time of it, the lithosphere livening up and letting itself go, oh yes, for we love to move, oh yes.

The seafloor sways away from the spreading ridge and we drag and suck down and even the sun and moon come in to play with us.

So you have decided to build on the ocean floor, have you? Well well, what a hair-brained idea that was! As if we would just settle down and stay still and never move again. But not party plates like us. We like to move, just when you think we are still and silent, that's when we'll be thinking about getting on the move again. Dear dear, when will you ever learn?

The sea washes away the shit and it breaks up into tiny floating, undulating pieces; some fall to the muddy bed and will settle there. It is only a matter of time, tide and time, before the bed is rocked awake again and then the surge moves forward to thrash upon the land again and the people, in the form of tiny particles of useless shit, are then brought home again.

Shit. Again and again.

24

I should have known. Monstaa at the door. Livid. He's raging. He's trying to keep his voice down but can't seem to manage it. The veins are veritably throbbing at his temples, like thin worms with heartbeats implanted under his skin. The score is 1-0 with his side on the losing end. And I had disallowed a goal too, offside, even though my assistant referee was a little late with his flag, I made the final decision, and I think I was right.

"Not good enough referee! Not good enough!"

The goons are at the door keeping an eye out. Hide and Takeshi are in the dressing room too, but aren't in the least bit perturbed, as if they had played their part to the letter. Monstaa is happy enough with them. They are all in on it. They are all in on this conspiracy, this fixing, this whatever-you-want-to-call-it. Sin. As if I hadn't known.

I'm saying nothing of course, which is adding to his anger. I don't even look at his face now. Why bother? I know the ugliness I'll see there. I just scrape mud from my studs with a blunt old knife, a thing that's been here forever, was in some kitchen somewhere once, maybe it got carried over here on a flood, and now has a different job altogether. Maybe I can find a new job, too, a new purpose, get carried away to somewhere better. I could always head off somewhere brighter and warmer and get a job there, couldn't I? Picking fruit off the heavy branches. Somewhere they say the sun still shines. What's the point of staying here? No daughter. No wife, really. What's the point of going on? I'm sure they could find another idiot to referee their games. All they need is to offer some cash. There'll surely be takers. It's easy enough. All you've got to be is fair. And keep the whole thing in order. That's easy enough, isn't it?

"Are you even listening to me? You know what will happen! There's a lot of money riding on this game!"

I couldn't care less. My daughter is gone.

Blow... begin... chaos... you must keep it in order, the whole thing must be kept in order... lines and demarcations... if you don't blow... if only everything in life where as plain and simple... drawing a line that you cannot cross... Maya... why do I always want to cross that line... shot well over the bar... Maya's glorious backside... what I wouldn't give... what would you give? waste of a chance... Monstaa will be furious... the two on the sides cannot keep their eyes off me... look at them waiting to see if I will give in...why do they come in twos... these pairs of evil... will I crumble... snap... he'll break me in two... and those two girls... what do they want?... Monstaa is not enjoying himself one bit... can see his wrath from the corner of my eye... he is like pus... like an infection... Asami has beautiful eyes... but I don't see them anymore... they are shut... Tombo has big eyes... Tomohiro... Tomohiro Nemoto... looks like an insect... the playground jeers... so what... could've been worse... my daughter is gone... my ears... my ears are bad since... Maya... fizzles... Maya's ass... is there anything else so perfect in this world... Marina too... beautiful... but she

has a cock now... my legs are tired... my mind is tired... how
would I know if she always had one or not... play on... is
she still beautiful? we are none of us perfect... mind tired...
too many thoughts... maybe Asami is right... just break
down... stay in bed... to hell with it... what's the point in
getting up... heap... heap of life... blow foul... heap of she...
heap... take it from there...a nother wasted chance... sails
over the bar... strong wind today... Monstaa is on his feet...
should be a free kick... Marisa... I am not a decent man...
why is she not already taken? I'd take her... why not... I have
no wife... I do... play on... I do have a wife... what do I do?
...run, run, running the game... up and down the length of
the field... thirty... who are you? ...not young anymore ...not
old either... just kind of stuck... this heap of... the land is
dying... 11... 12... 13... what's next... another idiot running
the country... waves and wolves... Asami's eyes are hidden...
need to be fixed... blow again... elbows, keep them down
boy... and I am married anyway... heap... bound to end in *a
grandiose fit of madness*... read that... father's download suggestions... Kafka... oddest moments... no... play on... I said
no... no need for reading now... those days gone... who has
time for all that... useless... keep my eyes off the crowd, the
yellow screams... they are abusing me now... I became a PE
teacher... run run running the game... eyes in the back of
my head... Tombo... dragonfly... insect... yellow screams...
they are abusing... have you got no eyes referee? are you not
seeing what's going on? always see it... going on all around
me... my daughter is gone... dirty game... they never let you
go... those wild dogs... all vice-grip... pit-bull terriers! Name
just came to me... oddest moments... always a summoning...
listen to the screams... are those from the crowd or are those
in my head? ...play on... run run running the game... no
yellow card yet... but it's getting dirty... my ears no longer...

at night I ramble... see it all there too... Asami's daughter is gone... corner... preposterous my flesh and blood... run run running the game... stop that pushing in the box... Asami would ask me in the morning what I wanted for dinner that evening... great cook... but how was I to know what I wanted later... play on... only know what I want now... I am a man... my flesh is foolish... Maya's posterior... blow again... free kick... spray... Asami looking at me... take a look at my watch... we are all of us summoned... groan... the sweat drops from my forehead onto the grass... *everything conspires, elements and actions alike, to harm you*... Cioran was... what? ...a favourite of my father... he had his points... a man... every man has his points... I am a man... play on... *I am disorder*... Sabbath... play dead... I don't know... useless... I am not a decent man... cannot help myself... watch... stay with...quest to find some order... all right... that's it... two added minutes up... blow... game over...

25

Barefoot still. What has happened to her shoes? What has happened to her? Did her family float away and did they sink? She stops a while and rests and looks at her cuts and sores. Some people cut themselves intentionally, she has no need, the world does it for her. Close to the bone.

Close to home now.

She walks on and sings something about the bottom of the pit and on and on shoeless and forlorn and on and on and on.

A girl walks on and

26

I should have known. Monstaa at my car. Livid again. The right thing to do now would be to get out of here as fast possible; I should try to run and save myself. But in which direction should I turn? And to what end? It's not like he wouldn't be able to catch me. He might be old, might be physically past it himself, but he has his minions to do his bidding: his goons would have their meaty hands on my neck in no time. Or the Eggmen. I see them there too, their louche loitering at the far side of the car park, waiting to cover my vehicle in their usual goo. I have no chance at all.

"Thought we had a deal, Mr. Referee. I was under the impression that we had come to a kind of understanding."

The game has rules. It's my job to be fair. To be fair and nothing else. This is what I want to say, but the most I can do is stutter and shake.

"I... I..."

I want to tell him too about the pain of living, about poetic moments, about my parents, my missing child, my loves and losses, Maya's ass, and how waking is the pain. But what sense would it make? What good would it do? It would all come out in one nonsensical belch. For that is the way my mind turns. Turns and turns and farts out its excess. The best thing would be for him to take out a gun and end me now. Does Monstaa have a gun? How far does his criminality go? I am about to find out.

One of them catches my arms behind my back while the other one punches me hard in the stomach. The wind goes completely out of my sails and I am collapsing, knees buckling – sometimes during a game, a ball, stray yet stealthy, gets kicked right into my stomach, or worse, finds its way to my privates, always a great spectacle for the antsy crowd, and it's a humiliating and painful experience, but this is double or triple that force, not stray at all but absolutely deliberate, and it is excruciating. To accompany the first punch, another one also lands on my nose, sending a spray of blood onto the windscreen. Not albumen today then, not eggy white but red red blood.

"You cost me a lot of money."

I am then bundled into the back of a van and driven away. I had not even seen it approaching, but suddenly I am in the back of it, and the beatings continue. My mind is just a noise, just thunderous noise, the blood rushing through me, a Niagara of push. They are tying me down too, they have got my hands behind my back and the rope or wire or whatever it is chafes my skin.

"A lot of money."

The van seems to be travelling at some speed. There are no windows to let me know this and I could not see out anyway, my eyes seem to be closing, either from the swelling or from the sheer force of fear. It may be that I don't want to see anything anymore; I just want this to be the end of everything. Would you, please please please? Is it at all possible? The final whistle. Blow. Blow. Please blow. They have gone to so much trouble, all this organization… it's not like they don't mean business. I know for sure I will be tortured, that they are only warming up; they might even decide to kill me. Please please please. And make it fast.

I accept my fate. I don't argue my case. I don't plead for mercy. This might be all a blessing.

Faces run through my mind, like it is an album of all my loves, flicking right in front of me: Ruby, Asami, my mother, my father, Marisa, Marina the whore, Maya my workmate. Only one male. This is rather pathetic, but then that doesn't surprise me at all. Why not even those buddies from child-hood? Why can't I picture someone helping me collect car-toon cards, collect frog spawn, collect risqué comic books, collect memories? Why…

We have arrived. I am hauled back out. I am treated to more kicks and blows. I am pain all over. I can feel blood drip-ping from my nose. Hot blood. Walking is the pain, living is the pain. Waking.

Still I hope they will do whatever they have planned swiftly, cut to the chase, Monstaa do your worst… I know I have become quite delirious, this is what they call "shock", I presume, the doctors in daytime dramas are always quick to diagnose. This must be it. *Shock.* But would I know it? Or am I just holding out for my demise? The colours that whirl around my mind are stupendously beautiful, mostly purple and shades of violet, as if foreshadowing the colour of the bruises that are already forming on my flesh. They act like a buffer too, this temporary blindness, protecting my from the pain that my body doesn't quite know how to manage just yet… yes, this must be shock.

The faces still slide on before my eyes, Asami, my beauti-ful wife: why didn't you ever get up? Why do you not take my hand when I offer it to you day after day?

They have positioned me on a chair. They have not come this far to skip on any of the details.

They have surrounded me and they are barking, wild and nonsensical utterings – they sound like the wolves that creep around the neighbourhoods at night, sniffing out living meat, when they are hungry and discontent and ready to hunt again this is the sound they make, barking and eerie, spine-chilling guttural groans. The blood still rushes between my ears and the sounds are too hard to decode: what is this tongue they use? This dislodges me further; I like to have things in order; I like to have my life…

Purple. Violet. Pulse. Album of my years, fading. Frog spawn? What colour is that? Clear, isn't it?

At last it is Monstaa only. His loud voice in front of me. I open my eyes now to see him. I can see. I am able to see. His sneer. His leer. And I can hear. All I need is to focus. Concentrate. Tell them what they want. They might let me go. But I don't want to be let go. Let go back to what? Better the idea of demise. Better go now, swift and swift and just out of here. These are not dark thoughts. Quite the opposite, these wishes for death are light, totally light. In colour and in weight. There is not the *darkness* of the thought of death, only the darkness-shutting-out -the-light-of-death, which is light (in colour, in my mind, warmly hued) and light in weight, airily light. Am I following all this? What is he saying to me?

"A lot of money."

This I have gathered is the crux of the matter for him and it seems an apology will not do. He asks me why I did not play his game, why I did not relent, why I was being so difficult. Again, I want to say to him that the game has rules. That it is my job to be fair. That it is my duty to be fair and nothing else. But I have not the strength. The colours in my head have gone back to red and yellow again. This somehow manages to settle me.

His goons come closer, wide-eyed, as if expecting something momentous to happen any minute – I might spontaneously combust, I might die right here under their very fists! – this makes them keen to inflict more blows.

Monstaa intervenes however. He sighs, as deep a sigh as I could muster myself, I am almost impressed. What perturbs the man now is how I could be so thick-headed, so disregarding of his will, disregarding of his might. Where would I get the nerve? How could I be so utterly stupid? But… does he not know that I am dead already? Already far gone. That only my body has been going through the motions these past years, and that my soul has long since flown. Does he not know that I am sorry for my life? I am sorry for your life. I am sorry for all our lives…

He sits on a chair in front of me – where have these chairs come from? Where – now that I think of it – are we? I look around this cavernous warehouse. There are signs, broad retail signs with apples on them, plump and gleaming red apples. It strikes me then that we are in a neighbouring village, not far from my home at all, a place where yes, apples, were the local produce and were quite famous; delicious they were too, until they were uprooted by one of the quakes or washed away by one of the floods or one of the manifold calamities – take your pick, something is always bound to get you. This place must have lain disused for years. Only Monstaa and his cartoon apes had imagination enough to use it for their movie torture scenes. I just hope he takes out a knife and slashes my throat and gets it all over with. I really don't think I can go to work looking like this on Monday morning. The principal, for one, will be quite alarmed when he summons me into his office for our brief chat. I think I'd rather the blade. Dead already. Quite long gone. Although I am in exquisite pain, I am also beginning to find this whole episode oddly funny, it must surely be the delirium, the mind playing its usual ghoulish games, like we don't have enough to contend with.

Monstaa looks tired. Maybe he sees the hopelessness in my eyes. Maybe he is hopeless too. Maybe his family was washed away or ravaged by wolves or sank into some hole or floundered under an avalanche of mud. It could have happened. Anything could've happened. Maybe he was abused as a teen, taken to some copse on the outskirts of the village and stripped and handled by vampires. Why not? Anything could've happened. This late in the game, what would it take to surprise you?

"You will never speak of this. You will never say what happened to you. No one will know. And you will never referee again. Get someone else to do it."

I want to tell him that I do not make those decisions, that I was simply called upon, summoned time and time again. That I just happened to have a license for refereeing that I took as part of my PE education, and that if I never blew a whistle again, it would be all right with me. Or if I never took another breath, then that would be all right too. Ruby is gone. My wife, in her way, is gone too. I want women who don't want me, whores and… and I am trapped and…

But the fight has gone out of him as much as it has gone out of me. He had simply banked on the wrong man. Maybe he thought *my* goons, Hide and Takeshi, had persuaded me to join their nefarious little clique and…

It's not because I'm morally superior or anything, I just wanted there to be a little order; if the game of football had rules, then the rules should have been respected; no moral high ground, the game should have been played the way it was set out. That's all. That's all I ever wanted I suppose. Fair play.

My father could've written a treatise on fairness. Maybe he had read such philosophical doctrines, morality, justice, fairness, but that was not my forte, I am nothing, I am nothing at all, just a man who sits in his kitchen and…

He does not look like he will take any knife to my throat. Nor does it look like he has a gun. Looks like I will simply be discarded. He has not even the energy to do away with me. I don't know if I am relieved or disappointed.

"A lot of money."

His sighs are as heavy as mine. And then he gets up and brushes himself down. He signals to his men and they lift me back into the van. This could be an act of mercy. I don't know what it is.

We drive for a few minutes and then, after a loud bang on some part of the van, a cry of "here" and a cutting loose of the shackles that bind me, the door is opened and I am flung out of the moving vehicle. I tumble and I roll and I wince in pain and when I open my eyes it is night, pitch black, and I am alone again.

There were male friends. Why do I think of them now? Alone. Here. Why not? As good a time as any. There was no frog spawn. But there were boys, boys my age; we played sports of course, and video games, and we climbed trees in the forests on the outskirts of the village, and we swung from ropes. Were there forests then? Why do I think of them now as sparse woods, skeletal trees, like they are skinny underfed girls who have been ordered to strip and are ashamed of their feeble nakedness?

Makio Nishimoto.

Hitoshi Izumi.

Masanobu Nakata.

Where have they all gone? They are no longer in the village. Did they do the smart thing and move on? Move out? Or were they washed away? Are these the only two possibilities?

I lie looking up at the stars. There are a few. I can just make them out. They are vague and slight but they emit light.

I am sore. Sore to my core. I am on this road.

And I am alone.

27

I am not alone.

A wolf mother and her cubs.

Is this what I really see? Or do I invent?

She is about twenty meters away from me, deep in the thicket, surrounded by thick brush and...

But it is her eyes that I catch, and hers catch mine too, both of us, looking; her green glare in the gloaming; I have to peer hard to make out her features. Perhaps my eyes are becoming more accustomed to this dark, but her form begins to make itself known, as do the three little cubs that nip at her snout, looking for more food to be regurgitated, for their little bellies to be filled, ever-hunger, ever-want, the ever-need of the breeding, breathing.

She knows I am here. Not only can she see me, but I'm sure she smells me: my sweat, the blood that bubbled to surface and now hardens at the corner of my eye. She surely knows that I am no threat, am derangement only, no ungulate for her pack to chase – where is her pack anyway, chasing elsewhere, or leaping over a fence with ease into a fold? They would tear me apart, too, of course they would, hooved or not, they have adapted, as we all have, to new circumstances, new days. She growls lowly, a deep rumble in her throat to tell me that ten meters is close enough, any further and her babies are at risk, any further and she will have to defend, or attack, however it would all play out. But I have no intention of going any further, am content to see her like this, her precious offspring snuggled up to her, safe, assured, knowing that their mother will do everything to keep them alive.

They feed on the old, the sick, the weak, these wolves down from the high ground to wrestle on the shores in these harrowing times; the scent of the rotting meat got all too much: the bodies washed up, what else were they to do? New days, new situations. Wolves will always find new prey. Midnight howls at every moon abound: *Canis lupus hattai* – my, my, where have you been so long?

I remember my father reading me old folktales when I was a boy, so many animals in the forests, each with wonderful episodes of their own, the cunning foxes, the sly snakes, the stock cast of beasts in any land, but the wolves frightened me, it was their numbers, their togetherness, the way they surrounded as one, all angles, manoeuvre and maul, what chance did you have?

In the stories the grain farmers would worship these wolves, making them almost deities, they would leave neat plates of food in front of their dens, calm offerings that would somehow beseech them to keep safe their growing crops in the coming season, and to fend off deer or wild boar who came to graze there. My father relished the details, explaining how these animals had forty-two teeth, some of them flat for the breaking of bone, some of them sharp for the ripping apart of skin and flesh. I was often sent to bed with these images, my mind distempered, and they invaded my dreams, the salivating malicious packs, sometimes they still do: when something is all around you, it seeps right in, right through: wolves, waves, women, and grief, grief for the missing, grief and dread. But why put such images in a young boy's head?

Dreaming is the pain as much as waking. Dreaming is the...

I leave her at it. This is not Dante's she-wolf, this is an animal surviving and helping her offspring to live and carry on, commendable beast. I should have been there to protect mine. I had only one. One girl. How could I have lost my one and only girl, how come my hand lost hers, slipped away and...

I take my battered and bloody face, my hurt limbs, away from the serene scene, away to find my own den, to discover what awaits me there. What will I find? What next? You graciously lingered, and still, still no sign of anything like a hero.

The road is long and my tired legs are barely up to it. I am daily, a fit, strong man, but I have had enough of this particular day, quite enough. Instinct, I presume, like any beast, keeps me on the right track, back to the village and the path to my house. I need no satellite, need no computerized navigation system, need not even the stars, I just sway my way, drifting like a dream, floating like a fog.

And there it is, still standing gothically grim, perennially dreary. Everything around it gone, dragged and dropped into the tumult of the sea. I walk up the incline and gaze upon it, wondering if it will ever give off any warmth, and if only houses with children ever give off warmth; who would dare to spend a night inside?

Marisa is watching out of the first-floor window and follows my plod up the path and my almost-collapse at the door. Actually, when the door opens, I do collapse, straight into her arms, as if it had been planned. I must be heavy. My life on top of hers must feel so heavy. Why is she not my wife? I can smell her congeries: cooking aroma, powders, pastes, and her own sweet perfume. Why is my wife not there to carry me, over the threshold? My wife smells only of decay.

Why is Marisa not my wife? Seriously, why?

Why is my mother no longer alive? Am I the only…

Her face is stricken with horror, she had not been expecting any of this. Me in this condition.

"What on earth happened?"

Her voice is shrill and bores into my ears even more. Sore my ears, sore.

"Rough game," I say, trying to make light of it, trying to make light of my life. I want to crack a smile, too, but it hurts too much.

I am on the same mat as I had been – how many hours previous? Remember that? We had lain on this bright blue exercise mat, this obscene cartoon-blue mat, and I had heaved and pushed and she had slid on top of me. Now look at us. She is bent over me, and whatever inkling of desire she may have held is overtaken by pity. Pity and concern. I gasp like a fish on a muddy bank, laboriously sucking air into my lungs, but my heart has at least stopped its furious racing, and my legs are happy to be stretched out and no longer pacing the paths and raking the roads.

My mother had prints and photographs of various versions of the *Pietà*, Michelangelo's obviously, but also Joseph Whitehead's *Mother and Son*, and it is the latter one I am reminded of now, for although I am not laid out across her, it is the way I imagine myself, her nourishing maternal presence overwhelming the mise-en-scene, and my piteous pose, inviting only sorrow unto the situation.

Swiftly she severs the scene to scurry and retrieve the things she'll need. Again everything done in a hurricane of hurry. She returns with soft cloths and a small basin, and the powerful smell of disinfectant is the most welcome salve of all, soothing and caring and loaded with memories of childhood heal and balm. She takes the cloth and wets it and dabs my maudlin face, my wounds, and I am happy to accept it all and grow soft and low in calm. This is as intimate as we will ever get, I know this now, and I am grateful for her, I am glad that she exists and is my family.

She whispers to me like she would a child, and I wonder if she whispers and coos to her own sister in the same way. How wonderful a mother she could have been. She still could be. How old is she again? I begin to hope it's not too late for her. Is it? I am in this moment reminded too of my preposterous erotic hankerings, not only for her, but for all the other women I have tainted in this telling – here though, what is clear, is that what pathetic man most needs, is someone to sanitize the wounds, or would you rather have us doleful creatures lick our own? She is delicate and for all her meatiness wraps around me with squirrel-like movements and careful administrations. There is such goodness here, I could lie here forever and take all this; and in the world too, must be, goodness there simply must be, how sad it is to see so much of it always washed away.

She washes away my pain, the soap singing its way up my nose, my breath finding slow and easy grooves now, and her smile is beneficence.

"Those girls," I say. "What happened to them?"

"I was able to clear them away. They need not trouble you, at least not today."

"But they will appear again, won't they?"

I do not know why I ask her this question. Maybe it is only with myself I am conferring.

"Yes, I think they will come again. You must close up that business too. A lot of these things you must stitch up. Wounds need to be closed."

She dabs again at my literal wounds, while her voice softens over the figurative ones. I hear whistles, I hear cries from soccer fans, I hear yellow voices, I hear wolves baying, hungry cubs wanting more, I hear my wife upstairs as she stirs in the bed – should I show my wounds to her? Tell her all I've been through? Let her pity me? Let her weep for me? Or has she wept enough? Someday soon I want to think that this land will be dry. That no more waves will come and no more mud will slide down and no more snow and floods and no more tears. At least that. No more tears for a while. This is the most I can give her. No, I will not show her my terrible face, my black and blueness, my soiled soak-throughness. My black heart.

For a minute or two more I enjoy the dabbing and the care, the soft cloth on my skin, my tingling, already-healing skin.

When she rises to take her basin away and fill it with clean water, I feel no need to stare at her hips, no need to eye-weigh her breasts, her smile is enough, and I realize (pathetic specimen of maleness that I have grown into) that I am mostly mistaken in most of my affairs, that I have become morally... waylaid, and I miss my mother, I do, and I must not give up on my wife. There may yet be time for a hero to emerge from all of this morbidity, and I think it may well be me.

28

"UUURRRRRGHE. RRREEEEGURRSSSSHAW."
These are the sounds coming from Bado as
Sado watches on. The girls are in Bado's pink bedroom and
her scissors are in her right hand aloft and dangling dangerously over her left wrist and her eyes; her eyes are saying that
she is threatening, that she is really threatening something
this time, make no mistake, this is the real thing this time.
But Sado has seen this charade before, has seen the hyster-
ics, the over-reactions, the theatrics. When Bado gets all upset
she makes horror-sounds and then she reaches for something
sharp, her hands manically patting the floor or rummag-
ing the drawers for a knife, or a box-cutter, or more often
than not scissors. The horror-sounds are copied from the
virtual-horror-games they play on the WaSc, where they put
their faces really close to the screen and focus on one solitary
pixel and switch on the headset and the frequency it deliv-
ers implants a solitary searing silent signal that travels to the
amygdala. The amygdala then fires its glutamate out into two
other regions of the brain, and thus begin the process of getting into the state of being scared, and thus goosebumps, and
thus beating heart, and then sweats and *UUURRRRRGHE*

RRREEEEGURRSSSSHAW: the sound of Bado (though Bado is nowhere near the screen at this moment, and these jaculations dire must be coming from her naturally. Parasympathetic nervous system will kick in soon enough anyway and reverse the adrenaline bombast, and soon the heart will beat at its normal rate again. Normal again normal: as if they were familiar with such words or concepts. Such fun they have in this room in this house in this forgotten village.

Bado looks like something from a horror movie right now (though Sado won't say anything of the kind), something that would have played in the old movie theatre that got flooded, when the silver screen ripped off its wall and went sailing out the door in strips, as if it had a snakey bisect-y replicate-y mind of its own, and shone with the day's radiance as it got carried away – it was its first time out in the daylight, that silver screen, it might even have yawned! Bado is face-hang and mouth-droop and her hair is no longer tied-up and neat but hangs in straight clutches of length like thick seaweed, and she is not looking her best at all, oh no, and Sado is beginning to think she is quite losing it. And that just might be the case. Plenty others have lost their minds before. Plenty. In this land, in this village, plenty. Why, Sado once heard of a marauder who went from door to door at night, entering through the kitchens of quiet households and savaging the slumbering souls he found within. A whole village full of them! Though that couldn't be true, could it? Are we expected to believe that? One man marauder. Really? This day and age. Although it might have been a previous age. When was it? Old wives' tales. Surely. And all the wives are old now, and all of them are dying off. Where are all the young people? Where have they all skedaddled to? Imagine, imagine if it is only Bado and Sado left in the whole place. Imagine that for horror. The loneliness of that! Not even Daisuke to play with. Or what if they are the only two females left and they are to repopulate the country. Imagine that! Save the land! Like superheroes. Like two superheroes, or maybe one superhero with one sidekick, which? Nice pink costumes they could manufacture. Two-girl firm. And they could take off into the sky and fly, fly like birds. Wouldn't that be something! Wouldn't that signify, wouldn't that announce to the world, to the ARCK people: *look, look, you might have taken over the world with your strong economies, but look here, we have people, we have young teens who can take to the air, and they can just fly, fly like birds! Beat that!* All this is nonsense. Right from the beginning. Their lives. What truth to any of this? Why have we stuck with all this so far? Sado knows she is hardly there at all, just a sketch, they can all be erased so quickly. Bado might well lose the plot entirely, not that there was ever much of a plot to begin with, an animal's trot without direction, never to canter. Such is their lives, scant and getting scanter.

Sado soon gets bored with the histrionics of howl and hair and looks to the Snake Box for something to soothe. But the Snake Box is getting quite empty, and one of these slow afternoons they will have to go on a raid, skipping off to whichever local shop still stands (Sado saddens when she sees the emptiness, the horizon so clear, with all the shops and houses taken away, so clear the horizon, which makes it scarier when the big waves start coming in again, vast they appear, vast) and filling pockets with whatever items still sell until their pockets are packed.

Sado saddens when the…

Sado saddens if…

If they don't get caught. They must not get caught. They do not want to jeopardize their final stay in the village. A blot on their good (actually, *fair*) academic record would mean that they could not get in to the college they want, and to get to a reputable college would mean getting out of the village, which surely is the aim of all the poor youths still left and clinging. But they have yet to get caught stealing. The ensnarers yet to be ensnared. Why would it happen now? They are too swift with their hands, like magicians, super sleighty, the candy bar and the chocolate and the gum quick to the insides of their jackets and their secret linings and secret pockets. There is a lot about their lives that remain secret. Secrets of the village. That is why Sado likes to get naked with her friend, touching her in her private parts and being touched in turn. No more secrets. There is freedom in it. Freedom in no more secrets. Freedom in the reciprocating touches, too. They are not lesbians, even though Bado often calls Sado a "little lesbian". Or maybe they are sometimes, actual lesbians, but it doesn't matter. It's not about the sex. They can do without all that. It's about the tenderness, about the satisfaction, about the intimacy between two friends. And how many adults can say that about their lives anymore? What couples left in the village are intimate? They can't be. Intimate? They can't be. That's why no babies are being born. They are cold. Adults are cold. Like Sado's parents. Throwing things. Going someplace to do things with other people (although she has yet to find substantial proof of this, hard evidence, these are hunches only, but she is not so stupid as to not suspect something going on, her female intuition, her nose for scandal, as keen as any teenage girl's).

"Not much left."

She could be speaking about anything: the world, the country, the village, personal dignity, but she means the Snake Box. And Bado isn't listening anyway, she is all glazed over in her eyes and is thinking of something else entirely and says with seriousness in her parched throat:

"We need to capture Tombo. We have only one or two chances left."

"Before what?" asks Sado, fearing to be one step behind.

Bado stares ahead, straight ahead, no weird sounds now, no flashing blades, no horror-movie gestures or gesticulations, none of that, but she cannot answer her friend, so deep is she mired in thought and forecast.

"Chances left before… what? Before what happens?" asks Sado again, possibly two steps behind now.

Bado hasn't thought this through. Not any of it really. From the beginning it has all been winged, of its own accord and bearing, only she knows that it is nearing the end, knows that soon enough it will all come crashing down, she can feel it in her guts. She's not quite sure *what* will come crashing, or *how* it will come crashing, but just that something *will*. If those waves have been coming in on them for years, chances are that they'll *keep on* coming in on them for years more, she has read – where? – that the land had often gone decades without quakes or spills or any dreadful drenching, sometimes decades with nothing at all but industry and hard work and contentedness and the respect *of* people *by* the people *for* the people. But that is all alien to her, to all her friends too. They know only catastrophe. The dark villages have been ignored, and have only gotten darker. That is why she has turned bad, *Bado*, and her friend is always sad, *Sado*. Isn't that the reason? You don't have to be a therapist, you don't have to be the school counsellor (and hasn't that fine lady been kept on her toes!) to work out the root of the traumas. It's because their land has not settled. Constantly awake with quake and break. The sea brash with its thrash and crash. Volcanoes boom with fume and doom. If the very land won't settle then how are the people ever to be expected to settle? How? How? How? The politicians are no good (her father says, when he can be bothered to say anything) because they, too, are men without hope, though they live in the cities, where things still work and people still cross the junctions in their thousands, with purpose and pride (impervious to the rise of ARCK and its insidious influence). But in the villages they have been forgotten. The people in the villages have been forgotten because the villages themselves have been forgotten, even the notion of them, long discarded. Ghost places. Phantom villages. Graveyards, with a few undead, or at least not-yet-dead-but-soon-enough, walking around them, like everything is bleakness and cheerlessness and… now that she thinks of it she might not wear that T-shirt inside her cardigan again. What was the point of that? Was she trying to be political or just somebody's pain in the ass? She takes it out of her drawer and begins to cut it up. She likes this. She cuts pieces of her skin, she cuts herself. No. She doesn't. She doesn't cut herself. You have to have guts to cut yourself. Need guts to cut. Guts to cut someone… anyone. And she is not there yet. She has thought about it – cutting herself or cutting others: her anger, her constant despising – but instead Bado cuts ribbons out of this stupid offensive T-shirt, cut cut and the fabric falls to the floor.

"Remember when we said we would become pop stars?"

"What?"

Sado is eating the last of the snakes. They are gummy and juicy and both sweet and sour at the same time, like being a teenager, and she is not listening to Bado as Bado cuts cuts and postulates.

"We once said we would become pop stars?" says Bado.

Sado swims in sugar.

"But pop stars aren't real people anymore."

"Yes, but we thought we could bring all that back."

"Yes, I remember now," says Sado, juice dripping down her chin.

"We thought we could dance on stage like they used to do years ago, when real performers danced and really sang. We had good singing voices," says Bado.

The scissors dance in her hands, snip snip, at the air. She likes to cut things.

"Yes, and we thought we could make pretty costumes too."

Bado rips some more of her homemade T. What you can make you can easily tear apart again. It's easy to destroy the things you create. Shiva and Kali. Didn't they use those names too? Creator and destroyer. Which is which?

"It could have been great."

"Yes, it could have been a revolution."

Sado sits back and pats her belly. The chewed up snakes wriggle inside, maybe they are reforming in there, growing again, maybe she will be sick from all this gorging on sugar. Her head spins.

"What?"

"Nothing. Just...our names. We had great names."

"We always have great names."

"Yes."

"Let's go back to our stage names."

"OK. Deucalion and Pyrrha"

"No. Not those, Bing Bang Bean and The Ting Tang Teen!"

"Oh, yeah. The Bing Bang Bean and The Ting Tang Teen. Those were good names."

"Not that the names ever meant anything."

"Nothing. Nothing at all. They never really do."

"We are always changing our names."

"Yes, it's nice to keep things fresh. Even though they mean nothing."

"We mean nothing."

"That's right. We mean nothing. Nothing at all. To anyone else. But only to each other. Only to each other we mean."

"Like leaves. Like ashes."

"What?"

"Nothing."

"Where did that come from?"

"Never mind."

"Have you been trying to read books again?"

"No."

"OK then."

"Bing Bang Bean and The Ting Tang Teen. Nice."

"OK."

"And if you are to be sick, please use the bin."

"OK."

"Are you?"

"What?"

"Are you going to be sick?"

"No. I don't think so."

The Ting Tang Teen grabs the bin and spews violently into it.

"That's what I thought."

"Sorry."

"No need to be sorry, Ting Tang Teen."

"Komodo Dragon."

"Yes, that's how bad you look. But we'll clean you up. We'll have you panda cute in no time."

The Bing Bang Bean drops her scissors and helps pull her friend's hair out of the stinking bin.

And then The Ting Tang Teen spews once more.

No slouch, but then no genius either, loping, shaven-headed Daisuke Karino, through the crackling atmosphere, realizes that he has had enough, and so walks to the school because he knows it is the highest building in the village. No one secures the school in the evenings, there is no need for security, and anyway there are enough people floating around there, like the adult evening classes –are those still running? – or Nemoto-sensei's karate class, what is there to pilfer, no trophies, no gold medals, even the technology is worthless, shaky as it is in the shaky atmosphere on this shaky land, and so he walks straight up the path and straight through the door. Even at this evening hour there will be some teacher inside, still marking papers, still preparing lessons, hunched with stiff shoulders and pinched nerves, still going through the endless reams of paperwork. Daisuke knows not very much about the adult world, but he knows that they are run-down, over-worked, all of them. He knows the principal is half-mad, and that most of the teachers are anxious, addled souls that are long overdue a holiday, a lengthy relaxing sun-soaked holiday that they will never get. His mother is exactly the same. His mother, forever cooking – why does she need to cook so much? Where is she even getting the supplies? Perhaps it gives her a sense of purpose. She feels good when she is feeding her only son, dishing stuff out on to his plate, a cornucopia of colour: green broccoli and spinach, orange carrots, white rice, yellow corn, red pickled ginger. Father left many years ago. Father was there one minute, gone the next. That's the way it is with mere mortals. One minute. The next. Did he go with the waves, or did he drive his car to the other side of the country, to the other side of life? Who knows? After the last quake he was gone, vanished, and so was his car, any trace of anything about him. There were clothes at home, suits and shirts and striped ties he wore to the insurance office. Cufflinks. Handkerchiefs. Leather belts. A battered briefcase unopenable, only Father knew the combination. Hard to say what happened. One minute. The next. But a man in an insurance company would surely know a thing or two about disappearances, claims, that kind of thing. Isn't that what most people think? Suspicions? Whatever. Daisuke didn't have much of a relationship with him anyway. Fathers don't anymore. Or people. No one cares enough about anyone else. Is that true? Is that really true? Hard to say. It's not that Daisuke feels guilty now, about... it's not... this is just something he has to do and they will all benefit from... his mother will be fine. She is half-crazed herself anyway and not long for the grave. They are all half, half done in.

Up and down steps, through the corridors, in that dark, un-sunlit section of the school, the stubborn stacks of trees outside casting impenetrable shade, the corridor all gloom with only a soft light coming from a flickering fluorescent overhead. Maya Yamanashi passes. She greets him and he greets her and they smile. Of all the teachers she was the nicest. She was the sexiest too. And if the drugs had worked properly, or at least if he hadn't taken so much of the "enhancing pills", then maybe he would have gotten more excited about the thought of her. He turns around to see the backside of her sway down the corridor. Beautiful. He will miss the beauty of the world, what little there is of it, what little time any of them take to look and ponder and admire. Up the stairs he climbs, up to the fifth floor. His legs are tired already, the walk from his house to here, all that way, but it is coming to an end. The closet behind the classroom has an opening, if you push through its skylight you can climb right onto the roof. The janitor had to do that often, as some sparrows often built their nest there, and he was sick of the hits of shit falling on his head when he was sweeping outside. He broke those nests, the sparrows must have flown to some safer environ. So much endless destruction. But where is safer? All the classrooms have bars on the windows, it is like a prison. For Dasiuke it *is* a prison. Not the building itself, but the whole village.

The land. If he was bright and courageous enough he would hitch a ride somewhere else, start again, somewhere sunny, where tender fruit weigh down the branches, find somewhere sturdier under the feet. He is wrong to be doing this, and his mother will be alone, but she must not have long either. Anyway, another set of waves will come along before they know it. Always before you know it. Unexpected. That's the way it is around here. One minute. The next.

Daisuke pushes out. Two hands on the plastic covering and push push and he's out, out onto the roof, the highest point in the village, he doesn't wail as he emerges, he doesn't gasp for breath, no one helps him to his feet. He can see for miles here. His eyes widen. It is like seeing for the first time. This place, this place he will soon depart. There are the sports fields, right below him, the baseball diamond, and the soccer pitch, where his teacher, the gloomy Nemoto-sensei (they cruelly call him Tombo because of his bulging, insect-like eyes) takes his charges, runs them into the muddy ground. There are the roads all radiating out from the village square in the centre, radiating out, as if they held promise, as if they held any hope. And the clusters of houses, dotted here and there, willy-nilly, a cluster, then a lone house, and remnants and ruins all around, those that were quashed and those that were squashed and those that were swept away and those that are now nothing but foundations, but who would bother to build again? Over there, the woods and forests, though hardly anymore, not woods and forests, just clusters too, copses, so many trees uprooted and washed away, nature's ruthless spoliation, although some steadfast stayed, some still up and growing to the hardly light, leaves cleaving, to keep alive, you have to hand it to them, such fight, such resilience. And further, further out you can see the coastline. His eyes are no longer that strong – the pills, too? – but he can just make out the coastline. And is that someone walking along? A small figure. A young person, surely, a young boy or girl, or a very little man or woman, walking the shoreline. If you are walking the shoreline then you must have hope. Shoreliners must have hope, must think they are going somewhere, or looking for something. Shoreliners are purposeful. Are purpose. Have purpose. Have. Have somewhere to go, have something to do, have, they have, these people who walk the shorelines, something to cling to, have. Daisuke wonders if he or she sings as he or she walks. Isn't that what you do when you walk the shoreline? You sing or you hum to yourself? Or else you contemplate the big questions. You wonder why you are here. Why are you in this absurd situation? What is the point of it all, this being here, and the breathing and moving and reproducing and all for what? These are the thoughts that run through you while walking the shoreline. And these are the thoughts too high above the whole village, where no one can see you. You speck. You speck in the universe. Because everyone is looking down, down deep into the cataclysm of their own situations, and none of them have the answer either. Daisuke, speck Daisuke. He has had enough. There's no point to it all. He'll leave behind those two girls as well. Whatever was their game? What were they up to? Did they have to come and pick *him* out of the crowd, pick on him? He almost made them happy, almost did what they required…almost showed himself to be a man. But not quite. Didn't make it. Daisuke didn't make it. Fell at the last stretch. Never mind. No need for any of that now. Right now all he needs to do his fly, for seven seconds, or however long it takes, just enough to be airborne and away from all of them with just the air surrounding him, weightless, only air and nothing else holding him, that's it, just for that briefest moment, away away, now, away, and he moves to the ledge and then away away, like a speck of lint that you flick off your sweater.

Marisa feels a brief jolt to her system. A spasm of the colon, or the bowel. Is that Irritable Bowel Syndrome? Or is it something that just actually happened outside of her? When her insides spasms like that she…

She also saw for a brief second someone fly. Was that it? Was that what it was? A vision? An angel? Some instinct she had? She has been in her own house all afternoon, not looking after her sister, and she has just now felt something, deep inside her. There is so much death around here. So much destruction.

The Ting Tang Teen has stopped her stinking spews. She has brushed her teeth and washed her hair, using The Bing Bang Bean's toiletries. The Ting Tang Teen is even wearing The Bing Bang Bean's clothes, because the vomit had gone all over her own, and even though they are a little baggy on her, she is glad to feel her friend's fabric so close to her. They are like sisters sometimes, these two. They are so close, sharing everything; neither of them have any siblings, so yes, they are both willing to be sisters, as well as best friends, as well as sometimes lesbians. They have a very strong bond and who would dare break it? Who would even dare?

"More than panda cute, maybe even *red* panda cute!"

"Aw, thank you. I feel so much better now. I appreciate all your help."

"Yes, well, it's time to get organized. We are coming to the end of it, I can feel it. Tonight might be our last time to ensnare Tombo. He has that witch to guard him, but if we catch him after his evening karate class, then maybe he will be unable to resist."

"Shouldn't we wear something a little more revealing?"

"No need. We can strip down when we face him."

"Take all our clothes off, you mean?"

"Of course. He will be unable to resist. Men are unable to resist anything."

"That's true. My father. Everyone's father."

"But isn't it a little too cold to take our clothes off?"

The Bing Bang Bean is delighted that The Ting Tang Teen is asking sensible questions, that she is putting forward the right ideas, and even if the thoughts and questions are to be swatted away, she feels like she is making a contribution.

"We shall be warm when he takes us in his arms and brings us close to the heat of his tough and hardened body."

"Yes, we shall be warm."

The Ting Tang Teen has a slight far-away look in her eyes. It might be sheer wistfulness, chimera, hormone-fueled lustful hope, but it is enough inspiration to spur on her companion as they finish preparations and take one last look at their headquarters before hugging tightly and then going into action.

29

It has been a strange day. Or maybe it has been just like any other. Maybe this is all one long, strange, tortuous day. Accursed time. Are you still with me? I thought you'd have left hours ago. Einstein tried to tell us, it's not linear, that's our imposition. But Einstein has long faded from everyone's memory, and science and philosophy not high on the agenda around here. Just how high to make the tsunami walls, that's as far as the 13th is willing to go. That's the science of this country. Cars are made in ARCK. Devices too. All things. But none of it, none of it is my show, I am only a simple...

I have been cleansed and cared for. My cuts and bruises have been soothed. Marisa left the house and headed down the road to her own lonely house – lonely? Why must I insist? I wanted to tell her to stay, stay, for the love of love, and for her to climb into bed with me and my wife for us all to lie there and cry together, to endure life's pain together, to be utterly unsexual, incorporeal even (is that possible, if we put our minds to it?), together but needy, needing each other, three nurses caring for three patients at the same time, all at the same time, finding each others' sore spots and quickly alleviating (is that what I mean? *Sore?* Not *pleasure?*), three lost souls but in search, and then emerging whole and strong and new and ready for that clean slate. The cleanest of slates. Was that possible? Is that such an insane idea? But I said nothing, nothing of that sort, kept it all to myself, as I have gotten used to doing – I just let her dab and daub and dawdle the way she does, endless streams of narrative that I can hardly follow, stories about Mrs. Shiroto and something about a guy with a long earring and a feather in it, like a Native American Dreamcatcher but hanging from the earlobe instead of over the bed of a child, that was the gist of it, and something about shopping bags, and premonitions and ghosts and the way the ground shakes and outer space and she wondered if the other planets have earthquakes, plates moving at the very heart of Neptune or Saturn, long sentences, long tales and talks and then more tales, her voice drifting harmlessly, but her voice, her sounds were sweet and welcome, and I ignored each word's meaning, right there I could've...

What will she do there tonight? What will...

Another ludicrous episode today.

No, let me account for the tragedy before the comedy. There hasn't been enough comedy so far, and to your credit you have stuck by and...

Maya is to get married. This is what she told the math teacher, and the math teacher (having the biggest mouth in the village, physically as well as figuratively, like a baseball mitt when it opens) is utterly unable to keep any kind of secret, no matter the magnitude, was sizzling with the news and passed it on to Matsuda-sensei as well as the three loquacious women who work as secretaries in the front office. The whole thing whirled around the staff room and finally got to me, and it smacked me right in the face. Yes, she is getting married, and I am utterly disappointed. When she does leave, at least I'll be free from the tyranny of lust, at least that, at least not looking at her...

She spent the day radiant and, of course, I had to congratulate her. I even had to look at the dainty ring and feign admiration, when all I wanted to do was kick all the basketballs, volleyballs, and every other thing that got in my path and scream. My number one fancy was fading in front of me, that's the only way I could see this, a sort of fading, a ghost walking through a wall *away* from me. If I was man enough I would swallow my jealousy and be gracious about her leaving – she would of course be leaving, the man, her man, it turns out, lives far away, where it is warm and sunny, and in a city, no less, where things are mostly operational, and where they don't get blasted much from the world and its awful energies and...

She told me what he did, this sweetheart of hers, for a living that is, but I quickly forgot, or I quickly erased it from my mind. I didn't even want to know his name, didn't want to know the slightest thing about him. I am a petty individual, bound up by insane jealousies and...

Have I mentioned that I am already married? My recumbent recluse. And that my sister-in-law...

I told Maya that her ring was beautiful and I wished her all the luck in the world and that she deserved it. I told her that I would miss her too. Which was the only true part, I suppose. I think she believed me.

I didn't have too much time to ponder my misfortune. Misawa, our legendary principal, finally went insane in front of quite a few members of staff and was witnessed buck naked in his office (the door is usually left open, an understanding that anyone is welcome, and that far from being intolerant he is actually approachable) shouting out (as if his nakedness was not enough) that he was following in the steps of the great Mishima and was getting ready to march to the Emperor at once and demand... something or other. No one quite got the gist of his rant, although Far Right incantations were gleamed, as well as the word "coup", repeated several times apparently. Eventually he was restrained and an ambulance called and he was taken away. Oddly, no one felt shocked about the whole scenario. The general feeling was that something like this was bound to happen sooner or later. Merely a matter of time. And that time turned out to be earlier today, at one o'clock in the afternoon, and word would inevitably spread around the village very quickly, like wildfire (a term which I shouldn't even mention, should my words invoke and it actually occur, with our record of disasters we must be careful not to tempt fate). But at least it gives me something else to think about. If I keep picturing his naked eighty-year old rump, I might be able to delete the memory of Maya's glorious tracksuited twenty-four-year-old sublime...

Or maybe not.

Comedy. Tragedy. So much going on here. And in such a small space. Whatever next? Aren't you glad you...

It is evening. The school is almost deserted. There is nothing but the shouts of my karate pupils and their hard feet slapping against the floor. Of all the students I encounter on a weekly basis I can actually abide these ones. There are only five of them, but all are tough little boys and obedient and polite and actually a pleasure to be with. There are not many humans left that I can tolerate, but these kids get a pass. We only ever have an hour or two together like this, but they get on with their practice with seriousness and aren't afraid to show who they really are. Unlike the soccer players and their crazy fans, these guys don't have much expectation. They are not champions, and although it is my job to push them to be so, I fail dramatically, and they don't seem to mind. They like the idea of having strong bodies and being able to defend themselves, and medals and honours don't seem to be too high on their agenda, much to the chagrin of the heads of the school – a club or team without ambition, am I kidding? Yes, I suppose I am. Nothing is that serious. The waves make everything transient. But that's the way they, *we* are, in our karate after-school class, that runs over time always, from the sheer enjoyment, and I like to savour their air of devil-may-care. The fact that they enjoy being with each other, push each other (again, physically and metaphorically) without ever anyone getting seriously hurt, and that they all seem to casually improve, well, this I admire greatly. They respect me, and because of their calm character, I think I truly like them. We sweat a bit. I shout a bit. The boys and girls all carry out their orders to the letter. They shout a bit, too, of course, mimicking my every move and thrust, looking deep into my eyes for guidance, for they must. It is, as always, a perfectly rewarding hour or two together: the slaps of bare feet on the floor of the dojo, all of us white-clad and kicking and turning like an army of well-turned out, well-drilled super-ghosts, powerful and in accordance. We say our goodbyes when our session draws to a close and the sweat begins to cool on our bodies. They trot off home to whatever comforts their parents can provide and I'm pretty positive a good nights' sleep awaits them.

But not me. I have just finished clearing up, wiping the sweat from my body with a towel that has seen better days, and no sooner am I out into the refreshing cool of the night air and heading towards my car, two things happen. Firstly, I get a call from Marisa, who sounds distressed.

"What's wrong?"

"I just felt something go through me. Something awful must have happened."

Her pitch is high, I can almost feel her nervous tension coming through the device.

"Nothing surprising about that, something awful always happens."

I'm aiming for levity, but it doesn't catch.

"A student. For some reason I feel it is a student of yours. Something bad happened. I could feel it. Please check it out. And please be careful."

I have heard of her "feelings" before, her sixth sense – she is like an old rheumatic dog when the rains are on their way, feels it all over, but at least has voice enough to explain herself.

I have no time to consider her request however for who should appear before me. I could have guessed.

The two girls again.

Why always *these* two? What have I done to warrant such attention? A schoolgirl crush is one thing, but this, this kind of inexplicable behaviour is something else entirely.

Their eyes, limned in the dark, are pins of phosphorescence, like cats, or like those crazed lynxes you might stumble across down south, all hiss and hysteria, and the skin of them, even more etiolated than last time, bleak in their bloodlessness.

Perfect unison, their ghostly voices again:

"You are the one! You are the one!"

This is all executed trance-like, monotone, grave. We have been here before.

"You are the one! You are the one!"

I don't know whether to feel afraid or shocked or disgusted or whether to simply burst out laughing at the whole ludicrous spectacle before me.

"You are the one! You are the one! You are the one! You are the one!"

"Girls, I don't know why you are here. But I think it is best that you head on home. It's late. I'm tired after practice, and I think the best thing we could all do now is go and get some rest. If there is a school matter you wish to discuss, then..."

"We are not here to discuss anything," says Shiori.

That is her name isn't it?

"No discussions," says her pal, Maki.

That is her…

"There is no time for discussions anymore. You are the one we have chosen, it is time for us to bring this to a close."

When she said *close* it sounded for a moment like the planet gave us one of its rumbles, perhaps it did.

"I'm quite serious now. This has all gone a little too far."

It is a cold October night – is it still October? Time passes so slowly here, it seems like this month has been going on forever.

I have to be careful. This is the only way to approach the unhinged. One spark might set them off. So quickly could the young lions roar upon me. Whatever their infatuation is – and I certainly do not understand the ways, wiles or wants of women, especially young women – I know I must be careful. That is about all I know.

Cold October, frosty bites in the air, but the two in front of me seem to pay no heed, my eyes nearly pop out of my head when they start to remove their clothing.

"I don't know what you think you are doing, but…"

"Tombo, it is time for you to take us, behind those trees over there, and satisfy us. Ravage us both, but *fill* me, fill me with your seed."

This is all Shiroi, the taller one, the one who is even more deranged (if that is even possible) than the smaller, impish one.

"It is you that holds the only hope for humanity. The rest of the world has forgotten us, but with you in control of everything, perhaps we can start again, a new order of things. You would like that, wouldn't you? Order? Set the world to rights. I can be your wife. I know your wife is down and no longer any good, let it be me. I have done my research. I know you need a mate. I know your needs."

I have no idea where they have gotten this stuff, this strange language, these outlandish notions – how do they know about my family? And those ghostly voices, how...

It is all unsettling, this moving from schoolgirl-crush-embarrassment to something actually quite... frightening. These two are only sixteen-year-old girls, I know this, and yet...

Where did they... how do they know about my wife?

"This has really all gone too far! If you don't put your clothes back on then I will have no other choice but to call to the police to come, and they'll..."

"The police, like everyone else, have been washed away. It's only us that are left, Tombo. It's up to us. You must make us whole. Fill with your seed. We will start again, this whole mess, a new village, a new land, with you at the helm. We can make crests. The dragonfly. T-shirts. I can cut up T-shirts very well. I can sew."

Sew? Helm?

Why are they calling me by that name? No one calls me that. It is not my name. My name is...

"Are you listening to us?"

"Your parents then. I will have to call your parents."

I want to tell them that they should address me properly, to call me by my proper name, inform them that this was once a land of strict propriety, of honorifics, but now hardly seems the time for lecturing, bigger issues are at hand. They are naked and it is getting colder by the minute and if soon they don't put their clothes back on they will catch their deaths.

"You will get no signal here, my love," says Shiori. "And how would you even get our parents' numbers? Will the numbers just fly into your head, like magic? Magic numbers, Tombo? Surely you do not have every parent stored there on your little device?"

The shorter one, Maki, she laughs. She is laughing at me. The elfish one. Is this what I have become? A laughing stock. That must be it. The whole of this. Right from the beginning. All of it. Go on, altogether now.

She is shivering too. This is not easy for her. And yet they both persist.

"Come now. Be with us."

Maki, yes, that's her name, Mikami Maki, shivering, but she is braving it. These are not your average teens. These two are tough. If only I knew what black rivers ran through them, if only I could…

I pat my breast pocket, search, all my pockets.

They want me to eye their bodies, their tactics so obvious. Instead I keep my eyes on their eyes. Moving from one set of gleaming eyes – what contacts have they inserted? Night vision? – to other set of gleaming eyes. Maki is grinning wildly, despite the shivering, she is untamed, untameable, looks like she would be happy to kill or be killed at any moment. What is it about these two? How come I can hold my nerve with every student in the school, and yet when these succubi appear before me, my nerves are wrung. What evil drive, what…

"Come now."

No red. I have no red. Not even a yellow. Where have my cards gone? What cards have I to play?

I almost go. I almost stumble. Almost fail. Almost succumb. For a second I almost lose my nerve. I *do* look at their bodies, I do glance quickly at the tight skin that wraps their young bodies, my eyes betray me, despite my best efforts, my eyes slide down their slender frames (are they rolling in my head my eyes? am I dizzy with confusion?) and almost, almost very nearly almost I relent. But I am saved. The nick of time.

My whore.

Marina comes to this dark wasteland outside the school,

the edge of another forest, where anything might happen, where fairytales might begin or most likely end.

Marina is there suddenly, seeming taller than before, and her long raincoat hangs from her thin frame like a superhero's cape, maybe she glides too, like Maya. All these good women are superheroes.

How?

Why is she here?

"I was just out taking a walk, Mr. Wazka. And I thought I heard young voices. I thought there might be some trouble."

Marina the whore knows all about trouble. Has a nose for it. She's been *in* it, of course, countless times; she *is* it.

But I am so very happy to see her.

"Is there a problem?"

It is only then that she notices the two girls, who have scampered and hidden behind my car, their two sets of eyes shining, peeping from the opposite side of the car, animal eyes revealing fear.

"Who are these girls? Are they naked?"

I don't know if Marina is going to laugh or not, the situation seems so absurd (welcome to my life), but her face shows only concern, and then anger, as if I am to blame for all of this.

"What is going on here, Mr. Walker?"

My name has changed again; I don't know who I am; or who anybody else is. This tale of woe.

"These two evil girls have been stalking me and they are trying to..."

Trying to what? I don't know really, I don't know what they are trying to do. I do look guilty. I must do. It must be all over my face. Isn't that how the innocent often look? As if they are to blame. Though they have done nothing at all. Just tried to get on with things. Isn't that what happens? One day you go for a walk. The next you are a criminal. These were the kinds of books my father read. Grim European tales of people caught up in all kinds of quandaries, and the poor souls never brought any of it on themselves. I was simply out for a walk. Just as I was when the waves…

Hissing then. The feral cats have not yet lost their fight. They have managed to put some of their clothes back on, and they have come around to face Marina. They hiss at her. They are like beasts come from the forest and ready to engage in toothsome battle. The shivering has stopped. They are suddenly like flames, whatever fortitude in this cold, whatever fire they have summoned, it is as if they are ready for fight and they reach out with thin arms, hands hooked and claw-like, long-nailed and baying for blood. Someone's blood. Anyone's. Marina's? Mine?

All I want to do is crawl into my car, have it harrumph into life as it usually does and warm up my weary bones. I have had enough of this, enough of all of this ridiculous story and am quite happy to get out of here, to drive away, away from this scene, away from *all* of my scenes.

But I remain frozen. It is Marina who has the wherewithal, who has seen battle before and will do so again, and if wherewithal happens not to be commodity enough, she has at least her umbrella.

The two female beasts circle the taller one. They give off strange heat, and strange animal sounds, they emit moans and mewls.

Shiori suddenly produces scissors. Where has she been hiding them? And of what use are they to be put? Is that all she has got?

Marina holds her umbrella like a rifle; she holds it aiming at them. Haven't I seen this before? Why all this repetition? That's the way it is in this land, everything comes back at you, you've seen one giant wave-wall, you've seen them all.

So which one is diabolical here? The witch with the angry face, umbrella aloft? Or these two harbingers of doom, these…

I remember this umbrella tip is sharpened to a deadly point. And she looks like she is not afraid to use it.

They continue their circles and their snarls and then they run at her. Marina beats them off with all her limbs, but they return. No sooner are they shaken off but they come back, as if they cannot get enough of this beating, as if it is good for them. They have their teeth on her then, Maki biting into her arm and Marina howling into the stark night. They struggle, all three of them, and I remain there, rooted. This is what we have become, characters in some gruesome gothic tale? Or is it nothing now but a salacious cat fight for me to…

I pat my breast pocket, and still I cannot do anything. If I am I to intercede then how am I to do so? With my karate body? With my PE-fit, referee-fit, up-and-down-the-pitch-fit, out-at-night-on-long-walks-fit, with my hardened body to jump into the fray and…

My ears are full, full-full of noise.

The cats continue. I see Marina's pointed tip graze Shiori's arm in a long line and quickly there is a red soak through her white shirt and onto the gravelly ground goes plip and plop. I think again of those cold, crisp autumn days, the grey sky a stark contrast to the splash of expressionist red in front of the kindergarten.

I want to shout *enough, enough*! Enough of the course of blood through life and us foolish beasts that strut the earth, enough for we know not what we ever do; I do not know if anyone can hear these silent screams; I only hear the gush between my ears, the forever falls, the Niagara of noise that picks up in times of intense stress.

The two young girls back away from the adult one. They may have had enough: Shiori whimpering, panicked by her wounds, and Maki a picture of fret. If this was all just play to begin with, it has suddenly become very real. That's what blood does to a scene. What might start off as nothing but tempers rising, when blood issues forth takes on a whole other dimension. My mother knew this. So much of it in her work, so much red on her canvasses, I'd watch her load it on, talking all the time about the red and yellow of Gauguin, "Jacob wrestling with the Angel", wasn't that her favourite of them all, the red ground beneath their feet, the white headwear and the yellow wings of the angel forcing Jacob down.

Maki still bares her teeth, but the fight is gone from her. Tears on her cheeks, our recurring theme of wetness; like this is all a bad dream someone is having, it is always thus: floods and falls and blood and tears and sweat and pus and piss and us... drowning in it all.

It is at this moment that we hear a rustle in the trees, and our hearts momentarily stop. Something, or some *things*, have gotten the whiff. Our red. We are not alone. The battle is not yet over.

Down from the sultry hills they come, braver with every year, through the forests these animals, thought long extinct, resurrected somehow, from the thick mists and humid airs they come again, as the heady whiff of blood and sweat gets all too much.

In swelling fevered packs they come at night, lope along the shoreline with tongues a-loll, breath a-pant, and desire in their eyes. And here they are now, three or four of them, we cannot yet see for sure, but here they come, you can smell and hear them before you see them, that acrid tang in the air, wet matted fur and the pungent lunge of their breath suddenly in our air too, getting under our nostrils, and then their eyes, their eyes there, shining in the light of the horror moon, and we do not know what to do, whether we should run or whether it is too late.

We are, all four of us, close enough to my car, but…

If I can…

And then I remember. And then at last I act.

Quickly I open the doors of the car and push the three girls inside. Marina wants to stay out with me but she has done more than enough. It is up to me now. We have been waiting on a…

From the back of the car I retrieve the principal's sword, slip it out of its scabbard and let the light of the moon fall upon it. If I die here tonight, then that it is fine, it has always been fine. Without Ruby, with my wife the way she is, it is all fine and just…

The time has come…

Time I protect…

The wolves edge closer and then edge back from me again, one step forward and then back again, as if they are unsure of themselves, or their tango is a calculation. Is it worth their risk? The two girls in the car are screaming in terror. They are only kids. I always knew this too. They have let their imaginations get the better of them. It happens. And when it does it is important that adults step in and be adults. Marina opens the door to come out and join me, but I kick it back shut, we will need more than her movie prop umbrella.

The beasts before me snarl, drool from their flews only add to our wet world. They have made up their mind, the blood has got them going and they want in. They have triangulated around me, a three-pronged attack, that is their strategy, but I am reckless enough to be game for it. I could be in that car and I could be driving. But I am not. I am standing, with sword aloft. Such weaponry I have seen brandished in such a short time: Marina's broom, Shiori's pathetic scissors,

Marina's umbrella, and now my sword, each phallic weapon more outlandish than the last.

One wolf makes a sudden charge low at my legs, but I am swift to the manoeuvre and quickly kick it away. They come in a pair the next instant, one from the front low at my legs again and the other with a leap to my lower back. But I am swift and circling and slice the sword through the air. The blade catches nothing yet, but they are wary of it. They have caught nothing, nothing of me either, I remain unharmed, their muscular body-lunges unable to knock me over – it will take a lot more than that, they will have to summon a much greater wave.

My ears still thrum. Louder know. The blood beats inside. Sweat drips into my eyes. But I *can* see. I can see them coming.

And they do. They come again. The three of them this time, all together, at once, and I spin with such speed and force that my blade does catch, its force strikes at the neck of the largest wolf and its head is almost knocked off. Not quite clean though, it hangs there from some skin or sinew or muscle, something holding it barely on, a cascade of liquid at my feet, a sudden blood puddle. The other two whimper, but they have not given up, and both are immediately at my legs again. I continually kick and spin, kick and spin, and the sword, sharper than I thought it was, swooshes through the prickly air, skimming off their backs and grazing them both. I can see clumps of fur on the silver blade, but they are not yet finished. Once more they gather, one from the front and one from behind, and I summon all my darkest energy to fight them off. I summon the wrath of the waves that wash over us time and time again, I summon the dark skies that rain upon us, deluge down and river rise, and I summon the earth, implore to its very core, its instability, its terrific tendencies to topple and tear, I summon the cries of my dead soul and my dead girl and with this strength at my back I raise the brutal blade for two more stabs into the black unknowing hearts of my enemies. King and invincible, my sword carmine and an eerie silence envelopes. This battle has been won.

It is another beast that is the first to congratulate me. It is not the misguided girls in their tortured teendom that come to my side, and it is not the foreign prostitute either, it is the raccoon dog, quick past my feet and slobbering over the carrion faster than a hyena or jackal might,

Has it been watching all along? What instinct has it that…

This pet needs a name. I will call it Atma.

We drive in my car, the three females and I, in my rusty car. Marina is beaming at me. She is in the front seat next to me, and while I look straight ahead down the ill-lit road, she looks at me in obvious admiration and not a little lust. But I have a job to do, as usual, I have to get these two girls safe to their homes and have them swear they never speak of this dreadful night again. I do not want to lecture them, but I feel I must make clear that…

"I think I want to walk home," says Shiori, suddenly.

I will have none of it. These people are under my care now. I have already fought off wolves for these people. I will see them home. I have already lost a daughter, I will not see more girls carried away – who knows what other wolves are waiting within this dark fairy tale, poised ever as we are, ever the brink, us and our situation, ever-edge of some event, some catastrophe near or nearing still.

"You will all stay in the car until I get you home."

I am enjoying my heroism. A humble man with a sword and vicious grey wolves attacking. It is not every day. None of this. None of this is every day. None of this should happen.

I decide to take a little detour before I drop them home. I drive to the graffiti boy to see if he is still at it.

"Down this laneway," I instruct the three females of my pack. "Keep going."

They know now to trust me of course. I am no danger. I am their guardian who will protect them from danger. My heart is buoyed, the first time in a long time, not drowning, not going under, buoyed.

He wears a balaclava again and those army pants again, like his activities are military manoeuvers, under the radar, covert. He works with terrific urgency again and he panics when he hears the rustle of our feet behind him. Abruptly he turns, ready to bid a hasty retreat, but when he realizes it's only me he relaxes, and casually nods, then continues again at his deft spraying. He doesn't seem to mind that I have brought an audience with me. And why should he, his piece is almost finished. And there it is:

It is an egg.

Just an egg.

On my nightly rambles, I have often wondered what it was going to be. And from a distance (I never got that close to him or his wall), I knew it was turning into a large, round or oblong... something. But from where we stand now we can all see quite clearly that it is an egg.

No, it is not *just* an egg.

That is not it.

Sometimes things are different from a distance, you have to get right up close and see. My mother used to show me pointillist paintings (French, from centuries ago) that she had stored in one of her art tablets, and my childhood self rejoiced in the far and nearness of them. Stand far from it, look at its complete shape, its overall form; go right up close and see... see what?

Kanji. Chinese characters. Words. But not just any words. Names.

"Are all these names?"

"Yes."

"Whose? Whose names are these?"

"These are the souls that have been taken from our village."

"Nice," says Shiori, with a depth of feeling you wouldn't have thought possible. I think I see her wipe away a tear.

Then, with an air of theatricality, the boy rips off his balaclava. I have never even considered his face, who he might be. It never even struck me. I didn't really care. But I am totally surprised to see that it is one of the Eggmen, one of the boys who regularly smears my car with runny goo. I am quite taken aback to be honest, but can find no other response than to laugh.

"You," I say.

He is smiling back at me, as if this has all been some grand scam he has been engineering and the play finally revealed.

I could get angry. I could question him as to his actions. I could even attack him (I have shown myself to be a man of not inconsiderable strength). But what's the point? I know who puts him up to it. I know Monstaa has all these guys under his thumb, and what of it. My car is nothing special. Neither am I. Only this egg on the wall is special. Complete, or almost complete, and...

"I'm sorry about your car. I won't do it again. It's just that the soccer supporters pay to..."

"Forget about it. It doesn't matter. Nothing really does."

I go in close to his egg again. I search through the names.

"She's not there. If that's who are looking for. Only the names that have been found. The people I mean."

"How do you know about my daughter?"

"You told me before, on one of your nightly walks. You told me that you were searching for her. Ruby, right?"

"Yes. Ruby."

"Like the jewel," says Maki.

"Yes, like the jewel."

"Is that her actual name?" asks Marina.

"No, it's just what we liked to call her."

"That's nice," one of them says. I don't know which one, my ears have gone all funny.

The girl came out of her mother red and glistening. I was there to see her shine like a jewel. We both knew right then (that peculiar telepathy of those deeply in love) that even though her name had been decided (Kurumi), we would always call her Ruby.

Our jewel, our gem, our precious...

I try to talk about her sometimes, I try to talk about Ruby and...

I find them all in a huddle. The three girls have surrounded this (admittedly handsome) youth and are asking him all kinds of questions about spray paint and art-terrorism and whether he has a girlfriend or not. They are delighted to hear there is no one, and it seems like Shiori and Maki's next battle will be *against* each other *for* his affections. Or maybe there is another eggy friend the same age who can manage to square things up. Marina stands and looks at them like they are her unruly but beloved children, and I am the granddaddy of them all; my ears are still full and my head is not sure what direction to take next. The day, as I have said, has been long, but I also have the feeling that it is not yet over.

I drop Shiori off in front of her house first. I watch her sidle up the little path and am only relieved when her door closes.

I was hoping that she would apologise for her, for *their* errant behaviour, and promise never to stray so waywardly again. But none of that happened. That's just the teacher and referee in me, always looking to eke out punishment and have people account for themselves. I don't know the kinds of homes they come from, the respectable families we *think* they have sprung from might not be that way at all. But I cannot spend my life, what's left of it, speculating, or peeking behind curtains to get glimpses of others'. I don't know what direction my life must take. But it can't be that anymore.

Marina is next, and there is a familiar face waiting outside her door when we get there. She tells us to stay in the car and that she'll walk to her apartment alone, but I insist on getting out and taking her by the arm – it is almost like I am walking her down the aisle.

Monstaa is at her blue door.

Monstaa.

I should have known.

He is smiling as he mentally prepares for what the evening has in store for him. He is another one of her paying customers, or… is he the one who gets paid, her pimp, another one of his business ventures? Who knows? Who knows what goes on anywhere. Every time you look through a window you are surprised, and I can do nothing but give this good woman away. I wonder briefly as to the nuts and bolts of their arrangement, and what will go where, now that I know the truth about Marina's anatomy, the physicality of it, the logistics. Windows: it's probably best stay away from them from now on. None of it is my business anyway. I was never brave enough to go with her, never brave enough to take her up on her offers, her discounts, her going rates, never would have been able to open my wallet to her, didn't have it in me. I had my chances, and so many I blew, acknowledged the temptation, but couldn't follow through. Just not that kind of man. What does that mean? What kind of man *am* I? A fantasist? Living alone in my addlepated head. She kisses me on the cheek then sweetly and tells me I should take the other little girl home, and that my heart is good, I have a good one, a rare one, and she likes me for it; but my heart is heavy when her door closes shut, and I hear his voice from inside, already gruff and eager. Doors, windows, this awful…

Maki is sobbing quietly in the car when I return to her.

"Are you all right?"

"Yes. Yes. I'm fine. It's just that man with the moustache. I've seen him before."

"Where? How?"

"It doesn't matter."

I get the feeling that for her it matters very much, and that not all our answers would be cleared up this busy night. I get the feeling that when the waves poured in upon us they left the ground beneath our feet nothing but quicksand, so easy it is to sink into it all, so easy to get swallowed up, how hard to grasp a branch and pull yourself out of it.

I cannot sleep of course. Too wound up. It would take everything for me to shake my wife and say: *Hey, listen to what happened to me tonight, you wouldn't believe what….* and that would, of course, be of no use. So instead I go out into the night again, a short walk I have in mind, and, when I have it in mind well then it must be; to the school again; this time I take my gym bag with me. I feel something pulling me back there, something I had glimpsed near that wood but had not fully processed, something in the corner of my eye was beckoning, but in the midst of all that had gone on (girls wolves blood wolves girls wolves blood girls death) I was forced to ignore.

Is this what Marisa had called about? Is this what she meant?

There is a pit. Let's call it that. A kind of pit. A shallow grave. It belongs to the wolves. They must have dug it; it is not the tidy work of men with shovels, no, it is a shallow groove in the land, soil dug up with scrabbling paws, and in that pit lie the bones – all that's left in it are bones, the bones of a what I think is a boy.

I think I know who it is too.

There is not much flesh on these bones. The flesh has been eaten away. For that's what the wolves do. They get hungry and they seize upon their opportunities. Quite how they got to this boy I don't know. But I think I know who it is. He hasn't been in school. This troubled youth. There were rumours in the staffroom. Oh, troubled boy. When I called his name in the roll book there came no reply. This boy who has succumbed to...

It is Daisuke Karino for sure. I'm almost certain. I know he was one of those they tested on, they gave him pills to see if they could strengthen him. Cheap energy vitamin pills that would improve stamina in all areas of life, this is what the Government said, the people in the still-standing Capital. The 11th first – or was it the 12th? – started the initiative; they were sure to make an efficient, improved workforce, but more importantly would be able to spur the lagging libido of men who were too tired after work for anything. They said that the boy took too many pills. The pills got the better of him. Grew he did, but not in the right way. Grew not strong but strange. Grew wrong.

Nothing but gnawed bones now. The wolves have fed and the cubs will grow with Daisuke's blood and sinew and hair and muscle in their bellies. Vessels of boy, cartilage of boy, corpuscles of boy, skin of boy all inside the warm satisfied bilious bellies of the grey beasts. That's the hard science of it. The tragic biology. I know what I have to do with these bones. It is a crazy idea, but so what, everything I have done and seen and thought has been only that, crazy, a crazy mind in a crazy situation, a crazy story, all of this. Nothing makes sense. Nothing since Ruby… I try sometimes to talk…

But this might make sense. This trick might make something happen. There may be magic in these bones. This might work.

I take the empty sports bag and I bend to the bones. With an old rag, I begin to clean them. One by one, I gather and wipe them until they are presentable. Yes, that is what I mean: *presentable*. The stench is bad, the whole copse smells of blood and waste and excrement. This has been the way for a long time now. But I have gotten used to it. In this region, we have all gotten used to the detritus of decay, the rancid air.

One by one, pulled apart from whatever of his body remains, I wipe and wipe and place them – like some high priest on an altar – into my old sports bag. It is not long before I have quite the collection, quite the collection of bones. These are things we think we will never hear ourselves say, never think we will think, let alone see ourselves actually do. Quite the collection of bones.

My head spins. My ears thrum. Blood beats. Sweat again. Wet again.

I begin to walk home, the paths again. Atma is following me, appears out of nowhere, all sniff and inquiry, like a loyal dog, curious as to what I am up to, or does he think I have something that will feed him?

What day is it?

I don't know.

Is it still October?

I pat my breast with my free hand. No cards. I have no one to send off today. Today I am no referee. Why do I get such a thrill doing it? Sending someone off. Seeing them march to the sideline, down the tunnel, head hung. Because they deserve it. Because they have usurped the order of things and therefore must be punished. I get some bizarre thrill out of this: the power I hold in my hands, in my whistle, in my melancholy head. I've already been hurt so much; they can do what they want with me. Who? Who can do? Today I am not a referee. I am a man with a bag of bones. A bag of boy-bones. Extraordinary to say, extraordinary to think, and what of the doing! The *doing!*

String me up. It might be a relief. Beyond it now. Beyond hurt. But I have a bag of bones here. Walking with a bag of bones for my latest mad endeavor. It just might work.

There goes the Barrow Man, asleep in his chariot. Only his boy pushes him now. The boy has gotten stronger. Look how much he has grown! Has this all been only days, or months? Where is the boy's mother, I hope that...

I am standing in front of the last drinking bar. The others, there used to be lots of others, but they fell down or were washed away. This one, like my house, still stands, and for that it must be applauded. I shall go in and drink there. I know who will be in there. I fling my bag of bones over my shoulder and I enter.

Drinking establishment. Full swell of man-smell. Beer and spirits and after-work sweat and cheap cologne on used collars, fried food and dried-fish snacks, soap when someone can be bothered to wash hands in the rank toilet area, ever-damp towel and lingering flatulence. Hide and Takeshi are in the middle of all this. Imbibing. They actually look up when I step in, they actually acknowledge my existence.

"Well, well, well. Finally we are deemed worthy of your company. Oh, all hail to the referee."

I say nothing. I go to their low table and sit opposite

them. They are pleased, and shocked, and for a moment no one quite knows what more to say. We are only faces looking at each other, familiar and yet very unsure. The truth is I don't know why I have come here myself. Because it feels like the end of something, and I am saying goodbye. That could be it. Or is it that I am just thirsty? That could be it too. Usually I am in bed by now, next to my hushed heap of wife. But I am here in a rundown bar instead, and suddenly there is a bottle of beer in front of me, and even more suddenly I find I am gulping it down.

"Thirsty?"

"Very."

"Well, well. What have you been doing that has made you so thirsty?" asks Hide, the ever-present spittle-glisten at the corner of his mouth a tiny bubble about to pop.

"Fun with little Marina?" adds Takeshi, leering and lecherous as ever.

"No. Far from it. Fighting. Fighting with Marina."

"Oooh, you like the rough stuff, is that it? She let you beat her up a bit. She likes that. Oooh yeah, she likes that kind of thing."

"No. Not fighting her. Fighting *with* her."

They look confused. We all have this expression so often. This could be the expression of the village, if the village were to have one face, seen from above, if the drones clicked one picture for posterity, to send in a time capsule, or for other alien races to discover, it would be this one, the face of confusion.

"Fighting who? Monstaa?"

Hide looks worried, his features suddenly creasing and cringing to that of a boy who might collapse and cry.

"No. Though she is with Monstaa now. No, no, we were fighting some wolves. Bastards."

I could explain more. I could go into specifics, which is

what they are after of course, but I am not the chatty type. Not with these two anyway. They are never on my side when I need them. Why should I give them anything now? I am happy for the moment to drink back the beer and look at them, their wildly animated faces; I look at them as if I once knew them.

Nothing in this place really interests me. I have no reason to be here. And my company is so bad I am sure that my pitch-mates will never ask me again. In fact, I doubt we will work together again. I cannot see myself running around trying to make order of a game. It has been too much of an ordeal. Everything has.

The décor. It is all so foreign to me. It shouldn't be. I should be a man who goes drinking regularly with other men. I should have my back slapped often and told what a card I am. But none of this has happened to me. Or I let none of it in my life. I married young and grieved young and am now a man who aches. When called upon though, when called upon, I am a man who knows how to use a sword.

Fujibayashi and his scissors and talk of war and…

That's why I am here. I am celebrating. I am the man who fought off the wolves and saved the girls. It did happen, didn't it? Didn't it? Then why can't I boast? Why can't I tell them this epic tale of sword and blood and moon and the gnashing of teeth and…

Because since Ruby was taken nothing ever…

Not even a good tale, not…

Heroism is that in which…

My father might have been some use to me here. Struggling with my own words, struggling to form any…

I must tell of Ruby. What happened that day? To clear my mind of…

I must try.

"What's in the bag?"

"Bones."

"Bones? What kind of bones?"

"The bones of a boy."

They look at me like I am quite mad. They have every right. Do they see the real me? Who is…

I pick up the bag of bones, drop money on the table and leave them to their bewilderment. It is late and I must go home with femurs and tibia and a host of others, the poor boy's smooth skull too, rattling over my shoulder. I will have to wake my wife and tell her what I've got. Or the morning. In the morning might be better. If there is to be a morning. You can never be quite sure.

30

Something about the bottom of the pit and on and on, shoeless and forlorn, what is that song, she doesn't even know herself, something her music teacher sang, when he strummed on a guitar, and on and on, and she remembers he had a lovely voice.

It is cold on the shoreline this late month of year. How is she not already dead? How come the wolves have not torn her apart? How has she managed to evade?

Shoreliners must have hope, must think they are going somewhere, or looking for something. Shoreliners are purposeful.

She sees a man pick up a shellfish, crack open its armour and scoop it out and smear it across his eager, salivating maw. He rejoices in his find, it makes him dance. It makes her hungry. She will need to find her own food. It's been days now. How much more?

Sings something about the bottom of the pit still, and on and on, shoeless and forlorn and on and on, and on and on and on

31

The 14th is not a woman.

The 14th quickly took office because the 13th quickly lost it. Lost what? Lost the plot, political reality, the trust of the electorate, his wife and children. It was the loss of his wife and children that probably hurt the most (though nobody even took the time to ask – what was his name again?). He looked even more befuddled in front of the cameras, and everyone had expected his wife and kids to stand beside him, a united front, and to say how they would manage to pull through this together, despite their troubles, despite the poor man getting lost along the way, forgiveness and understanding would surely the be the way forward, that's how they did it in the West, surely here they could get past the shame. Yes, this is the way political rascals have done it over the previous century or so, but the West's model was not going to cut it here. This land has taken a lot from the West, and most of it not good, but when it comes to shame the land stays East: the wife took the two teenagers to a soccer game instead of appearing at the press conference, and instead of forgiveness for his three-year affair with a twenty-year-old intern, they shouted at the lazy centre-backs and the incompetent midfielder and anyone else who took their fancy. It is said the oldest teenage son, fifteen now, has shown some skill on the soccer pitch himself, and there are interest from foreign clubs. Western!

He wept. The 13th openly wept. Not that anyone really cared whether he did or not. They were not prepared to forgive him, only ignore him, for that is what most people do these days. Ignore. And they are a little apprehensive if the truth be known. They know that the 14th is heavily involved in the acquisition of military hardware, and has been in cahoots with such "businesses" for a long time. In his first few months he has spent most of his time attending defense and security trade shows and trying to establish ties with some rogue nations who for some reason think this land undoomed – such must be the power of the 14th's persuasion to convince other attending delegates that the waves will come no more and the plates have put up their last fight, that the land is secure and that economic renewal is nascent, the country would indeed become glorious again. Only a matter of time. He talks a good military game in fact, and has already managed to increase contracts for the manufacture of tanks, drones, military helicopters and police riot vehicles all to the surprise (though not outrage) of the general populace. The villages, of course, hear almost none of this, so tardy is the communications infrastructure these days, and only the big cities really resound; the villages have all but been forgotten, those that still remain and have not been washed away have no voice, only the howls of the wolves that roam in great increasing packs. Something must be done about the wolves and the waves yet, the 14th knows it, but military might must come first. So they will make it for themselves. And they will sell it to others. This is as detailed a plan he has of yet. But it will suffice. It's not like anyone really cares about them anymore anyway. Who cares what ludicrous policies he will implement? He has stopped bandying about the phrases of old: "proactive pacifism" and "interoperability" and is prepared to call spades spades. He is out to make and have (lots of): fighter planes, submarines, missiles (send them back the other way for once), maritime patrol aircraft, rockets, escort ships, ammunition carriers and tanks and banks and banks of munitions and will not stop till they are there and are at hand and in abundance.

The 13th is no longer allowed access to his kids, and the sexy intern has left for a Western Banker, and the kids never much liked their father anyway (was never at home, was always working), and there is only one way for him to go. And so he will find a sword (will probably need it sharpened) and do the honourable thing.

IV

hurled to and fro

Try.
OK.
Ruby was...
Again. Deep breath. Ruby was...
OK.
Ruby disappeared two years ago. Our jewel, our gem, our...
Try.
Deep breath.
She was eight years old. She had been walking home from school, her hard leather *randsel* schoolbag strapped on her back, walking in that slow, slouchy way she had, long legs, like mine, long strides on the footpath, kicking stones into the drains, blowing the fluffy heads off dandelions.
This is all a lie.
Start again.
OK.
Ruby was...
Again.
Deep breath. Ruby was... with me.
We were together.

Say it again.

We were together.

Again.

We were together.

There.

We were together when the last earthquake struck and together when the tsunami started its course upon us. For so long I have been avoiding all of this. Avoiding stating this. Coming to terms with... coming to... just that I have been cowardly, that's what it amounts to: afraid to admit what happened. It's...

Deep breath...

That I could not save my girl. I could not save my girl. I could not even save my little girl.

That morning had been as any other. Breakfast with toast and cereal and she licked her little yogurt cup clean as usual, her tongue almost saurian into the corners. Blueberry. I remember. The sun outside high and shining, so much promise in the air: in hindsight such connivance. Asami was busy in the house – so many things to do, though she seemed to enjoy her tasks. I always called her "busy-lady" in the morning, or "busy-bee", as she was always buzzing around, clearing plates and wiping the table and vacuuming the house and dumping the laundry into the washing machine, then taking buckets of water from the bath to fill the machine, ever the recyclist – that red bucket is still there, under the sink, always ready for emergency. I used to take Ruby to school, sometimes we would go in the car if the weather was bad, but if the weather was good we often walked the twenty minutes – her elementary school was adjacent to my high school, in this land convenience always prized above all else. I enjoyed that walk a lot more than going in the car. When we walked together I got to hear all about her life. She'd tell me what she was going to do that day, and all about her friends and the things they got up to. Some days she'd be quite chatty, other days she'd have nothing at all to say and it was me that was rampant with pointless talk. Spring was our favourite time for these walks and talks, and the two of us would slouch our way forward, often she, yes, she would talk of flowers, there were flowers after all, yes, there were, how they continue to spring up through the mud around here, I will never fully understand, you've got to hand it to them, the boast of their blooming, a tulip head would almost turn one to religion.

She'd tell me what was in store for her in school that day, who her new friends were, and those that had been her friends and were no longer: the tender dramas of the young classroom was ever morphing and hard to keep up with, but I would listen to her talk about anything and be pleased, and oh what would I give to hear your voice for even one minute now – do I remember what it sounds like? How abominably sad is that, to start to lose the sound of your only child; I think I'll have to go and find old video recordings of her, scenes from picnics and sports days, just to hear the lilt of it again, but can I face it?

We had been walking along enjoying our time, enjoying the sun and the warmth on our morning faces. I strode the narrow paths like I was above it all, never questioned for a moment the future, never tempting the fate of our doomed village. When you have your own beautiful child by your side, you may think yourself immortal, indestructible, but the universe always finds some way to redress, there's always a breaking of what seems like the natural order, for then, just then, on an ordinary day, in an ordinary hour of ordinary lives, the rumble. The massive rumble throughout the land, as if the planet had given up its ghost and was preparing to say goodbye to its place in the solar system and spin off its axis completely; a belching, a rupture, then the plates rubbed against each other, like giant palms in gleeful anticipation, sirens sounded, all around our village, and even from neighbouring villages too, you could hear, alarm everywhere, it was an earthquake, we didn't need to be told, had been down this road so often, but it seemed bigger this time, the land didn't simply sway or rock for a few seconds, but jolted and shuddered and buckled and even jumped, throwing us a little into the air, we knew, we somehow knew that this was the mother of them all, or this was end times, this surely was the end of everything. And so the waves started on their course towards us. Ruby and I ran, we both saw and heard the monstrous wall of water, we both heard and saw, our panic instincts instantly fired into action, our bodies filled with fear and adrenaline flooded us. I remember her looking to me, looking to me for guidance, in which direction exactly were we to run, Father answer me with your eyes, this is what you are here for, parent, save me from this, I am only a child.

To a high place. That's all I knew. We had to get somewhere high. We had all been trained to remember this. I remember wanting to call Asami, but hoped, and maybe knew, that she was going to a high place too, the hills behind our house, only half a kilometre or so away, but you could get there, if you ran, and if you were fast, if you could make it to those hills, they should be high enough, and you could breathe.

The waves had other ideas, they came, a huge approach, and we took off sprinting as fast as we could, back down the road we came, our hands clasped together, our eyes on the hills. Cries all around us, the mad sheer cries of terror, wails whirling over the pound and roar of waves – they kept sounding in our ears, waves and wails.

You think you have time but you don't. In any of these situations you think you have time to think. To react, to cope, to deal. But you don't. You have to be as natural and instinctive as any animal, no time for fear or a moment's ponder, you must just flee – your body knows this even if your mind is slow in picking it up, your body panics and ignites its desperate engine.

The wall-wave was growing ever near, ever frighteningly close, and my heart thumped with fear, doubt filled me before the water did.

On. On we ran. But already I could feel her slipping. Her legs weren't as strong or as fast as mine, and I could feel her begin to lag. Her hand left mine, and I shouted at her to keep going, to not give up, we were going to make it, the hills were close now, we would only have to scramble and climb and they'd surely be high enough for us, for us to lie and draw breath, but she was struggling to keep up and I remember being angry, and at the same time begging, please Ruby, hurry, please my love, for we must, and crowds of people were leaving their houses with the same thoughts as I, all frantically moving forward and upward but then, then too soon, the waves were all upon us.

A sudden whack at my back, knocked over and gurgling, the wind out of me and my mouth full of salt water, my brain a sudden shock of purple, my eyes seeing nothing but murk... but Ruby was still with me. I could feel her presence, and our eyes met briefly, our heads above the surface bobbing, and we were pushed together and then apart and then together again and apart again and she was all I was thinking about – get her head above water, make sure you keep eyes on her and get her head above the surface, but things hit us, big things, maybe wood or hard slates or even other bodies, I don't know, the water was full of things, and the dirt and brownness of everything was making it so hard to see. And suddenly a bigger surge of panic inside me: I had lost sight of her. I kept thrusting my head up taking huge lungfuls of precious air, but she was gone. Where? In which direction? Where had the waves taken her? I saw other bodies, some already surrendered to the force, eyes open staring at me, their last seconds nothing but terror, and I remember swimming and pushing my body forward, the only things on my mind my daughter and my wife, nothing else mattered, not the sun that still shone above nor the land that bore us all, find them, find them, find them. But how? Ruby had slipped away and I was now clambering over the side of a warehouse or some shed, a red roof, clinging to its corrugated surface; it was slippery but I could get a footing and hurl myself upon it and got myself above the crashing surface of water and breathe. I breathed. I gasped. My eyes stung and my ears were hearing nothing. I shook my head but my ears were taking in no sound, only the inner tumult and whir. I shouted my daughter's name but I could not even hear my own voice. My ears had stopped working. And I could just about see through my tears. I scanned the whole scene with my weakened senses and saw nothing but floating things, there was nothing but floating things on the now calming water: wood and felled trees and umbrellas and bikes and bags and buckets and even cars moving slowly in the currents, and dead animals, them too, was that a floating black Labrador, or was it a bear, could that have been?

But where where where where...

I screamed at the sky. I called my daughter's name even though I could not hear a single note. I screamed and I screamed again. I could still feel her phantom hand in mine, her thin hand with those elegant little fingers, but how how how had I let go? I had only one job to do in this life...

Deep breath.

Try.

Only one job.

Deep breath. Precious air.
Only to keep her alive.
Try.
Nearly there.
I had only-
Parent.
But I failed.
Her hand.
Her hand.
Somehow I had let go.

V

awake, arise

32

U p the stairs. A series of photos on the wall. Me. Asami. Ruby. I stop and stare and there, there she is, my beautiful wife looking back at me, her eyes open, wide and glowing, looking at me straight, unflinching. How gorgeous she is, leaves them all in the muck, this beauty, not one of them has anything on her, surpasses all, surpasses everything. This one was taken when Ruby was three years old. When a girl reaches that age it is traditional to go to a shrine and get a blessing from a monk. We followed local customs like everyone else, the people here might have lost their way somewhat, but they, we, do not forget our customs and continue to do the same things, together, year in year out. At New Year we go to whatever shrine still stands and pray for a better future – which we invariably won't get – in summer we visit the graves of our ancestors and lay offerings of food to appease their wanting spirits, and when a boy is five, and a girl three or seven, we go for that special blessing.

So, there we were. The family of three. Ruby looked adorable in her little kimono, her hair all done up, and her two proud parents standing either side of her (it's hard to find a photo more radiant). When people stopped and bent to ask her name she would say "Kurumi", just like she would in the classroom, but when alone with us again she would whisper "Ruby" to us and giggle, like it was a wonderful secret we would never reveal to ordinary mortals. We had gone out to a small local restaurant after the blessing, Ruby had wanted *okonomiyaki*, delighted with the creepy movement of the fish flakes on top – she always got what she wanted from us, we were always going to spoil our only child, we were always going to give her everything she needed, and I suppose, looking back, I'm proud to say that we had made her short life a happy one: she never saw us fight, Asami and I, she couldn't have, because we didn't, the world provided suffering enough without the two of us going at it, we were a team, wife and husband, and we had an immaculate daughter, it was a beautiful little family.

That little restaurant has of course been washed away, and that shrine too, and the photographer's studio where we got that perfect picture framed. All gone. As you'd expect.

I stand outside my own bedroom door for a minute or two, deep in contemplation. How come I have continued to get in beside her night after night, week after week? How come I have stuck with it? What have I been *expecting* – a very dangerous word around here that one: *expecting*. Have I been anticipating a sudden rise from the bed, for one day, or night, for her to just get up like in some Biblical miracle and embrace me and tell me that she is ready for us to live again, for us both, together, to live again? Is that what I have been hoping for? *Expecting?* I know I am a foolish, indecent man, and all those hours fawning over others, the now tiring fantasies, were all a way of passing the dreadful hours, the dreadful time, or, more honestly, a way of not dealing with the true matters.

The truth. What matters. What I mean is, what I mean is... I tried to escape from the mourning of my girl, the rambles, the nightly rambles, what I was doing, where I was... I searched... and all in... and forever the hope that my wife would somehow rise.

This is all outside the door. This moment, and a mind trying to untangle. The bedroom door: blank, white, and relaying it all so vividly before me.

There is a bag of bones over my shoulder. I am standing outside my bedroom, our bedroom door, of a house that remains, a house that has been rocked but somehow has not fallen, and I have a bag of dead boy's bones over my shoulder. This is a very peculiar position to be in. If you asked yourself at fifteen, or say twenty, would you ever be standing outside your own bedroom door to greet your silent wife whose eyes you have not seen in months, with a bag of bones over your shoulder, a bag of bones you took from the pit of the wolves, what do you think you would say? All this, this preposterous story, but no more so than any other story happening to any other man in any other stricken place, all of it patently absurd and yet-

They are not heavy. These bones. They are light. All of life, I realize, is like this. You might think at first that it's all heavy, but really it's all light as a feather, it can be taken away so quickly too, all of it, a feather on the wind.

Adhaesit pavimento animea me: It's just come to me, that line I say as I walk, that nightly chant, I've just remembered what it means: *My soul is attached unto dust.* Oddest moments. Must surely have been Dante. Must surely have been him. *My soul is attached unto dust.* Why my mind clings to such...

Deep breath. Deep breath and I am ready to go in.

Am I?

Yes, I am.

Enter.

Heap. Heap of being on sweating sheets. Heap of she. This is to be the end of it. Have had enough. This is the last, no more of it, am taking charge and I have my presentation. I can take no more of the life we have had. This has to be it. The final try. The final attempt at getting some semblance of normalcy back into whatever life we have left. How you have stuck it out so far – you are only to be commended.

Normalcy?

I can smell her. She has not washed in a day or two. Heap is there on the bed. Heap of grief on sweating sheets. Perhaps she expects me to go to my side and plank myself down on the bed and undress and put my pathetic pajamas on and slide in and close my eyes and surrender to the night. But tonight is not the same as any other night. Tonight, I must make clear, is either the first night or the last night. I know this now.

My heart is racing. All of this, or none of this, none of this might work. But I am nothing if not persistent.

I can hear her breathing. It is shallow. It is as if she is awake, as if she is just waiting for me to slide in before she succumbs to the darker hours. How much can she sleep anyway? How many hours of the day and night…

I am trembling. For so long I have gone about my own rotten business, enmeshed in my own private hours, my crazed, salivating fantasies, have I forgotten her? This was her wont of course, but no more of it. Be done. She is my wife. She is the one I married, the one I chose. She is my wife, and she will be reclaimed.

"Asami."

She hears me. A slight movement in the bed lets me know. She hears me call her name all right. But will she ever respond?

Her mind, who knows the condition of her mind right now, or the way it has been for months, for years?

Marisa knows.

But I suppose I don't listen to her either.

These women I have abused, I have had no right, though I must admit I have been fortunate in that I…

I have never quite succumbed. Give me that. Give me something.

"Asami, I have something for you, for us."

There is still not a word. But her shoulders move, acknowledging my existence. This is a start.

I try a third time.

"Asami, I… I have found Ruby's bones, I need you to see them."

These frightening words I had not expected to say, these tortuous…

I don't know how or why this trick, this mind-con, descended upon me, but here I am saying it to her, this ghastly proposition.

She moves even more in the bed now, surely intrigued, and very slowly, almost glacially, she turns her body towards me.

My face is facing her face. This is the first time in a very long time. She looks like death. She looks like a skeleton. She looks like a ghost and every horror image you can think of. We used to be so good at making those movies in the past, our artisans, terrifying gothic images, lank hair and wan, haggard faces, they could have used this one that lies before me now, they could have cast fear into a million hearts with a single frame of this.

And yet, there is yet a something else, get past the sunken cheeks and the unkempt hair and there is a something else there, it's in the eyes, that same gentle loveliness there always was, a tiny spark just there yet, or the faintest ember, all it needs is a little oxygen.

Her face facing my face. She is active now. She is human and with her human eyes is looking at me and her faint humming seems to be asking me what is going on.

"It is all over, Asami. We have come to the end. Ruby is never coming home."

No words yet, but her hum seems to say: *How on earth do you know that?*

"Because I have her bones here. This is what we need to let her go."

No words still, but her hum and her human eyes seem to say: *Tell me all.*

She has pulled herself up to a sitting position now and her wide eyes look even wider than I remember them, wider in her gaunt face.

"You see, sweetheart, every night I have gone walking in search… to see if ever any trace of her was left. And finally, one night, I found this tiny necklace on the path in front of me. It's Ruby's. Do you remember it?"

Her eyes follow the little red stone, but she is wary, as if I am a conjuror about to hypnotize her.

Her hum manages to change to a word, the word I make out is: *Yes.*

She is all upright now and looking at the bones as I take them out one by one.

"It is time to let Ruby go."

Grief needs a dead body, the cold corpse of your loved one laid out and stiff, that's what grief needs to get itself going. You need to *see* first, recognize, then you will be ready to let go.

Bones will have to do.

It is all a terrible trick to be playing on a scrambled mind, but it is all I have left, this subterfuge, and for all its dastardly nature, seems to be working – her mind might right itself after all, she can be brought back from the edge, my wife reclaimed, I have been looking in the wrong places for some alternative version of life, it is up to me to save my wife.

Her eyes move quickly, darting from my eyes to the necklace to the bones emerging from the sports bag. And then they well fully with tears and she sobs, slowly at first and then violently.

"It's OK my dear. This is how we move on. On and only on. She would not want to see you like this."

Asami is nodding. As she sobs and chokes and wipes tears and snot from her haggard face, she nods at me, as if she understands, as if she has always known. She puts her thin arms out to take the bones. She rubs them, one by one, like they are dolls, like they were Ruby's own plastic playthings, smooth, delicate, refined.

"Really?" she asks.

I nod to her, to tell her to trust me, to believe in my ruse, these are the things we must do, us lost folk, if we are to cope.

She puts them all around her as she continues in her grieving spasms and when finally the sobs begin to subside she puts her hand out to mine, reaching for me, reaching, and she finds me. It is the first time our hands have clasped for two years, and my heart soars. I could sing.

For a while we sit alone and gradually she moves closer and closer, her head near my chest, her body frail and fragile and relying on me for support. I will be there for her. I want her to know this. Despite my wanderings (of legs, of mind), I have always really been only here and it has always really been only her.

"Wait," she says suddenly. "I need..."

"What?"

"I need you to give me a moment to finish something."

I lay back on the bed waiting for my ears to fill with their usual tumult. But the barotitis media has left me, the affliction vanished completely perhaps; I am at once uncharacteristically optimistic; I hear clearly, I almost hear the atoms merging in the air.

She lays back too. Her eyes close. She is going somewhere.

Every land needs a hero. And you have come to assume that mantle. A prophet. No, a messiah. A saviour. Saving them from slow drowns in the malicious waves, or slow chokes in the smothering mud, or falling down the cracks when the earth opens up hungry again, needing appeasement, and you can be dead sure that the earth *will* do it, it *will* just open up again and again. Out of their misery. You put them. But now, Nai, it is time to go.

Yourself.

You must yourself, do it. You understand. There comes a time for all. And you, you, Nai, must always have known this.

End it now.

You take your ladder to the apple tree and you tie your rope around it. The rope is strong enough and the tree is strong enough and you are strong enough.

You are found hanging from that apple tree, a lopsided grin on your raven-pecked face; you had no one left to kill, even the grim and ragged scarecrows had been hacked down in your rampage.

But thank you, Nai, thank you for the consolation, for the steering through the soul-dark nights.

I undress and climb in fully beside her. No pajamas: I have no clothes on, not a stitch. She opens her eyes to see me and she smiles. She is beautiful. She is my wife. She holds me. My name is Tomohiro Nemoto.

33

A girl walks the shoreline on and on and sings something about the bottom of the pit and on and on. It was a song her father used to sing. She can't remember exactly how it goes, only there was something about the bottom of a pit.

The singing of this song helps her remember her father, and the mother she once had too, who accompanied on violin. *For the nightingales to sing along with*, she used to say.

Father and mother.

The girl does not cry. She sings.

On.

She might find them all again. There might be a reuniting. She must keep going. There might be music again.

(It is not *her* of course. It is not the one we have been expecting. *Expecting?* No. It never was. This is the way of the world.)

Shoeless and forlorn and on and on, and on and on and on she sings.

34

K itchen. Morning. Toast and cereal and something sizzling in the frying pan. Asami eats what Marisa prepares. Her hair has been washed and, even though it is only
days since she has risen, she looks healthier, stronger.

Marisa has told her about the two strange girls, and about
eggs, the Eggmen, about the wolves in their packs that grow
larger and the raccoon dog, their new pet, Atma.

Atma sits outside the window on a ledge now, looking in.
We feed him, and he is content. It *is* a he. Yes, we checked.

There is of course a lot more to fill her in on: Monstaa,
Hide and Takeshi, Marina the foreigner and her umbrellas,
the hordes of vulgar soccer fans – *hordes?* This is only a village. Did I imagine all that? – and the truth about the bones.
But she has heard enough for the time being. What she really
needs to hear is how the future will look, what it will bring,
but I cannot answer that for her, I can only offer assurance
that I will remain with her, and that I am strong.

We could escape, we could flee to a warmer clime, to a
steadier land, but where's the honour in that? The honour is in
the staying-put, the putting up with, and the putting manners
on the boo-boys and bray-girls, blowing the whistle on foul

play, guiding the lonely boys and wayward waifs, in pulling bodies of men and dogs onto roofs when the waves come, and finding space for us all to breathe – you can be sure they will come again, the catastrophes of flood and mud, and we will battle again. We will need to fight back too, against the irascible neighbours who torment us, and the world who might choose to ignore us; the 14th might not have all the answers, or even *any* of them, and the 15th or 16th may follow suit, maybe it is down to ordinary men in ordinary fields, trying to keep some kind of order.

I am a referee and a husband and a teacher and a father.

I am a husband and a father and a teacher and…

All of these things. All of these mortal things.

I am not a decent man. Some of the time. Most of the time.

Given to flights.

Given.

But I can…

Yes.

I am Tomohiro Nemoto.

And I have sung.

ABOUT THE AUTHOR

Colin O'Sullivan lives in the north of Japan with his family and works as an English teacher.

His short fiction and poetry have been published in various print and online anthologies and magazines, including *A Living Word* (anthology of Irish writers), *Staple New Writing*, *The Stinging Fly*, *These Are Our Lives* and *Cork Literary Review*.

Colin O'Sullivan's first novel, *Killarney Blues*, captivated critics and readers alike and has been translated into French.

"Colin O'Sullivan writes with a style and a swagger all his own. His voice – unique, strong, startlingly expressive – both comes from and adds to Ireland's long and lovely literary lineage. Like many of that island's sons and daughters, O'Sullivan sends language out on a gleeful spree, exuberant, defiant, ever-ready for a party. Only a soul of stone could resist joining in." —Niall Griffiths, author of *A Great Big Shining Star*

"His words swagger with purpose, never meandering too long on a scene, always moving the story forward, even when it goes back in time, like a faded photograph coming into view. Lyrical to a point, one word flowing to the next, hardly stopping." —*LoveSexAndOtherDirtyWords.com*

"Marvellous novel, endearing, moving, fascinating. I adored it. O'Sullivan is a real writing talent." —Jean-Paul Gratias, literary translator

To learn more about Colin O'Sullivan, visit *http://osullivancolin.wordpress.com* and *www.betimesbooks.com*

www.ingramcontent.com/pod-product-compliance
Lightning Source LLC
Chambersburg PA
CBHW020632260626
47157CB00008B/2702